Welcome

To

Outcast Station

To BETH —
I hope you enjoy
The adventure!
Best wishes —
[signature]

Jeanne Adams
Nancy Northcott

Welcome To Outcast Station

The Accidental Plague is copyright © 2017 by Jeanne Adams
The New Badge is copyright © 2017 by Nancy Northcott

ISBN-10: 1-944570-93-4
ISBN-13: 978-1-944570-93-4

Cover by Lyndsey Lewellen, Llewellen Designs
Copyedits on The New Badge by Elizabeth MS Flynn, Flynn Books Words & Ideas
Formatting by Libris in CAPS

Published by Rickety Bookshelf Press

Table of Contents

DEDICATIONS

The Accidental Plague is dedicated to Andre Norton,
Robert E. Howard, Anne McCaffrey, Edgar Rice
Burroughs and
all the science fiction/fantasy writers from whom I
learned to love the genre. Here's to space, the unlimited
frontier!

The New Badge is dedicated to Carol A. Strickland,
a wonderful friend and a brilliant writer and artist.
She introduced me to fandom and
to the idea that the far future could be my imaginary
playground.

THE ACCIDENTAL PLAGUE

By

Jeanne Adams

CHAPTER ONE

Finally, a posting!

Ravi strode through the doors from customs, happy to be in station gravity again. The trip had been fine, given that she'd been in stasis sleep through most of it. She didn't feel the lingering drag she sometimes had with shorter hop space travel. Ravi moved out of the flow of disembarking passengers, scanning the post-decontamination waiting area to see if there was a guide for her. Elation caught her in a wave, as it had been doing since she'd gotten her assignment.

She was eager to get to it. It didn't matter that the job was on Paradise Station—sarcastically called Outcast Station for its edge-of-territory position on the space trade routes—Ravi was just happy to finally have an official job in her field. She'd noted the out-of-date security and decontamination radiation arches, and some of the facilities had near-defunct tech compared to the inner regions of traveled space. To Ravi, it only mattered that she was officially a BVax Scientist, ready to work on a station.

Outcast meant hope to her. The way people talked

about the place, you'd think it was derelict, rather than a brightly lit, well-populated space station. The fact that it was on the edge of nowhere, and supposedly populated with misfits, didn't matter to Ravi. Maybe, finally, she'd fit in.

Besides, the best finds for BVax scientists tended to be in remoter areas of space. Most BVax-ers made one or two major finds in their careers, either in the area of cures or plagues. The memorials for the plague-finders were nice, but since you had to die to get one of those, Ravi hoped to miss that honor. She'd rather have her bronze memorial at BVax HQ champion a cure.

"Scientist Trentham, BVax?" The voice that hailed her was soft, but it carried over the ambient noise.

Ravi turned and looked up, then tilted her head back a bit more. The being greeting her was a Tilden, and a male. Tilden were from Terra's allies, the Five Star Consortium. Fivers and the Nine Planet Guild had been some of the first Others to contact Terra for an alliance. Of course the fact that Brigitte Ramirez Banderleigh the First solved the riddle of the Superium Space Plague was a pretty good impetus for contact.

Ravi touched her BVax shoulder insignia on her jacket with a rush of pride. She was an official, posted BVax scientist. It was real, real, real.

Ravi nodded and said, "Trentham, I am, good Tildensir. My journey master, are you?"

Her counterpart wore the same patch on his station uniform, the icons commemorating that first fledgling company, Banderleigh Vaccines, founded in terrifying need and molded into BVax, one of the largest, most important and far-reaching companies in the galaxy.

4

The male smiled, showing rows of serrated teeth and crinkling, narrow-pupiled green eyes that contrasted with the short, cream fur that covered his face and hands. The darker cream hair on his head was drawn back in a short queue, which bobbed when he shook his head. "Tildensir to you, I am not," he replied, but with humor in his tone. "Know me as Cragrral. I am also Scientist, BVax."

Masking her surprise that she was being met by the top station scientist, Ravi gave the Tilden a half bow of respect.

"Outgoing BVax Representative, am I," he continued with evident pride. "Bound for Himea Research Center in the Clunch sector. A chance to work with Scientist BVax Maxim Degeurro, have I."

Impressed, Ravi smiled and pressed her hands together in the Tilden celebrational gesture. "I'm so pleased for you," she said. "Many luck coins must be in your jar, and may many more join them."

It was Cragrral's turn to look impressed. "My thanks, Trentham." Cragrral's speech was more formal, in the Terran syntax this time. "Are you rested or tired?"

"I'm rested."

"Would you tour the station now or settle in and tour tomorrow?" he asked, obviously spacing the words carefully for correctness. "Scheduled you are, to meet the station administrator, first thing in the station day."

"Excellent." Excitement sizzled in her veins again. "I'll look forward to meeting him." She turned to look around the waiting area. "If you'll direct me to my quarters, I'll change to my uniform and be glad of a tour."

"The pleasure, it is mine," Cragrral said, smiling a toothy smile.

She hadn't expected the courtesy of a tour from her BVax counterpart onstation. Then again, she never expected courtesy anywhere in the galaxy. She was from McKeon's World, and most guessed her origins with a simple glance at the regular, wave-patterned blush of skin that circled her neck like a crimson tattoo, and from her thick, blood-red hair.

The Tilden, however, didn't seem the least concerned to be escorting a McKeonite.

"A complex place, is this Station, Paradise," Cragrral said as he led the way through the wide station corridors with their soothing, muted colors. Deck Six, where most of the official station-to-station vessels docked and were received, was a soft cream above the midline, a little worse for wear, and a dark blue-green shade below it. "Color marks the decks," he said, gesturing to the walls. "Some can see the differences, others cannot."

She nodded as they rose three deck levels in an otherwise empty in-station personnel lift. Cragrral was silent for the ride, but as they walked down the deck nine corridor, he tapped the edge of a cross corridor. "Turn here, we do, at Spoke One, on the knife-hand—" he broke off, snapping his teeth. "My apologies. To the left."

"Got it." She smiled. Cragrral seemed to be trying to amend his speech patterns to the human norm. She wanted to tell him it didn't matter to her, but she didn't want to offend.

"The BVax facility large, here is. Many workers.

Many hydroponics technicians," he amended. "We, alone, are Scientists." He gave the word a title's emphasis. "The charge of BVax we hold here."

It was a reminder, though in this case a proud one, that BVax was sometimes all that stood between expanding space exploration and death. BVax was the first line of defense when it came to the terrors of spaceborne illnesses.

They passed two station personnel who happened to be human. Both gave her an up-and-down look and, when the male saw her neck coloration, he curled his lip before the two moved on. Ravi's insides quivered, but she kept her back straight and her head held high. Nothing encouraged bullies more than letting them see their contempt upset you.

Cragrral gave her a curious glance but said nothing. "Here, the assigned BVax quarters are."

He pressed his clawed hand onto an identiplate, and the door slid silently open. Cragrral bowed, motioning Ravi to precede him through the door.

It was one of the first times in her adult life that someone hadn't shoved her to the back of the line.

Of course, there wasn't much of a line to come to Outcast Station.

"Thank you."

"BVax welcomes you to Paradise Station," he said, moving to a bank of electronics. "Here to be placing your hand, please."

When she did, he keyed her into all the systems in the suite, making her an administrator. "Into the computer, we have now logged you. Hydroponics, separately must be done. The suite here, three sleeping rooms has, plus personal lab and office spaces. Occupying one section, am I. You the other. Third was created in hopes this station would be pivotal." His wry smile was the first indication that Cragrral was aware Outcast Station wasn't the prime posting in the universe. "Go, I will, within the month, and there will be one again," he said, as if she needed reminding that she would be the sole BVax scientist for a whole station.

"Have you had much trouble in the time you've been here?"

"One standard contract term have I spent, with little to distress my work. The usual Emergency Responses, coming on a regular basis, are, but nothing much else." He gestured to the unoccupied rooms. "On some odd trade routes are we, which provides interest. With the Drachans, we now have peaceful contact. Exciting that is. But most are routine. With some agro planets are we working, the crops to improve," he enthused, "this mostly is the hydroponics division's work, however."

Cragrral made a broad gesture, indicating the two doors leading off the main living suite and its bland sitting area. "Choose your room, to be staying. Generous are our quarters," he said. "Your time, please take, if you wish. Then, when ready, change to station uniform as you wished. Here, I will be waiting. To hydroponics we will go, then, to be logging you in."

It didn't take Ravi long to get into one of her crisp, new, specifically tailored BVax station uniforms. When she reappeared, Cragrral tested the login to the suite's protocols and securities by having her open and relock the doors as they left. The BVax quarters, like the BVax storage areas he showed her next, needed strict security.

Their offices and personal labs held medicines and components for medicines that were highly prized on the black market throughout the galaxy. Once they'd seen the setup and she was officially logged in, Ravi and Cragrral locked the doors again.

"A standard location for all things, there is, in every station," Cragrral said, pointing to the quarters, lab, quarantine area, and storage, highlighted on the map of the station he'd pulled up on his handheld station communicator, or statcomm. "For BVax, every need is met, and all equipment in best condition, is. Even in these outer places, where older equipment is for everything else, great care is taken for BVax."

"Plague knows no class, category or status. Plague knows only death."

"BVax knows no class, category or status. BVax saves lives." Cragrral's smile was wide and filled with a predator's sharp teeth. It would have been frightening had she not known his personality a bit already. "Know your BVax motto, you do."

"I knew it from the first xeno class I took."

Cragrral beamed. "Same, was I. BVax all I wanted, as a youth was. Now, that dream I have realized."

It was Ravi's turn to beam. "Same, was I." She echoed his phrasing. He'd dropped into a less formal and friendlier Tilden pattern. "And regardless of where we're stationed, we are BVax."

Cragrral nodded. "Well do here," he confided. "Other places you will go. Example am I. One term here and I am moved to a better place. Moved will you be too."

Somehow she doubted that a McKeonite would have

9

the same luck, no matter how smart or how successful, but hey, she could dream, right?

Cragrral hesitated, and she knew he wanted to speak. Her stomach lurched. She should be used to it. She was about to preempt his question and say, *yes, I'm a McKeonite*, when he rushed to say, "Trentham are you, who wrote the thesis on biogenetics of Carpathian worm slime as burn and wound regenerating material?"

Surprise lit her from head to foot. "Yes. That was my doctoral thesis for xenogenetic medicine."

He beamed. "Read it, I did. Wondered things. Ask, may I?"

"Of course."

They spent the next forty minutes sitting in the storage room discussing xenogenetics and wound treatment, and advances from several core worlds. Cragrral was enthusiastic about her work and kept probing as to why she hadn't continued the research.

"Promising thoughts there were, yes. I intend to continue the research as soon as I can," Ravi concluded, "but I didn't have enough samples to commercialize it at that point." Students had to get outside funding for major studies, even while in school. No one had wanted to fund a McKeonite. Once placed, however, BVax scientists continued their personal research projects on BVax time, as well as the required research they had to do on the plants, animals and other materials from the planet where they were based.

"Work toward that, will you now?"

She nodded. "Yes. I'll have to share with BVax, of course." They had to split every commercial application or patent on a seventy-thirty basis with the company.

That seventy percent was a heck of an incentive for scientist to continue their research. Ravi would have done it even if the split were the other way.

"Problem, is that?" Cragrral queried, his furry brow furrowed in question. "Most find it useful, BVax backing to have."

Huh. Ravi realized she would now be submitting the patents as a working, posted BVax scientist, rather than a McKeonite science student. The anonymity would give her both access and camouflage.

Something unfurled within her. A tiny seed of hope.

"I guess being BVax would help," she finally responded, smiling. "For the research."

A chime sounded and a disembodied voice spoke. "Deck nine mess is now open."

Cragrral snapped his jaws open and shut several times. "Good. Eat we will, then hydroponics tour we will before evening rest. Food here, it good, is."

"Sounds like a plan." Ravi steeled herself for her first encounter with the larger population of station dwellers. She would have preferred to get a meal sent to their quarters, but she walked proudly into the mess. She refused to let herself be drowned with worry before there was even a drop of rain, as her mother would have said.

Dinner was, however, predictably uncomfortable. She and Cragrral got their meals and sat. Others already at the table took one look at her neck and hair coloration, knew her for a McKeonite, and picked up their trays and moved away. Cragrral was visibly shocked.

"Understand this, I do not." He gazed after the retreating station workers.

"I do," she said as despair crowded out hunger in her

belly. "I'm from McKeon's World."

Cragrral looked puzzled. "Are you poisonous? Do you bite or emit offensive odors? I have not noted anything noxious about you."

His true bafflement made her laugh, and her knotted stomach relaxed a fraction. "Forty galactic years ago, criminals from my planet committed a severe terrorist act on our origin world. It was long before I was born. My parents were about twelve, I think." For nearly forty years, since ten plotters had blown up the IMEXTEX Galactic Headquarters on Terra, those from McKeon's World had been the pariahs of the galaxy, at least the humanoid portion of it.

The fact that McKeon's planetary government continued to champion the killing of five hundred men, women and children didn't help.

She cut her meat and took a bite. That nearly distracted her from Cragrral's reaction. He was right. The food was good.

"Hold another's actions against you, they do? Two generations later?"

"Yup."

He said something guttural and, by its tone, expletive laden, in his own tongue. The translator was programmed not to repeat expletives directly, and it usually substituted the word "expletive." Whatever he'd said must have not had a corollary in Basic Trade Tongue. Or he'd deliberately murmured the words so as not to be translated.

"Great gifts, many humans have," he began, spacing the words out as if he were trying to phrase his thoughts carefully. "And flaws. Disconcerted am I, by that attitude."

Ravi gave a jerky shrug. "I'm never welcome." She met his gaze. "You're the first welcoming being I've met virtually anywhere in my travels. Thanks for that, by the way." She gave him a wobbly smile.

He frowned ferociously. It took all her willpower not to recoil. When a Tilden frowned, it looked like attack mode. She knew that and forced herself to breathe normally, but her gut said, "RUN!"

"Scientist, you are," he said, punctuating the statement with a thump on the table that made both their trays and cutlery jump. When she didn't say anything, he growled. "Well? You are?"

"Yes, I am. A good one."

"Settled then. Matters not where you hatched. BVax posting says you are better than good. Science trumps origins."

He thumped the table again, then shot a glare around the mess. He sought out those who'd moved from their table and showed his teeth. "Scientist trumps birth," he growled again, and his resonant voice carried throughout the room.

Embarrassment flooded through her, but she refused to duck her head and shrink away. The carrionbirds circled in to feed if you showed weakness. So she held her head up, focused on Cragrral and continued to eat.

When most people in the room had stopped talking to look at the pair of them, he said it again. "Scientist trumps planet, birth, age, size, shape. Scientist BVax is your safety. Never forget it."

Several people nodded and most of the non-humans in the mess looked as baffled at Cragrral's words as

Cragrral had at the negative treatment Ravi had experienced. When Cragrral turned back to his food, the conversations around the mess gradually resumed.

"Thank you, I guess," Ravi finally said. "Maybe they'll stay healthy so they don't ever have to trust their lives to a McKeonite."

"Stupidity. BVax hires no bad scientists. BVax reputation, it does, depend upon skill." He pointed his claw her way. "Skilled, are you?"

"Yes." She never said anything else. People seldom believed her when she said she'd graduated with her first advanced degree in xenobiology at fourteen. Her second degree in galactic biochemistry and biogenetics had come a mere two years later. School had been her haven, but even with seven advanced degrees, two at the third doctoral-ribbon level, the only jobs she'd been able to get before this posting were dishwashing, cleaning crime scenes and construction work.

If the powers that be on McKeon had let the memory of the IMEXTREX bombing die, it wouldn't be so bad. Sure, there would still be those who remembered, but forty years later, who would care? No, it was McKeon's insistence that the bombers were heroes that drew the galaxy's ire.

"Science, let us discuss," Cragrral demanded. "Calm, I must find."

Ravi was surprised and warmed by his defense. "Have you heard about the latest material found on Valoo Seth? It's out by Station XcLatttretttrat. They found a moss-like growth on one of the moons. BVax Central thinks it might be a potential new dermal contact base material for vaccines." She'd brought all the latest updates from BVax Central with her. She'd been devouring them in every spare moment since she'd gotten the posting.

Cragrral's frown eased and the fur on his neck settled. "Heard of this, I have not. Tell of the science!"

They spent the rest of the meal in discussion of proficiency of vaccine bases and rare disease vectors. As they returned their trays and recycled their dinner packaging, they continued the discussion. Ravi was so fired up to be discussing her favorite topics, she just said an absent "excuse me" when she bumped someone as they exited the mess.

"McKeonite scum," the man growled, rounding on her. "We don't tolerate your kind, ring-neck."

Before she could formulate a response, Cragrral's long arm shot out and grabbed the man's collar. He bent the man nearly in half, pressing his face into the BVax emblem on Ravi's black cargo pants.

"SCIENTIST FIRST," he bellowed, and everything in the mess, once again, stopped. Tildens were famous for their vocal abilities, and Cragrral's statement bounced back from the walls like he'd shouted it in a canyon. "BVAX HAS NO PLANET OF ORIGIN."

"True, and we trust that if BVax has vetted our station Scientists, he, she, or it, will be the best in their field and keep us healthy."

The mellow voice was as carrying, though not nearly as sonorous and loud. The man who spoke, as he moved to stand next to her, was of middling height, but was broad and muscular. So muscular that his biceps and chest strained the regulation-issue uniform he wore. The Federated Colonies Chief Station Marshal placed his hand on Cragrral's taut arm and squeezed once before he turned to Ravi.

"Was this station citizen bothering you, ma'am?"

"Racial slurs, this statcit spouted," Cragrral stated, calming marginally in the face of law enforcement. "Objectionable! Discord it sows. Unacceptable onstation. More egregious to so speak to Scientist, BVax Trentham.

"Yes, he was rude. I'd as soon let it pass." She cut a sharp glance at the marshal as her stomach churned with stress, threatening to bring up what little dinner she'd eaten. "Perhaps he had too much to drink."

The marshal thrust out a huge hand and she forced herself not to recoil. It took her two heartbeats to realize he meant to shake her hand in the Earth-style custom of greeting. She gingerly placed her hand in his, praying he wouldn't crush or damage it. She also wondered when he was going to demand Cragrral let go of the mechtech still pressed on to the rank patch on her trousers.

The marshal shook her hand with brisk welcome. "Welcome to Paradise Station, BVax Scientist Trentham. I'm Chief Station Marshal Braddon Carruthers. Friends call me Brad. Do you sing?"

The non-sequitur confused her.

Cragrral chuckled, and the warm sound was incongruous in the tense standoff. "Miss me, you will, Swordsman?"

"Damn straight. Hard to get anyone to sing with me," Carruthers replied without taking his eyes off Ravi. "Or spar with me either. So? Do you?"

"Yes," Ravi replied, still confused, still worrying about the mechtech. "Mezzo soprano."

A smile blossomed on Marshal Carruthers's face. "Couldn't be better. Cragrral," he drawled, "you might want to let that guy breathe."

"Ah." Cragrral released the hapless bigot and the man stumbled back, rubbing his throat. Fury ripened his features to true hatred as he now focused on the marshal.

"Pressing charges," he gasped, gripping his abused throat. "Assault. Damn McK—"

Before he articulated "McKeonite," Cragrral's hand shot out again.

The marshal blocked it, which impressed Ravi no end. The marshal was far stronger than he looked if he was able to block a Tilden.

"Enough, Cragrral." Carruthers cocked his head toward the mechtech. "Buddy, you've got a problem. You're a bigot and a trouble-maker. That don't work too well on stations anywhere in the galaxy."

Carruthers was right about that. If a station employee got a rep for being bigoted, he or she lost status, and that meant getting worse and worse postings.

Then again, Outcast Station was pretty much a last chance kind of place, from what Ravi had been able to find out.

Carruthers crowded in on the man and tugged on his uniform, straightening out the name and rank tab on his chest. "MechTech Rankin, report to your posting or quarters. The maintenance supervisor will hear about your conduct."

"My conduct?" the man blustered. "Mine? What about his?"

The marshal grinned, and Ravi suppressed a shiver. She wouldn't want that look turned on her. It wasn't as

17

vicious as the Tilden's bared fangs, but it held plenty of malice. Of course the sweet and gentle type seldom ended up in places like Outcast Station.

"Whose conduct? Cragrral's? A respected, multi-degreed individual who happens to be our BVax Scientist? Most Honorable Dr. Cragrral of BVax, would you like to lodge a complaint? I do believe a complaint of bigotry from BVax would be taken *very* seriously." The marshal kept the man pinned to the wall with his gaze, and the mechtech's eyes flitted from Brad to Cragrral with equal unease.

"You can't do that," he whined finally. "I know my rights."

"Rights?" Cragrral hissed the word. "Rights you have *not* to be accosting any station personnel with slurs. Contrary to all policy, it is."

Ravi touched Cragrral's arm. When the Tilden looked down at her, she gave a minute shake of her head.

"I'm sure it was a misunderstanding."

Cragrral's glare softened as he looked her way, then, with seeming effort, he nodded just as minutely. He turned back.

"So," he began, and in a lightning-fast move, his head shot forward and into the maintenance bigot's face. The move was so swift and menacing that the man shouted and cowered back against the corridor wall. Standing where she was, Ravi saw that all Cragrral's teeth were showing. "A misunderstanding, yes. As long as this humanoid realizes that BVax Scientist to be respected, is. No higher calling than BVax. Save even your bigoted life, one day."

Cragrral pointed a clawed hand at the mechtech's

chest, and the man tried to get even farther away, despite the marshal's restraining hand. Cragrral poked him with a final word. "Remember."

When the Tilden shot back up to his full height, the marshal drawled, "I think you can go now," as he waved a hand at the mechtech, shooing him away.

The man scuttled down the corridor, but not before he shot a last, hate-filled look at Ravi and Cragrral.

Great. Just great.

The marshal shook his head as he watched the man's retreat. "Stupid. Here are my station communication codes," he said, tapping his statcomm to hers, where it rested in its case on her sleeve. "Emergency code is Sigma91 on any statcomm, public or personal. As BVax, you have quarantine and shutdown authority, so we'll need to get you up on CentraComm, which is deck fourteen/purple, by the way, and get you registered."

"She meets with StatAdmin in the morning," Cragrral offered.

"Good." Brad Carruthers smiled at her. "Welcome to Paradise."

Emboldened, she said, "I've heard it called Outcast Station more than I've heard its real name."

"Yeah, well, that's because we're a long way from anywhere, which does make us the outer rim of the galaxy's outcast net. May the Fisherman Bless us all," he added, making the sign of the fish.

Ravi was surprised. She'd never expected to find one of the Emmanuels on an outlying space station.

"I'm okay with Outcast," Carruthers continued with another grin. "It works for a lot of us."

"Yes, work for us, it does," Cragrral agreed, his

demeanor returning to amused calm. "Singing we must be, soon, yes, Brad?"

"Absolutely, Cragrral."

"Then goodbye for now, I bid you. To hydroponics we must be going."

The marshal tipped an invisible hat, which seemed odd on the station, where no one wore hats, and bade them goodnight.

"Sing do you, truly?" Cragrral said, his tone a bit anxious as they continued on their way. "Mezzo…" He seemed unfamiliar with the term.

"A medium soprano. Higher than a contralto, lower than a true soprano. Highest note for me is here," Ravi pitched her voice to an A, two octaves above middle C.

"Ahhh." The Tilden smiled. "This is good. Very good. Come." He gestured Ravi ahead of him once more, pressing his palm to the identiplate in the nondescript wall. When the door opened, he entered a sequence of letters and numbers and gestured again. "Hand, please to be presenting."

Ravi pressed her hand and felt the scan and the prick of the DNA match. Within seconds, it beeped green. "Now, access code you would use, please, to enter."

She entered a number sequence she knew she'd remember, and again the scan beeped green.

"Excellent. Yes. Now enter the airlock, we do. Scanned for microbes, we are." The lights strobed over them with a subtle green glow. Cleared, they entered an observation chamber.

"Oh! Chrysanthemums." Beyond the plasglass were row upon row of trays with every color of Terran *Chrysanthemum Morifolium v. Celebration One.* The cheery faces and spicy scent of the specially hybridized flowers never failed to make Ravi smile. The plant wasn't much changed from its Earth origins.

The same couldn't be said of some of the other greenery. The corners of the hydro-tank were veritable forests of modified bamboo—T. *Chamaedorea Seifrizii v. PatelHowe*—which towered over the racks and trays of ru-weed—JC. *Chenchrus Urgradorsa parallis v. Cllck*—from the iron-rich mountains of Jennan Cham, and a Colonial Martian-grown varietal of paragrass—M. *Poaceae Xtee v. Eredecia*—arranged throughout the room. Hovering over the bamboo, a green metallic drone harvested smaller stalks, while another stripped dried or yellowed leaves from the topmost areas of the towering forest.

The standard *bacca* plants—T. *Nicotiania tobaccam*—used throughout human space in the development of vaccines and stimulants, glowed with health in its multi-level rows. Its broad green leaves spread wide as they branched off the individual four foot stalks, providing oxygen as well as stock for their work.

Floor to ceiling growing structures with the mutated, variegated climber B. *Epipremnum aureum v. BetelgeuseOne,* affectionately known as Beetlejuice Ivy, were being sprayed with a mist that hazed the air around them. *K-Zu847*, the variant of kudzu, T. *Pueraria montana v. lovata,* one of Earth's most invasive plants, draped in lush mounds and twined through various structures and shapes throughout the growing chamber.

In the center, a squat, broad k'urpurt tank swarmed with the spore-heavy, bulbous presence of the station's main air stabilizer, U. *K'urpurt Genesis v. RogueOne.*

That plant was one of humankind's keys to distance space flight and colonization. As an oxygenator, it had no equal. It had been found on the derelict ship of still-unknown origin that entered Earth's system, the one that had allowed Terrans to reverse engineer faster-than-light star drives.

Of course, that ship had originated Earth's first space plague too.

"The hydro-engineers, responsible for all this, are," Cragrral broke into Ravi's mental categorizing of the plants. "We, however, have access to all, research to be doing at our desire. Often too, plants are coming from agro worlds. Some promising, are, for medicines." He pointed at a mass of shiny, white-stalked plants with bean-like pods hanging in profusion from the top of the stalks like a maypole. "These, found were, on Rhessau. Curing some non-nerve based paralysis, it is."

"Fascinating!" Ravi exclaimed as Cragrral explained the distillation of the pressed oil from the pods and its use as a curative.

While many of the plants were Earth-based, others that originated in the Nine Planet League system, the Five Star Consortium and other allied regions or worlds. There were uhru plants—P. *Chaldiss Uhru v. Americana* from Pareau—aplenty around the edges of the room, probably for BVax use for experimentation onstation. The planet below them—also known as Paradise—held its own biodomes, which grew uhru, bacca and other mediums for vaccine trial and production.

"Are there testing media in stores?" Ravi realized they'd gotten so engrossed in the discussion of biomarkers and slimes before dinner that she'd forgotten to ask.

"Yes, large stores, there are." Cragrral smiled. "Well prepared, this station is, for any contingency."

"Good. That's good." Standing amongst the plants, Ravi let her muscles unclench and her body relax. Somehow, despite the bigot and others like him, she would make Outcast Station work for her. She would make her mark.

"The singing," Cragrral said. "We must talk of this."

Before she could reply, there was a pounding on the glass. A hydrotech waved at them, frantically motioning them toward the hydro command center.

At the same moment, both of their statcomms went red and shrilled an alert.

"BVAX SCIENCE PERSONNEL TO AIRLOCK 35, FIRST WAITING AREA, DECK SIX B. LOCKDOWN PROCEDURE INITIATED."

Singing would have to wait.

CHAPTER TWO

Ravi and Cragrral raced to their quarters and into their personal biocontam suits as if they'd rehearsed it in tandem every day of their lives. She let Cragrral lead the way to the personnel lift, and once they descended, to the decontamination waiting area by airlock forty-five.

"In or out?" he asked as they ran. "With which do you do better?"

"Out."

"Done."

They reached the quarantined area in a rush. Unlike accidents or other disasters, potential plagues had people vacating the scene as quickly as possible, rather than staying to gawk. Ravi and Cragrral synced their statcomms and Cragrral bent for a retinal scan before stepping through the pulsing red scanner of the quarantine gate blocking the waiting area airlock. That sealed behind him, and she slapped her palm onto the plate, reinstating the outer seal against breach by anyone other than the Chief Marshal, the Station Administrator or herself.

Beyond the secured quarantine doors, people were

sitting in clumps. Those not sitting were gesticulating wildly and, she guessed, demanding they be let out of the quarantine to go on to whatever important business they were about. Six harried-looking station intake stewards were handling them, and two security techs from the passenger line lurked should anyone make an active move to escape.

"Good luck with that," she muttered, smiling a little. "Look out for Guzos."

"Will do."

There would always be those who thought they were immune and should be allowed to leave a Q-Zone. BVaxers called them either TMs, for the long ago Typhoid Mary on Earth, or Guzos, for plague-spreader Terrance Guzo from Alpha I.

As potential carriers, they would stay put until Ravi or Cragrral declared the emergency over, or everyone in the Q-Zone was cured or dead.

BVax was in command of this area of the station now, as if they were a vengeful God. They could have someone killed, spaced, restrained, or arrested, and never face a single charge of any personnel code, space law, or reg violation. Not one blot would ever appear on any BVax record for restraining a galactic citizen or a statcit who might be a plague carrier. One thing every race in Treaty space had learned in the last several hundred years was, if you let BVax handle disease hot zones, more people lived than died.

If you ignored them, a whole hell of a lot of innocent beings—sometimes entire cultures—were lost before you got a handle on a plague or disease.

"Trentham," a voice snapped behind her. She made a

half-pivot to see the marshal through the face shield on her suit.

"Marshal Carruthers," she acknowledged him. "Cragrral is assessing. Options in ten."

"Got it. Need anything?"

"Not yet." To her surprise, he waited with her until Cragrral logged into the exchange port, linking their statcomms.

"Status?" she snapped, activating the incident recorder.

"Yellow. Four people with high fevers, one with delirium. Rapid onset at quarantine waiting area."

"Single species or multiple?"

"Multiple. Humanoids of three planet types, oopalateans from Nine Planet Guild."

"Marks, hives, pustules, itching, rash?"

"None, on any species yet."

"Mucous membranes?"

"Inflamed, color is red in humanoids, green in oopalateans."

"Secretions or excretions"

"None."

"Chills, convulsions?"

"None, even with fever."

They ran the whole checklist as if they'd trained together for decades. At one point, she saw that Cragrral was grinning, and she answered it. They both sobered as the data unfolded, but it was exciting to be doing what they'd trained for.

"Discussion." Cragrral spoke, continuing the protocol.

"Initial blood scan showing bacterium similar to IL-

23 outbreak on Eamdium Theta. Symptoms presenting as an influenza-type, close-contact contaminant."

"Possible," Cragrral said, his tone considering.

"I pulled this ship's manifest and it lists nine passengers from that area of space, and all passengers had contact at airlock support waiting area and the decontamination waiting area. Captain reports no one was ill prior to opening the initial ship airlock so it has a short incubation period. Station stewards confirm all incoming passengers were stable upon entering airlock support." Ravi was processing the data from the reports and lists as she spoke.

"Other options?" Cragrral pushed a button to text on his statcomm as they continued their verbal rundown.

Confident, I am, that this is IL-23 or variant thereof. Damp cold skin of humanoids. Complaining, Ooplateans are, of internal discomfort. Classic symptoms.

She nodded, but they ran the entire protocol list. She called up the stores list of available vaccine for that disease, found the storage point, and did the passback to Cragrral.

"Inoculant available for IL-23, should it be our bug."

"Excellent. Test strips printing now, are," he said, retrieving a series of paper based strips from the BVax exchange point on his side of the barrier. "Testing, I will commence."

"Palliative measures for IL-23?" Ravi continued the protocol.

"Inoculate, hydrate, rest. Initiate first steps, you should."

As Cragrral moved to the stricken individuals, Ravi checked the availability of medbeds in this sector of the station. Each quarter ring of every deck area had a section that was outfitted for triage or hospital care. They could have it staffed within ten to twenty minutes.

"Marshal Carruthers, whom do I contact to authorize three station Medstaff to go active at the deck six B, airlock 45-50 medspace?"

"Station Master Quiana Shupe in CentraComm. She's channel Alpha75 on the statcomm."

Ravi picked up her statcomm and keyed in the necessary data. "BVax Scientist Trentham to Station Master Quiana Shupe, Code Yellow, airlocks 45-50, deck six B."

"Copy BVax Trentham, this is Station Master Shupe, actual. Go ahead."

"Requesting authorization Code Yellow ER Medstaff for medspace, deck six B, Airlock 45-50."

"Duration?"

"Unknown, but forty station hours is postulated."

"Cause?"

"Probable cause is IL-23 variant strain, currently at yellow status."

"Understood. Hold on, BVAX," Shupe said, and the comm went silent. When it clicked back on, the words were crisply delivered. "Roger, BVax Trentham. ER medteam authorized via ChiefMed Officer PurrlTeeLaa. Cleared for 40 SH. By the way, welcome aboard."

"Thank you, Stationmaster Shupe," Ravi replied, even though she was distracted when a whirl of blue and green flashing lights initiated within the quarantine area. That meant a medspace was being activated.

"Fast work," she said to Cragrral as he returned to the BVax exchange port.

"Shupe, competent is," he agreed. "Confirm IL-23, official, via test strips printed at this port. Variants, none apparent. Numbers, five cases severe, four cases moderate, five cases mild. Twenty-seven, exposure factors have, so quarantined must be for twelve station hours."

Ravi repeated it back, as per protocol, adding, "Medspace is organized, patient transfer to begin shortly." She glanced at her statcomm. A text flashed on screen from an unknown sender but it read:

Medspace prepped at Airlock 45-50, deck six B. Ready for patients at 19:00, standard station time. Ready to receive patient IDs, and BVax recommended length of stay at your convenience.

She replied in kind and tagged Cragrral per protocol. "BVax Scientist Cragrral, Medspace is prepared for patients. Are you ready to break Quarantine lock at ER Medpoint and transfer?"

"BVax Cragrral, ready is. Transport, initiate at 19:00 SST. Observe, I do, ER Medstaff personnel at Q-lock Medpoint Transfer."

"Initiate Q-lock transfer at your command, BVax Cragrral."

Ravi stood with Marshal Carruthers as Cragrral organized the transfer of the afflicted through the secondary Q-lck into the activated Medstation. With each patient, he imprinted a hand on a tablet and the medical personnel did the same, transferring each patient officially to Medstat care and out of BVax control. With the disease identified and confirmed, with a known cure, they were ready to pass it off.

When the people designated as active carriers were

moved, and the others settled in the quarantine area and inoculated, Cragrral strode back to the command point. With his back to the Q-area, he grinned at Ravi. "Excellent response time, BVax Trentham. Worked your first E-Rep, you have, on Paradise Station. Broken in right, you have been."

Ravi grinned back, knowing Cragrral's bulk would shield her inappropriate—from a patient's viewpoint—glee at having successfully managed her first Emergency Response or E-Rep. "Indeed I have, BVax Cragrral. And please, call me Ravi."

Cragrral's eyes widened, and he made a gesture of both respect and thanks. "Honored, I am, BVax Scientist Ravinisha Trentham. I will treasure the knowledge of your truename. I will share it with no other. I will keep it in my heart next to the names of my truekin." He nodded to Marshal Carruthers.

Carruthers surprised her by adding the response another Tilden would have given. "Honored am I, to witness the gift of naming."

Cragrral bowed slightly to Carruthers, then more deeply to Ravi.

"And to duty, we return, BVax Ravi. I, remain here, will, for my rest period. You must also now take a mandatory rest period. Tired you must not be, if you must relieve me before the twelve hour quarantine lifted, is.

"Per BVax protocol," he stated more formally, "you will relieve me at 04:00 STT."

Ravi had forgotten this part of the protocol. She now had to leave off anything she might have been doing and go lie down. It was the way BVax protected its assets in a plague situation. A scientist in the middle of a plague—or an Emergency Response—had to take mandatory rest periods so BVax didn't lose critical assets that could solve the emergency.

"Per protocol, BVax Cragrral, I am returning to quarters," she replied, letting her palm rest on the scanner at the command port on her side of the quarantined section. "MedStat personnel have ordered consumables for all beings within the quarantine area, which will be delivered at 19:45. Signal me immediately if there is a further outbreak or if you need support of any kind."

"Acknowledged, BVax Trentham," he intoned, his formal delivery at odds with his toothy smile.

They both put their hands on their respective identiplates and confirmed the status of the event going from Yellow/Active to Yellow/Abating. With a flick of a button, Cragrral had an emergency cot extruding from the wall material. "See you, I will, in twelve hours."

"Sounds good."

"I'll walk you home, Doc," the marshal said as she broke the seal on her suit and turned to leave. When she frowned, and would have demurred, he shook his head. "My protocol. No BVax scientist goes anywhere alone when they're exhausted. You qualify."

"But…"

"I'd do it for Cragrral if he were outside and you were inside."

That decided her, but she was still surprised by the marshal's attention. They moved down the corridors and while some humanoids still gave her a wide berth, there were a few nods of acknowledgement and one brief smile from another station dweller.

"BVax knows no race, color, creed or planet of origin," she murmured.

"No, and Cragrral was right to put that guy in his place," Carruthers stated.

"I don't want any trouble."

"Trouble and BVax go together," the marshal said with a smile that transformed his craggy features into handsome ones. "Find one, you find the other."

"True." She returned the smile at the thought. BVax Scientists lived exciting lives, and hers was finally beginning, as today's event proved.

They rode up the personnel lift in silence and Brad stopped at the cross corridor. He was about to speak when his statcomm beeped a fast, urgent tattoo.

"Carruthers, actual. Go."

"Marshal, we've got trouble on deck nineteen. Deputy Marshals Brrrtrarrr and O'Reilly were dispatched, but neither is answering their comm. Stationmaster Shupe said there's been a CO2 leak there, but Brrrtrarrr should respond even if O'Reilly was overcome."

"Send Clingman, Pierce, and ma'Gonese. I'm heading there now." He reached out, squeezed her shoulder, and called, "Rest well," back to her as he dashed off.

For a moment, Ravi stood where she was, absorbing the sensation of having been touched, willingly, by someone who wasn't another McKeonite.

A movement caught her eye and she saw a station worker coming down the main corridor. Not wanting to spoil the simple joy of being dealt with in a friendly way, she moved down the cross corridor and into her quarters.

That's when fatigue hit her like a bellowing gar running from a king beast. Had it only been this single station day that she'd come onto Outcast Station? She looked at her statcomm and realized that she'd now been awake for more than a station day cycle. Twenty-six hours was too long to go without sleep.

Pulling her gear bags all the way into the room she'd chosen, she set her waking alarm. Her trunks had been delivered too, but she didn't have the energy to haul them in. It took everything she had to make up her bunk. The sooner she did that, the sooner she could give in to the dragging tiredness that had her leaning on the wall to take off her clothes. Ravi slid into her bunk and was asleep before she tugged the thermal cover all the way up.

####

The insistent *pingpingping* of her statcomm's wakeup alarm jerked Ravi from sleep, throwing her into disorientation worse than any dream. She was hollow with hunger and recognized nothing about her surroundings.

"Outcast Station," she croaked, her throat dry and mouth cottony. Her brain caught up with her surroundings. "Cragrral."

She leapt to the comm and palmed into the system. "Status, BVax Scientist Cragrral."

"BVax Scientist Cragrral is resting in the quarantine zone. He has instructed that the quarantine be lifted in two station hours," the computer informed her in a clinical tone.

Those in the Q-zone must have recovered quickly once inoculated. They were probably restless and complaining even more vociferously by now.

Ravi hurried through a chem shower, grateful for the warm drying cycle. Like most humans of Terran stock, she preferred water, but stations with communal baths limited water showers to once a station week. After changing into a fresh BVax uniform, she paused before the mirror in her quarters. Looking back at her was a BVax Scientist who had managed her first E-Rep onstation.

"How about that," she murmured, touching the BVax patch. Her smile lingered as she made her way to deck six, munching on a protein ration bar as she went.

Hours after she'd relieved Cragrral, she stood up to stretch. Most of the patients were released from quarantine and the paperwork begun, and nearly another station's day had passed. Ravi noticed that more station personnel were giving her nods or smiles of greeting. Either Cragrral's words, or her satisfactory performance in the E-Rep, had gained her a modicum of respect.

Ravi basked in the moment, knowing it couldn't last, given where she was from. It never did, so she'd learned to enjoy the brief periods of approbation whenever they came.

"On call, you are," Cragrral said as he came out of his quarters in mid-afternoon. They had both filed their paperwork on the E-Rep. "And to your postponed meeting with Station Admin, you must be going, but after, for dinner we will meet. Then, singing we will be, if not needed. Soon enough, tomorrow is, for beginning your research work."

Startled, Ravi wondered how Cragrral had figured out how eager she was to get started.

He smiled and nodded. "Would be my choice, first, as well. Long I won't be here, however, so singing we will be."

"It will be a pleasure." Ravi said, and meant every word. She hadn't sung with other people in so long. She'd hadn't been home in eight years. Which meant she hadn't sung anywhere but in empty bays, in her quarters, or under her breath since then.

"Is my uniform correct?" she asked him about an hour later, after knocking on his open lab door. She turned around to show her perfectly pressed BVax uniform, tucked into her older, but still serviceable and polished, station boots.

"Do BVax proud, you do," he replied, his dark eyes serious. "This is routine, so you do not need luck wishes. However," he added, "you will do better with them, so I give you luck wishes for your luck jar."

"Thank you," Ravi managed around a lump in her throat. She double-checked the route to deck nineteen, the station admin level, and got there ten minutes early. Another humanoid, an enormous male with pale lavender skin, waited in the reception area with her. He gave her a nod of greeting as she sat down, his eyes resting briefly on her hair. She, on the other hand, was fascinated with the full-color holo as well as life size posters of a massive plant in an elegant pot.

"That's lovely," she commented, noting the plate-sized orange blossoms and the fat, pollen-filled stamens inside. She didn't recognize the plant at all. It wasn't like anything in the lexicons she'd studied. "Is it a hybrid?"

"It is. We received export clearance through this station." The man smiled, and the expression gave his otherwise bland visage a disturbing hint of mania. "These blossoms have healing properties," he claimed, leaning forward to touch the holo with a fat, caressing finger. Jewels winked on every digit, and the nail of the finger he used to slide down the virtual petals was painted a revolting shade of puce, totally at odds with the glory of the orange petals.

"Kept in the sleeping chamber, they prevent nightmares, clear the sinuses, and improve the complexion. Used in mines, they cleanse the air of heavy metals, and pull excess CO_2 from the air. Protean has an excess of both."

"Truly?" Despite the man's disturbing expressions and appearance, anything claiming to heal was of interest. "What is its origin?"

"Protean Mining Colony, at the edge of Drachan space. The main plants grow in the mine shafts. Miners there never suffer from iron sickness or nickel poisoning. Protean mines produce erban ore as well, and no miners on Protean have ever gotten the erban ore sores. This hybrid won't propagate, as per the Federated Colonies galactic science laws for hybrids, but are hardy for several years before they need to be replaced."

"Fascinating. Has BVax had a chance to study it?"

The man drew back with a hiss. "BVax? No." He seemed to suddenly realize she wore a uniform and drew back even further when he noted her insignia. "Inspect it no further. BVax may not have it."

"No offense intended, citizen," Ravi stuttered, hands

raised in the universal gesture of release. She was taken aback by this completely different prejudice. Usually it was directed at her personally. This was for her employer.

The man made a series of grunting noises, which her translator either didn't know or didn't have a correlation for. "None taken, youngster." He finally spoke again, still grunting softly in between phrases. "I'm sorry to alarm you. I've had no good experience with your company."

"My apologies. This is my first posting."

"I recommend you do your time and get out." The words snapped with stiff distaste.

The receptionist came back at that point to call the man in to see the station administrator. "They are thieves, those BVaxers, the lot of them. They want to keep everything good for themselves," he muttered as he rose to collect the holo and his paperwork. Ravi was perversely offended that he hadn't included her with BVax, but didn't think it was politic to say so.

"Consider Protean, if you are a good researcher." He growled the words, passing a connect-chit to her as he passed. "We always need good help."

The receptionist rolled his eyes behind the man's back, and Ravi suppressed a smile.

Twenty minutes later, the miner's representative exited, looking satisfied, without holo or poster. The station administrator had apparently liked the miner because when the receptionist showed Ravi into the office, the holo of the plant was on an ornate stand by a lighted panel made to resemble a window, behind the desk.

"Administrator Cractor Bashink, this is incoming BVax Scientist Ravinisha Trentham." The receptionist announced her, then shot Ravi an encouraging smile as he ducked out the doors.

"Ah, our new BVax representative." Bashink's voice was high and scratchy and instantly grated on Ravi's nerves. He made the formal hand gesture of greeting, one that didn't require touch, and retreated behind his desk.

Ravi hated this kind of interview. It usually turned into a one-sided commentary on McKeonite politics.

Instead, the administrator surprised her. He plunked his thin, angular frame into the chair as if he weighed as much as the miner's representative and said, "Glad to have a human in the position again."

That took her aback. Most planets had moved past the human-only prejudice centuries ago. Too many good things came from other species and planets.

"Yes, sir." Nonplussed, Ravi kept it to that.

"Sit, sit." He waved her to a visitor's chair. "How was your first E-Rep, eh?"

"Per protocol, sir," she replied. "BVax Cragrral is effective and efficient. We handled it without incident."

"Excellent. I'm sure that will be a constant with a human at the helm. Getting settled in?"

"Yes, sir. It's a good posting."

He laughed, a sort of braying sound. "It's the armpit of the Federated Colonies Galactic Space Service, young lady. You'll move on long before any of the rest of us, so don't be smug."

"Yes, sir." Ravi nearly choked on that idea. She'd probably grow old and die at her post on Outcast Station, given where she was from. "I mean, no sir."

He brayed again. "Exactly. So. Not much to do or say about all this BVax stuff. You know what you know, and do what you do." He waved a dismissive hand toward his cluttered desk. "I'll handle the other stuff. Hopefully we won't have any emergencies that require you to take over from Shupe or me, and I won't have any complaints I have to investigate. Right?"

"Yes, sir." Administrator Bashink was going to think she was an idiot since all she'd said to him was yes, sir or no, sir. "We'll hope both our terms here are uneventful, and bring us both merit with the GSS."

"Merit? Well, that would be good. More likely you than me. So, if that's all, Trentham, we've done our duty and met, let's both get back to our jobs, eh?"

She stood and, taking a clue from his earlier actions, made the gesture for happy leave taking. It didn't require touching either. "Thank you, Administrator, for your welcome. May you have a prosperous term."

He gave her a sharp look, as if to check that she wasn't being flippant, then laughed again. "You too, BVax Trentham. You too."

He rose, and gave a half bow, a courtesy she hadn't expected. She returned it and pivoted to the doors to take her leave. They opened with alacrity, which meant the receptionist was listening at the door. Not much had been said, though, so Ravi wasn't worried about the eavesdropper.

"Station Manager Shupe was hoping to have a word," the young man said with a bland expression. "Do you know the way to CentraComm?"

Ravi consulted her statcomm. "Deck fourteen,

purple, so down six levels. Anything else I should know?"

"It's really noisy," the young man said. "Enjoy."

"Thanks." She got onto the empty car, and as she turned to face the doors, the young man waved. As the doors closed, she waved back.

Ravi hardly felt the drop of the personnel car until it slowed to bring her level with CentraComm. She was busy pondering what it meant that the man had waved. Had he meant to be friendly?

How odd.

To her further amazement, Ravi got several welcoming nods as she walked down the corridors. It pleased her tremendously and helped her weather the equal number of more familiar hostile stares. The admin receptionist was right, it was incredibly noisy. Most of the machinery that ran the station had control points in CentraComm. Engineering offices, repair and refit offices, mechanical systems offices. Why they should be so noisy, she had no idea, but when she arrived at the reception desk, she had to raise her voice to be heard.

"Station Manager Shupe asked me to report in. I'm the new BVax rep." Ravi touched the insignia on her uniform to ensure the older woman understood her.

"Trentham," the woman shouted back. "Yeah, she said you'd be coming." She stood and leaned over the desk, pointing down the corridor. "Down there, where the fake wood starts, that's the station manager's office. There's another assistant, like me. Tell her what you told me. She's got the same notes."

"Okay, thank you." The noise ebbed a little, so Ravi's voice seemed unnaturally loud. "Sorry."

"No worries.," the woman said in a more normal tone. "Happens all the time. This area wasn't designed for all the equipment we test here, so there's no way to insulate the sound."

At the wood doors—visibly faux, as the assistant had indicated—Ravi caught sight of another assistant disappearing into a cubby behind a desk. Ravi waited and the woman reappeared within minutes.

"Oh, sorry. Here to see Q?"

"Yes. BVax Trentham."

"Oh, right. Hi. Welcome to Paradise Station. I'll let Q know you're here."

The meeting with Quiana Shupe was as briefer than her time with StatAdmin Bashink, but more pleasant. Stationmaster Shupe was a tall, angular woman with mink-brown hair and equally brown skin. Her snapping blue eyes were, therefore, striking. Ravi and Shupe bonded immediately over the stationmaster's collection of decorative stone carvings from around the galaxy. One in particular caught Ravi's interest, and she asked about it.

"Drachan, and very rare," the stationmaster said. Shupe suddenly seemed nervous when Ravi asked more about it. So nervous, in fact, that Shupe shifted that statue to the back of the collection. "The Drachans don't give them up to just anyone. Religious reasons."

"The stone is so deeply colored." Ravi marveled at it, even as she recognized Shupe's discomfort. She didn't want to get off on the wrong foot with the stationmaster, but didn't know how to redirect. And the carving was most curious.

"It's one of a kind," Quiana said briskly, then,

thankfully, changed the subject. "Everything okay in your quarters? You're finding everything you need?"

"Yes, BVax Cragrral has been most helpful in showing the station to me."

"He's a good one, that Tilden." Shupe sat down and waved Ravi to a specific chair. She noted that Shupe arranged it so Ravi was seated with her back to the collection. "We've been incredibly lucky to have someone of his talents, and yours." Shupe leaned back and the springs of her well-worn chair creaked ominously. Shupe ignored the sound. "He was fresh as a new hatched chick when he came to us, and Tilden. Tilden's not one of the Guild planets in high favor at the moment."

"Really?"

"Trade stuff mostly. Politics. But I knew we wouldn't keep him. He's too good, and that kind of thing, the trade stuff, changes like the wind." Shupe pointed a calloused finger at Ravi. "And I was right, wasn't I? Off he's going to work with somebody famous. But now, we got you."

"Yes." Ravi kept it simple. That was always best.

Surprisingly, Shupe cocked her head to one side. "That's it? Yes?"

"Yes. I am, obviously, here."

"Cragrral says you're really good," Shupe persisted.

"I'm grateful for his praise." Ravi wasn't sure what answers Shupe was looking for.

"Uh-huh. Are you?"

Puzzled, Ravi reviewed the conversation but couldn't figure out the question. "Am I what?"

"Good at what you do, at being a BVaxer? Smart

about disease and plague vectors and all that?" Shupe crossed her arms, her posture challenging.

Ravi sat up a little straighter. "I am very good."

Shupe nodded. She stared at Ravi for another minute before nodding again, then relaxed into her chair. "Figured. I know you're McKeonite, so quit worrying about what I think about that. Don't care. Old news, and stupid to keep bringin' it up. That said, I trust Cragrral. I didn't figure you'd be stupid. Stupid don't get a full station posting, even a backass station like Paradise. Then again, I didn't dare hope for top smarts, not here. Figured Cragrral was a fluke."

"No, they don't. They end up in research groups in the Malay Sector," Ravi said, a wry twist to her lips. She'd thought she was going to have to finally take a posting there herself. Everyone thought Outcast Station was forgotten and isolated and filled with misfits. It had nothing on the Malay Sector, at least for scientists.

Shupe threw back her head and laughed. "I've heard about that. It's like a hamster wheel, right? Lots of white coats filling test tubes and passing time recreating old research to check for variations. Like watching space gas expand."

Ravi nodded, liking the stationmaster more and more. "Yes, exactly."

"So you're here instead," Shupe said. "Good. I got caught in a Protocol One before. On Xltttratttt in League space. It was Rosen's Falling Sickness. Took twenty percent of the population before they even agreed to let BVax on the planet. Another ten percent died before BVax got the titers done and vaccinated everyone. Lost a few more, even then."

The silence thickened as Ravi waited for Shupe to continue. When she didn't, Ravi broke the silence.

"I'm so sorry. You lost friends." There was no other reason for the hard lines that carved their way onto the other woman's face as the memories surfaced. Ravi recognized grief more easily than most.

"Yes." They sat for a few more heartbeats with that acknowledgement between them. Shupe took a deep breath. "So. That's why I always want to meet the new BVaxers." The expression on her face eased and finally she smiled. "You'll do, BVax Trentham. You'll do."

"Thank you, Stationmaster."

Shupe laughed again. "You're welcome. And I mean that. You need something, you let me know." That seemed to be the end of the interview, because Shupe rose, standing in front of her collection, blocking the view toward them until Ravi thanked her and turned to walk out the door.

"I'll be sorry to see Cragrral go," the stationmaster said as she walked Ravi to the lift. "But you're most welcome, never doubt it." She briskly shook Ravi's hand, as Brad Carruthers had done. "Anything you need, let me know. We support BVax all the way."

"Thank you."

Bemused by the mix of defensiveness and welcome, Ravi made her way back to her shared quarters.

Cragrral was beaming. "Went well, it did. I can see this."

Relieved that it was behind her, but pleased with the outcome, Ravi nodded. "It really did."

"Good. Then to dinner we will go, then to singing. Shall we?" Cragrral once again motioned for her to precede him.

They left their quarters together with no thought but for dinner and music.

####

The identiplate on the BVax quarters was easy. He wouldn't try the one on the supply room or the labs. He didn't need it.

"Filthy McKeonite and that damn furry Tilden," he grumbled, propping the door so it didn't shut behind him. It took mere moments to dump the McKeonite's luggage. He'd get to the trunks she'd left in the common area last. He scattered her things, and smashed the crystal figures she'd set on the desk. With a laugh, he slopped machine oil out of its container, onto her bedding.

McKeonites were so despised, the marshals might question him, but he already had another mechtech ready as an alibi. That made him laugh harder.

It was fun to destroy things.

He was twisting the seal on the second container of oil when he sensed a movement behind him. He spun in place, then relaxed when it wasn't the ugly McKeonite, or worse, a marshal behind him.

"What are you doing here?" he said, suddenly nervous as he realized who it was. Why would the big boss be *here?*

"You draw too much attention to yourself, Rankin. Negotiations are too delicate for you to be exposing us. This…" The other man looked around at the destruction. "This was stupid."

Rankin looked around at the oil-soaked bedding, the smashed figurines, the torn papers, and laughed.

"Nah," he said, trying for nonchalance. He'd only met the big boss once, when he was recruited. "No one will know it's me, and besides, no one gives a damn about a McKeonite."

"They *will* know it's you. You made a scene. You're the first person they'll look at. And she's not some random McKeonite no one will care about, she's BVax. Too. Much. Attention." The other man spaced the words deliberately. "I can't have that."

"B'Landruv is gonna say we were together drinkin' and watchin' king-beast racing at Marco's all night. I'm covered. But you're not." He hooked a thumb toward the darkened doorway with a sly smile. "You're the one who can't get caught. You better go, pronto. I gotta finish up and get outta here, and so do you.

"No. You're done." The words were decisive.

Belatedly, Rankin remembered that the big boss liked to do his own dirty work.

Rankin spun around, but sharp claws scored his neck. Blood gushed and spilled. Shock and betrayal faded with his vision, and he fell, dying, onto the crystal shards littering the floor.

CHAPTER THREE

"Stop," Cragrral ordered as Ravi's hand hovered over the identiplate.

"What? Problem?"

"The door unsecured, is."

Ravi looked more closely and saw what Cragrral had. There was a thick bolt propping the door open. It was placed in such a way that you wouldn't see the opening if you glanced down the corridor, nor even notice until you were right up on it.

"The marshal, I'm calling." Cragrral used his statcomm to page Brad. Before Brad arrived, however, two other marshals strode down the corridor.

"Problem Cragrral?" The first man, a beefy Oltonian with faintly green skin, looked from Cragrral to Ravi and back.

"Greetings, Marshal Trendte. Meet BVax Trentham, who taking over from me will be," Cragrral said first. "Trouble we had, earlier with a maintenance tech. Now, the door unsecured is."

The other marshal grunted. "Stupid for that tech to hit your quarters. We'll look right at him if there's damage."

Ravi's gut clenched. "I'm a McKeonite. This kind of thing has happened before. There were no repercussions."

The second marshal, whose nametag read ma'Gonese, shook her head. "Yeah, I heard." She didn't delineate whether she'd heard that Ravi was from McKeon, or whether she'd heard about the tech. "That's stupid, but stupid is routine 'round here, so let's take a look." She moved forward, nodding at Ravi. "If you'll step back, we'll see what there is to see."

Ravi noticed ma'Gonese's long, smoothly furred tail twitch as the marshal moved to the door. The cinnamon colored fur on the tail matched the long, cinnamon colored braid of hair that was coiled in a tight spiral at the back of the marshal's head.

Ma'Gonese pulled a container from a cargo pocket and covered her short, smooth-skinned muzzle with her hand as she sprayed a fixative onto the plate and the wall beside the door.

"For prints." She pointed to the wall. "You'd be amazed how many idiots we catch because they lean one hand on the wall there while they fiddle with getting past the locks. It'll give us a layer for each set of prints."

Three layers formed on the plate, and several more on the wall. ma'Gonese peeled off the quickset gels one after another. She slid the print plates into a flat container from another pocket, slapped on a seal, and she and Trendte both initialed it.

"Good." Trendte's crisp tone and nonjudgmental expression made Ravi believe he too might be fair. "Let's see what's up."

ma'Gonese hadn't shrunk from Ravi being a McKeonite, but she'd not looked favorably at Ravi either. Still, neutral was better than antagonistic.

The moment the door opened, ma'Gonese hissed. "Dead."

"What?" Ravi turned to Cragrral. "What does she mean?"

"She smells death inside." Cragrral's hackles had risen on his neck and his lip curled up to display his fangs. He put an arm across the corridor, keeping her close. "I smell no other, but behind me, you should stay. For safety."

Ravi shivered. What had someone left in their quarters? Her heart sank. She'd had such a lovely evening, singing with Cragrral and Brad Carruthers. She hadn't had anyone to sing with in…forever. Now this.

The second marshal, Trendte, came back out. "Your quarters are the ones on the left?" he asked Ravi.

She nodded.

"There's a dead mechtech in there. Looks like he was in the process of trashing your things and someone killed him for it." The words were blunt, straightforward and expressionless.

Shock coursed through her. "D-dead?" she stuttered. "But why?"

"No idea." He turned from her to Cragrral. "One of you want to see if it's the same mechtech who gave you two a hard time?"

The Tilden shook his head in the negative and laid a restraining hand on Ravi's shoulder. "No. Leave identification to his supervisor, will we. Hard pressed, would I be, curse markers not to put on his corpse for what he has done, if him it is." Cragrral looked even angrier than he had when he'd confronted the mechtech in the corridor. His hackles were fully up now and his guttural growl was such that even Marshal ma'Gonese gave him a wide berth. As senior officer, he did, however, look in long enough to confirm that only Ravi's quarters had been damaged.

Boot steps echoed in the corridor and Marshal Carruthers and an investigative team with a gurney arrived.

"This is ugly trouble," Brad said, shaking his head. "I'm sorry it's been heaped on you, BVax Trentham and BVax Cragrral, especially on the heels of an E-Rep."

"A pleasant evening it was, until this," Cragrral snarled. "Many of the things of BVax Trentham destroyed, are. Reparation must be made. Uniforms replaced, cleansed, and repaired, must be. Destroyed, her treasures are, according to Trendte." The growl from Cragrral's chest rumbled through the corridor, and the investigative techs plastered themselves against the wall, trying to be very small and very still. "Base and unmannerly. *Disrespect* has been paid to BVax Trentham."

Uh-oh. It was Ravi's first thought. Those two syllables kept on repeating in her mind. Tilden were, for the most part, a sedate race. Respect and peace were the two watchwords of their culture. However, if you were disrespectful, or you disturbed the peace...well. Tilden were the apex predators of their planet for a reason.

Ravi wracked her brain for how to respond, to diffuse.

"Cragrral, you speak the truth." Marshal Carruthers

made no move to soothe Cragrral's mood, but spoke calmly and succinctly. "Whoever did this, their pay will be docked to replace all of BVax Trentham's items. What can be cleaned will be. What must be replaced, if replacement is possible, will be."

He turned to Ravi. "Of the things in your quarters, what would you consider irreplaceable?"

A weight settled on her chest. "Nothing. I learned a long time ago never to carry that which is irreplaceable."

His features set in anger, like carved stone. "This has happened before?"

"At every job I've had, and at every school I've ever attended."

That bald statement rang in the silence.

The Tilden's growl intensified.

"I agree, Cragrral," Brad said, his voice tight and his mouth in a thin line of fury. "It won't happen again."

While she appreciated the sentiment, Ravi had heard it before.

"Thank you for the thought," was the only response she mustered. She couldn't tell him she believed him, or that she thought it wouldn't happen again. She didn't.

Good intentions had yet to keep her or her belongings safe. She'd taken every self-defense class available to avoid beatings, or worse. Nothing had kept her from humiliating scenes, embarrassing or dangerous pranks, and generally being shunned and ostracized.

Carruthers tapped fiercely on his statcomm, as if the pressure would transfer some of his anger to the pad. "There are two clean and ready crew quarters on deck twelve. Marshal Pantagul will meet you there. Pod 5752. Go up and get some sleep, both of you. This is going to take a while."

Cragrral, still growling low in his throat, gestured for Ravi to proceed down the corridor. It was all she could do to walk sedately with the tall, menacing predator at her back. Even telling herself that he meant *her* no harm didn't stop the atavistic fear of having a toothy, growling carnivore behind her.

Ravi was surprised by the smile from the human marshal waiting for them. "BVax Trentham," she said, "sorry to meet you under these circumstances." She gestured to 5752's identiplate. "It's already set for temp login."

When Ravi activated the plate, the marshal turned to Cragrral and repeated the process. "Sorry for the trouble." She held up a hand and crossed two of her six digits. "Here's hoping you get plenty of rest and we don't need you until this is resolved."

"From your mouth, it is," Cragrral said, the growl finally dying away. "To the ears of the Universe being heard."

The marshal nodded and, bidding them another good night, strode away.

"Ravi, to be sleeping. I, first shift will take tomorrow if necessary, checking all labwork and filing. See you in the BVax research area, when waking you are." He shook a long, clawed finger at her. "Not sooner. Sleep until you wake."

Ravi mustered up a smile. "I thank you, Cragrral. I enjoyed singing with you. It was one of the finest moments of my life."

Before he managed a response, she turned and went into the empty, sterile quarters, and cried.

####

"This is a mess," ma'Gonese stated as Brad signed off on the body's removal. Hands on hips, tail still wrapped around her thigh, the Gallupian marshal showed her distaste with a curled lip and another hiss. ma'Gonese was both supervising the collection of evidence and attempting to process the cabin for cleaning. The lubricant the dead man had tossed about made footing dangerous, and the crystalline shards on the floor had already penetrated one of the law enforcement tech's boots, necessitating a visit to the medstation. Now, the LEO tech's blood was having to be isolated from the other crime scene evidence.

"The only blessing in the whole forsaken pile of pil-droppings is that she'd covered the bunk with the thermal blanket, so the bunk itself is dry." Ma'Gonese gestured to the built-in desk. "Oh, and he hadn't yet opened the drawers where her data files, cubes and crystals are racked. Whatever she stored there is fine."

Brad's tension abated, marginally. "I'm not going to have this kind of harassment of any statcit on my watch. No one deserves it, especially not an innocent scientist trying to do her work." Like Cragrral, he didn't give a good damn about her origins. The fact that Ravi was soon going to be their sole senior BVax officer made it imperative she be protected.

"I don't want to think what would happen to a ship or station without its BVax officer." ma'Gonese's ears flattened against her skull.

"Yeah," Brad shuddered. "Outcast Station has

enough issues without having BVax pull its rep due to harassment. They'd have every right to, if we can't protect her."

As humankind colonized the stars, it was BVax that kept the population from being decimated by plagues and diseases. Any first-contact situation with new species or bio-material was fraught with peril, and not only for humans. The naïve notion from early space travel that germs didn't jump to a "foreign" or alien host had been decisively proven wrong by the initial Superium Space Plague. For centuries now, BVax had managed to keep everyone as safe as possible, so it wasn't an option to have their BVax rep in fear for her life.

"Part of me wishes they'd never made a McKeonite a BVaxer, but if she was the best person for the job, then she was the best for the job." He abhorred the continued bigotry toward a planet whose citizens were guilty merely by association.

"The biggest issue is their distinctive markings. It makes them readily identifiable and therefore easily targeted. Otherwise, the McKeon incident would have faded into obscurity, despite their government." ma'Gonese shrugged. "Those neck markings and hair color are distinctive."

"Yeah, too distinctive," Brad muttered, pausing as he caught sight of something amidst the shards on the floor. "Now this is interesting." He showed the broken-off tip of a metal claw sheath to ma'Gonese. "Would this correspond to the death wound on the throat?"

She held out an evidence bag. Once she sealed the claw sheath tip in, the bag began its analysis. Within seconds, the readout showed the composition of the tip—primarily stensteel but augmented with pavnium—and the fact that there was no biological residue inside the item.

"So whoever it was wore sealant under the sheaths?" ma'Gonese posited. "Or their claws where sterilized before they put the sheaths on."

She extended her own claws, held them up to the clear side of the bag. "Too small for mine."

"Good to know," Brad said with a smile. "Then again, you were with Trendte, so you're in the clear."

"Always wise to be sure, Marshal Carruthers. McKeon isn't the only planet whose people are persecuted. For many years, if you had these—" She flashed out all ten claws, with gems winking on several of them. "Or this—" She pointed to her thick tail. "You were considered a lesser being by some in the GSS."

"The GSS evened out its hiring four decades ago. But yes," he said when he saw her protest forming, "I get your point." Like ma'Gonese, he knew the pro-diversity quotas and even-hiring practices were working. However, there was a reason that he, the humanoid, was in the minority on Outcast Station. Non-humanoids were frequently shunted off to lesser posts on human-origin stations and planets, no matter how good they were at their jobs.

"Just so. In time, McKeon will be known as another humanoid subspecies and all will fade. Not fast enough," ma'Gonese added. "But it will fade." She smiled, and her elongated canines gleamed. "Maybe this one will help it along. I have a good feeling about her."

"Good. I do as well," Brad agreed. "Now, let's holo

this, and get maintenance in here."

They used the holo reconstruction unit to get the positioning of the mechtech's body and ran three scenarios before the holo gave them the most likely.

"He's facing the desk, getting ready to dump oil on it, and someone comes at him from behind." The image of the tech pivoted. "He turns. Slash, slash, and he's down and dead."

"Two slashes, from an upward angle. That's interesting. A hesitation," Brad interpreted the reading. "Maybe two arms on the right side?"

"Huh. Possibly. There are a few Reclands on the station. We'll check their whereabouts for the attack. The other option is an unfamiliarity with the strength of the claw sheaths," ma'Gonese offered. "Why else would you break one so easily? They have some tensile strength, but these aren't built for serious fighting, they're for fashion. This particular type are for creatures with non-retractable claws."

"How do you get that?"

"The tip is pavnium, but the stensteel base is probably from Marrakesh VI. It's poorly refined, and a lot of people are allergic. I'd say these were meant to be purely decorative rather than having any defined weapons function."

Brad nodded, but said, "And yet, they functioned just right for this."

It was ma'Gonese's turn to grimace. "Maybe that was the point. Use claw tips to turn our direction to a clawed being. This type might fit over humanoid hands."

"They'd be unwieldy," Brad argued. "Too awkward for most humanoids." He held his hand out as a measure.

The claw tips would have engulfed his fingertip to the first knuckle, but been uncomfortable on his overlarge hands.

"Yes, but if you only need it for one strike—" ma'Gonese pantomimed a downward slash. "—then you don't need them to be particularly strong or close fitting."

"Good point." Brad walked around the frozen holo, noting that the slash marks looked dark and real on the image. "There is that hesitation and second strike, though."

"Yes, another point toward it being a humanoid wearing claw sheaths to direct attention to a clawed being. Most clawed beings have hunted. We have no hesitation when it's time to strike."

Brad nodded again. "True. But if she's the target, why kill this guy? She wouldn't have been in here destroying her own stuff. In this case, she was in plain view in the deck nine mess, singing with me and with Cragrral and the rest of the deck nine group. Why not leave her quarters alone and kill this guy elsewhere? Then she's the first one we look at."

"Implicate Cragrral? He's got claws."

Brad thought on that for a few moments. "Possibly. But again, he was with us, and in a highly visible place." He hated the idea of it, but it could be. Neither Ravi nor Cragrral were particularly popular at the moment. Ravi for being new and a McKeonite, Cragrral for supporting her so vehemently.

There were also those who believed BVax held too much control over GSS in general, and station policies in particular.

"I guess we'll have to see what happens next."

"You should never have let her see it. Now what do we do?"

"Nothing. She doesn't know anything and more, doesn't care. She's young, mid-way through her third decade. She's a plague chaser, nothing more."

"She was interested in it."

They stood amidst the darkened cargo storage bay, with product lined up like soldiers around them. "In a few station weeks, we'll ship 'em out. No harm, no foul, and no one the wiser."

"Okay, okay, if you say so. I'm nervous, that's all."

"Stop it. Get nervous, you screw up. Settle down and do the job. Then we get paid. Just like always."

Clicking the locks they left the cargo area, and went their separate ways.

The planet was a surprise.

"This is…different." Ravi didn't want to criticize, but the planet's barren aspect shocked her. At the spaceport, the soil was volcanic, a dark and glittery gravel, with very little growing to relieve the stark black and grey. Beyond the boring, square plascrete buildings, lay the town of Micah's Junction. It was green and had trees and flowers where the spaceport was stark, but the landscape's drama lay beyond the town. Dramatic, steep mountains rose high into the sky. The jagged rims of the towering, extinct volcanoes and the rugged tops of other rocky peaks were covered with a rime of frost or snow. It was fall onplanet, but the breeze was still warm.

"Do they really ski in these mountains?"

"Yes, skiing, they do, and boarding and other snow sports, popular are. Water sports, too, popular are," Cragrral said, punctuating that with a broad gesture toward the rocky cliffs. She knew they overlooked a darkly churning sea that wasn't visible from where they stood. "Much wildlife viewing, there is, as well. And gliding, from the cliffs, many are. Serious sport."

Cragrral raised his head and sighed. Ravi caught the scent of a salty sea and wondered if that was what he was reacting to.

"Do you like to glide? Or hike?" she asked, wanting to continue the conversation. Reading about all of this on her trip out didn't make it as real as seeing the place and imagining what Cragrral had described.

Cragrral showed his many-fanged grin. "Hunt is my favorite. Lizard they grow here, large. Very tasty. Hunting preserves, they have, near the quartzite mines on the other continent, and on this continent near the bronzium mines."

"A lizard? The reptiloid or lizard-like lifeforms on my planet aren't edible." She winced at bringing up McKeon's World, but relaxed when Cragrral took no notice. "What does this lizard look like?"

"In the flitter, I will show you pictures," he replied, waving her toward the hired hovercar. "Come. To the farms we must be going."

At a local business, they left the dusty and antiquated hovercar and picked up the on-planet flitter assigned to them. It wasn't in much better shape than the hovercar, but it was definitely cleaner.

With each transaction, Cragrral stood watchfully by, waiting for any slight directed her way. He was practically bristling with aggression when one of the mechanics looked too long at Ravi's neck, noting her distinctive McKeonite coloring.

Ravi touched his arm. "Let's go."

With a last glance at the mechanic, who beat a hasty retreat, Cragrral joined her in the flitter. He took the controls. "Fly the return, will you. Shuttle license I know you have."

She smiled. "I do. Now," she said, "I want to see that lizard."

Ravi accessed the scans of Paradise's pekomodo lizards, noting their black and gold scales. "They're very prettily patterned."

"Very dangerous," Cragrral commented, putting the flitter on auto-nav long enough to point a clawed finger at the lizard's feet. "Claws, poison have. Plus, teeth are serrated and angled back, your flesh to be tearing if catch you, they do."

"Nice," Ravi commented, with dry sarcasm, and Cragrral chuckled. "Any other fun surprises?"

"Avians," he said. "Rocs they are named. Predators with wide wingspan, tooth-edged beaks. Very menacing." He made a snapping sound with his teeth. "Chomp you, they will."

She glanced at him and caught the glint of humor in his eyes. "Ah, yes. I'll make a note to avoid the chompers."

"Good, good," he added, chuckling again. The sound

was warm and friendly, and Ravi decided that Cragrral was becoming more of a friend with each passing day.

It was also obvious that he was brilliant, and not solely in his capacity for research. In the greenhouses and breeding farms, she got to see the well-designed housing for the hybrid geese and makker birds from which they produced vaccines when needed. Despite every technological advance, no synthetic had yet replaced avian eggs for producing mass quantity vaccines for humans.

Ravi also got a thorough education in the operation of the biodomes and farm machinery from her companion, something no course ever thought to teach.

####

After an amazing day of touring, Cragrral mentioned going to one of the port bars for dinner, but she demurred. It had been such a good day, Ravi didn't want to spoil it with another incident. Spaceports weren't as civilized as stations, and she didn't want to have to pull out any of her martial skills, nor see Cragrral's teeth or claws in action, and said so.

"Correct, you probably are," Cragrral agreed. "Food is better somehow, however, on planets. Still, it is rib-meat night in our mess."

"You think with your stomach, my friend," she said on a laugh.

"I do. I am a Tilden, after all." He patted his midsection and made a slurping sound. "Ribs a favorite, are."

Laughing, they returned to their flitter.

"Thank you for introducing me to everyone, showing me the ropes." Cragrral had also signed her in on all the systems and changed the primary contact record for any disease issues or problems to her name. Everyone she'd met, from the Dome Manager, Merka Chalmers, to Stock Master Leila Masters-Bujokutan, were pleasant and welcoming. Not one of them even glanced at her neck or commented on her origins.

After such a great day, Ravi simply wanted to get back onstation in one piece and savor the lovely day.

"Is the whole planet this sparsely settled?" Ravi asked as she took the controls and flew them back toward the spaceport. "I thought they grew a type of rice and had buffle herds here. That was in the briefing materials, anyway."

"Have them all, they do, both crice and buffle. Some things native here, are growing as well. Most, however, grow best away from the spaceport. Come again, we will, and go out to a big land station—called a demense—before leaving I am. See, you will, the variety."

Cragrral pointed out various retailers and city landmarks as they came in to land. Low single and double housing units, stores, and other businesses stretched in rows down several curving streets. Beyond the port, barracks and various Galactic Services headquarters rose in multiple three- and four-story buildings but, other than the port, they were the highest buildings she saw.

"The agro and mining stations," Cragrral said, waving at the landscape outside the windows. "Agro, in fertile areas are. Large, some of them, in the valleys are.

They farm. Produce crops and animals for food. Five resorts, there are. Skiing, the largest is. Next largest for water-based sports and events, is. Mountain sports, mostly, though, are taking the lead. Mining, in the southern continent is, mostly. The planet is not entirely self-sufficient. Soon, though, it will be its planet debt paying off. More it will be able to accomplish in the Colonial Council."

"We're a long way from the core worlds and the GSS and Colonial Council's power," Ravi murmured, glad of it, since it meant less oversight, and fewer who cursed her McKeonite heritage. They continued the conversation as they reclaimed their hovercar and headed back to the port.

"Difficult it is, yes, to be in the outer areas." Cragrral spoke slowly, as if considering the lack of council power out in this outer arm of the galaxy. "Difficult it is, to police, so Brad says. Smuggling, there is."

"Here?" Ravi was surprised. Paradise didn't seem like it would be a hotbed for smuggling. She glanced out the windows of the flitter. From this view, it didn't seem like a hotbed for anything at all, really.

"Here, everywhere, smuggling there is. Still," Cragrral said, holding his BVax ID out to the spaceport base guard. "Find good cures from the smugglers, we sometimes do."

"And, more often, we get plagues from them. They don't take precautions," Ravi retorted, enjoying the start of another debate. Cragrral was the first being since her early college days who'd treated her as a colleague, simply another scientist with whom to converse. "They can keep their few cures, as far as I'm concerned. There is more trouble to be found with them than help."

"Right, you probably are," Cragrral agreed, with a genial flash of his fangs. "But doing badly, we would have been, without the cure from Ulauu, provided by smugglers as it was."

"One instance. If BVax had been there quicker, we wouldn't have needed it."

"A point, you are making, but disagreeing, I am," Cragrral replied, equally delighted with their conversation. They continued to debate the value of smuggled vaccines all the way to the shuttle.

"So, changing the subject am I," Cragrral said, when they'd begun to reiterate their respective viewpoints. "Think you, that progressing will be the latest research on the Minotaur plague?"

She was about to reply when a cargo tech appeared at their seats and bowed. He asked if Cragrral would be willing to assist him. "We need an extra hand," the man said, smiling up at the tall Tilden. "We're short a cargotech, which doesn't matter to the shuttle run, but I don't quite have the heft for a big agro package we got and it'll throw us off schedule if we wait for a servidrone or another cargo tech. With you being here so early, I can get it loaded if you'll help."

"Help, happy I am, to provide," Cragrral replied. To Ravi, he said, "Right back I will be, and continue arguing, we will." She laughed at that and sat down as he ducked thru the door to the cargo area.

"Coming from another trade partner, is this?" she heard Cragrral ask as he and the cargotech vanished through the hold door. The crew member agreed.

"Second one this week. Plants for some client on-station."

She heard Cragrral sneeze, and the cargotech said the usual, "Blessings."

The minute they cleared the door, another crew member, a small reptiloid, jumped into the seat next to her. He was a male, and a Pertard from Xlathl, judging from his neck frill.

"Quickly, I will say it, BVax Scientist Trentham. I work for two companies. This here," he indicated the station-to-planet shuttle service, "and The Company." The way he said it made the capitals evident. "There are many good extra credits in it for you if you accept supplied products and forward to The Company. We don't care who you are or where you're from," the male said, flashing its teeth and ruffling its wide, colorful neck frill. "We take care o' our own, with pride, no matter their colors." He looked around, checking for other embarking passengers. "Show o' good faith. You tell me something you need. I'll get it. And hey, I know you don't gotta worry about that mech-tech now, right? But there're others. We'll help. So, I'll find you onstation soon. Think about it. Tell me what you need, I'll make it happen. You let me know, then I'll tell you how you'll help us."

He jumped up, grabbing the upper luggage deck straps, and perched there as comfortably as he'd sat in the seat. He looked at the doors, and she heard the noise of the returning crew and Cragrral. "I'll be in touch."

He disappeared as quickly as he'd appeared, making his way to the back of the shuttle along the luggage decking, and disappearing into an aft cabin with no one the wiser.

Surprise surged inside her. Had someone overheard her talking with Cragrral about smuggling? Did Cragrral accept things for this Company? Aid smugglers?

Cragrral's arguments seemed to believe there were benefits to smuggling, even if he didn't condone it.

Cragrral sneezed again as he sat down and refastened his flight harness. "Good to be early, going back. Dinner, ready will be, for the time we arrive."

"Blessings."

"Thank you. That is a strange humanoid custom, you know."

"Yeah, I know," Ravi acknowledged, thinking furiously. Should she tell Cragrral she'd been approached by smugglers? What had the Pertard meant about receiving supplies? Should she tell the marshal? What if it was a test?

Her brain finally processed all the Pertard had said. He'd mentioned the murder, the mechtech. Did he know something? That, she really should tell the marshal about.

But how?

Uneasiness coursed through her. The comment could mean the smugglers murdered the tech to ensure her cooperation.

No. Surely not.

It was too great a risk for the mere possibility that she'd help them.

Other travelers boarded the shuttle as she pondered. Most ignored her completely. A few glanced at her hair and neck, or her BVax insignia, but none made any comment.

One newly embarked Tilden passenger engaged Cragrral in conversation. After introducing Ravi, the two males shifted to Tilden for a brief exchange.

Anger warred with bitterness in her chest as Ravi returned to her musings. Who were these smugglers, these strangers, to try and put her in their debt? If they'd killed the mechtech, that was a blood debt. She had no desire to mix with that. But was that what the Pertard was saying, or was he alluding to something else?

He'd merely said they'd protect her, not that they'd already done so.

"Quiet you are, BVax Ravi," Cragrral observed, with a yawn after the other Tilden bid them good journey and strapped in further down the row of seats.

"A lot to process," Ravi offered with a smile. She knew it sounded idiotic, but she didn't know what else to say. Part of her wanted to blurt out the whole story and see what Cragrral advised. The other, more cautious part, bid her hold her tongue. What if Cragrral already worked with this *Company*? They had to have approached him too.

She reminded herself that, as comfortable as she was with him, and as much as she liked him, Cragrral was still a stranger to her. He wasn't kith-kin or any other bond. He was friendly, but was he her friend? He seemed to be, but any McKeonite knew not to take that to heart.

The questions circled and circled like carrionbirds over a feast and she didn't know how to get out of the loop.

"A nap, I will be taking," Cragrral said, yawning again. His teeth glinted white in the shuttle's bright light. "If minding, you are not."

"No, I don't mind." It would give her time to think. He nodded and within moments was asleep.

The shuttle left the planet's gravity well with its usual lurching tug and Ravi let the g-forces hide her grimace. She wished she knew what the heck the Pertard had been hinting at when he mentioned the dead mechtech.

Ravi forced herself to set that aside and consider the offer. Any cooperation on her part with smugglers was dangerous, not to mention illegal. But notifying the marshal's service of the contact, and the wording, would draw dangerous attention.

Ravi didn't believe for a moment that the smugglers wouldn't throw her—the already suspect McKeonite—to the wolves if anything went awry. Then again, if she was damned anyway, shouldn't she get something out of the deal? It was a cynical thought, but the marshals weren't likely to follow up on a lead about a random Pertard approaching her anyway. It wasn't as if she knew the creature's name or rank. He'd had no insignia or identifying marks on his shuttle cargotech uniform. There were so many Pertards working on any given station that his planetary origin would do her no good whatsoever.

The thoughts played in her head as they docked at the station.

They arrived at deck two, disembarking through the radiation ports into the primary waiting area for the required thirty-minute wait. Cragrral's stomach growled as they sat. Others worked with statcomms or perscomms, without any concern. Ravi always wondered how people could be so nonchalant as they waited for any of hundreds of space-borne illnesses to manifest. When none did, and all passengers were cleared for the station proper, she and Cragrral made their way through the shops toward the personnel lift.

"A snack, we should be getting, to hold us 'til dinner," Cragrral said, his nostrils twitching as the scent of cooking meat wafted to them. In the way of the translator coming upon an unfamiliar term, she heard the word he said—*rassah*—as well as the closest translated equivalent, snack. Her stomach was still knotted up from the contact with the smuggler, so she demurred. What was she going to do?

"You get something if you're hungry. I'm okay for now." She caught sight of an oddity amongst the wild variety of supply shops on deck two. Flowers. It gave her an excuse to move away for a few moments, and gather her thoughts. "I want to look at the flowers."

Cragrral looked at where she'd pointed, then nodded and headed eagerly toward the small eatery with the sizzling fare.

As she made her way to the flower shop, four Pertards drove a jack toward the receiving door next to the shop. The typical large wall slot opened in the smooth surface of the wall when they keyed in a code, and they proceeded to offload several parcels, some small and two over-large ones, from the jack as a drone appeared to check in the shipment.

Even as her thoughts whirled around what to do, Ravi had to admire their efficiency. It also allowed her to see if the Pertard who'd approached her was among the stevedores. After a few minutes of watching the action, Cragrral appeared at her side. He held out a dish with slices of meat and bread on it, along with several small indented areas of the plate holding spices, sauces and something Ravi couldn't identify.

"Having some kerr with spices, will you be?" Cragrral offered the plate. It did smell good, but since she had no idea what it was, she declined. She didn't think she could eat anything anyway. Her stomach was tight, thinking about whether or not she should approach Brad with the information about the Pertard and his mention of the dead tech.

"I'm not hungry, but thank you for offering," Ravi finally responded, hoping her wording wasn't offensive.

"The flowers, are they familiar to you?" Gesturing with his claws, Cragrral indicated the parcel that was being processed by a drone at the receiving gate. "Cargo it is, from the shuttle, I helped to lift. Growing medium for new plants. Perhaps this one." He gestured to the flower. "Cleared by GSS, it has been, for sale."

The flowers in the front window of the shop were the same ones she'd seen in the holo in the statadmin's office. The bright flowers were impressive, several handspans across, with orange petals that darkened to a deep red heart where the massive stamens rested almost like a fruit in the hollow of the petals.

"I've seen one in a holo, when I met the statadmin." A luscious fragrance—fruit-laden with a hint of musk, and an oddly iron-rich blood-scent—wafted toward them. "It has a strange fragrance to me. Is it odd to you?"

Cragrral bent toward the flower, then sneezed unexpectedly. His breath shook the flower so that some of the heavy pollen floated into the air and down onto the soil. "Fragrance it has," he mock-growled, a much lighter sound but still a rumble. "Like it, I do not."

She laughed despite the doubts still circling in her mind. "Let's go, then, and get you away from it."

"I will move away, and wait, if you would like to examine it, Ravi," Cragrral offered graciously. "My dislike does not mean you need stop your perusal."

She smiled up at him, doing her best to let go of her worries. She didn't want Cragrral to see how preoccupied she was. He was an astute being and he would want to know why. If she told him, he might confirm that he worked with the smugglers and she didn't think she wanted to know that.

She almost sighed, but kept it back at the last minute. What was she thinking? Cragrral would be gone within a statmonth. What did it matter if he worked with the smugglers? What business of hers was it? And why would he even care what a McKeonite would think?

"Ravi?"

"No, it's fine, Cragrral. I'd rather get back. Still," she said as they walked away, "I've never seen anything like that flower, have you?"

They discussed hybrids as they returned to quarters. They checked incoming data reports and Cragrral showed her how to log and file all the latest incoming sector alerts. He had her seal and code the station-block sector alerts for Paradise, and send them off.

"Full day, we have had, my friend Ravi," Cragrral said, stretching his impressive length in the chair next to her. She didn't notice how big he was until he did something like that—reaching with the full length of his impressive arms toward the ceiling, extending his claws to their fullest.

"Yes, we have, Cragrral. Thank you."

Cragrral looked at her, as if he were considering saying something.

"Yes?" she said, wondering what he was holding back. He'd held something back the previous night as well, in the temporary quarters.

The cynical part of her decided he wanted to tell her something terrible, but didn't know how to add insult to injury. The more hopeful part wondered if he was going to compliment her work, or even her singing, since he was so keen on it.

"Thinking I am, of the song you mentioned. Looked it up, I did."

"A Space Pirate's Folly?" Somehow that hit a little too close to her worries, and Ravi struggled to keep suspicion from coloring her voice. Had Cragrral heard the Pertard?

"That one, yes."

"It's fun, and has a join-in chorus I think a lot of people may know. I like doing the ones that get others involved."

"Yes, as do I." He stretched again. "Going I am, to my quarters, to read the words again. Perhaps sing it, we can, tonight."

He rose and moved away without another word, leaving her oddly bereft. She mentally rebuked herself for being an idiot.

In her own quarters, she found six new casual outfits in her size and three newly arrived, in-package BVax uniforms. A note from ma'Gonese informed her that if she found anything unacceptable, to contact ma'Gonese.

It gave the marshal's codes, and a numerical receipt code if she needed a different size or color.

Sitting on her bunk, Ravi's emotions went on a rollercoaster ride.

One minute she was elated that a being other than Cragrral had reacted in a friendly manner. Cragrral seemed blind to her origin. Ma'Gonese had acknowledged it, but remained unconcerned. Brad acted as if it were of no import. The next minute, she was flooded with memories of how often she'd been snubbed, shunned or attacked the way the mechtech had attacked her, and worse.

Was it really that easy? And if it was, didn't she owe it to these people to tell them about the smuggler's offer?

Pondering that, and the nature of friendship, followed her through dinner. When Cragrral and Brad motioned her to join them for singing, she nearly demurred.

It hit her, though, right in the gut.

No matter what he was, Cragrral had accepted her, an outcast in virtually every situation. So had Brad. She had been asked to join them, to sing in a group. For the second time.

That meant something.

"Thank you, gentlemen," she said with a smile as she walked to the section of the mess that was acoustically domed for performances. Another musician, a harpist, brought his instrument onto the stage within moments. To her shock, a lithe figure in a bright orange robe stepped onto the dais.

"Ma'Gonese," Brad exclaimed with warm surprise. "You've finally decided to join us?"

The woman nodded, and to Ravi's surprise, ma'Gonese ducked her head a little. The other woman had seemed so assured in her job. Perhaps she wasn't as confident in her vocal skills. They made room for her on the platform, and everyone tuned up and agreed on a playlist.

The five of them spent more than an hour trading songs and harmonies from a dozen different worlds. To the delight of their small audience, they sang "A Space Pirate's Folly," which Cragrral had learned. That drew more listeners and a good group to sing the rollicking chorus.

No one watched her with malice or singled her out. No one turned away from the music, even when they sang "Oberon's Fate," which was a popular, but very old, song written by a McKeonite before the troubles.

Ravi was flying high on the music and acceptance as they wrapped up their impromptu concert for the evening. It had been a good day. She'd resolved to take Brad or ma'Gonese aside and ask about the smugglers the next day. It was the right thing to do.

"Do you and Brad know the song 'Wicked Good Space Ale?'" she asked as the three of them turned down the corridor to the BVax quarters on deck nine.

"Know it, I do not," Cragrral said. "Most willing to learn it, however, am I."

Ravi jerked to a stop when Cragrral growled. Not that she could have gone further with Cragrral's arm blocking her path. The corridor opposite their quarters was splashed with bright red paint. Words in seven different languages proclaimed her a McKeonite whore, traitor, bitch, and other less well-known expletives.

Her heart, so light a moment before, plummeted to her shoes.

It hurt even more when she realized that a man lay below the painted words.

A dead man. In a mechtech uniform.

CHAPTER FOUR

Yet again, Ravi and Cragrral found themselves in the temporary quarters on deck twelve. They were opposite a quieter shopping sector and in amongst other crew quarters, so it wasn't as bad as it might have been. Most stations had overflow crew quarters in out-of-the-way places outside engineering or control, or in odd corners of the retail sectors.

There was an ongoing battle in the GSS about decommissioning Outcast Station and two others, so staff was dwindling as vendors downsized to the bare minimum in personnel, just in case.

In the common area of the larger, five-person living pod, Cragrral bid her goodnight, adding, "I must calm myself. Exercises I will be doing for a goodly while."

Defeat hung around her like a cloak. "How will I ever manage this, Cragrral?" She slumped into one of the forma chairs that lined the walls of the common area of the living pod. The chair conformed to her shape, supporting her despite her despicable origins. If only the station were like the chairs.

Fury rode the Tilden's features once more. "Manage

it we will," he stated, banging his fist emphatically on the wall. "The marshals, Brad, finding this culprit will be, and stopping this nonsense. Impossible to do your job, it will be, if this keeps up, and do your job you *must*."

Ravi dropped her head into her hands. Her fat, red braid slipped over her shoulder to coil into a heavy weight in her lap. "I can't change what I am, Cragrral. I'm McKeonite and that's that."

"No," he contradicted, anger still ripe in his tone. "BVax you are. Of no country, or clan or nation. BVax alone. Does not the Oath tell you this? Did you not take it?"

"Of course I did," she snapped. "No one other than us seems to care about that."

"Most do," Cragrral insisted. After a moment though, he sighed. "Be back to work, we must, tomorrow. Show you the research ongoing, I must. Three more standard station blocks am I here, then gone."

Twenty-four days.

Ravi rose with a bleak nod. Three statweeks and she'd be on her own with the hatred, bigotry and unwarranted prejudice.

Great.

"Have allies, you do," Cragrral said at last. "Obviously." His tone turned wry. "Protecting you, even in such an ugly way, someone is. Your enemies, think twice will, or three times, before harassing you. If the result is this—" He drew a claw across his throat, a universal sign of death most races had adopted from humans. "—then bother you, they will most assuredly not."

Ravi hadn't thought of that. It wasn't someone trying to kill *her.* It was someone killing people who bothered her.

"Oh, dear," she said as the realization hit her. "Not exactly the allies I need."

Cragrral disagreed. "If safe it keeps you, and from the terrible treatment you have described, then welcome them, I do." He crouched to take her hands. "Friend I am to you, Ravinisha Trentham. Safe and happy, I would leave you, when I go."

She nodded, unable to speak. She was still processing the fact that this wasn't actually a threat to her. She was being protected.

How incredibly strange.

"Thank you, Cragrral. It's odd to be…"

"To be?"

"Protected, however harshly."

"Indeed. I would fight for you, if need be, Ravi. As would Brad. And others." The gleam of his many fangs in the room's clinical light was mitigated only by his words of comfort. "You will win hearts here."

He released her hands, stood and stretched. "With this realization, calmer I feel." He yawned, then bent to pat her shoulder. "I will wish you goodsleep."

"Goodsleep," she murmured, still trying to get her mind around the death, the blood.

"Ravi," Cragrral began, but when she turned to face him, he simply shook his head. "Goodsleep."

Ravi realized that once again, Cragrral had hesitated, and withheld whatever it was he'd been thinking of saying. Instead, with a wave, he strode into the borrowed space, and the door closed behind him.

Scenarios revolved in her mind about who could be protecting her, and why. She wrestled with her decision to warn the marshals about the smuggler approaching her. It seemed ill-advised. It was best if she kept her mouth shut and not draw any more attention to herself. Heretofore she'd had to assume that everyone was an enemy to a McKeonite.

That seemed to have changed on Outcast Station.

There was her murderous protector.

And Cragrral. And Brad.

Other names popped into her mind as she continued to sit, belying the feelings of isolation and persecution she'd harbored her whole life.

Trendte. Ma'Gonese. The harpist, Pluvia San. Even Stationmaster Shupe and StatAdmin Bashink arose to conflict with her notion of being a stranger in a hostile landscape.

Rising, she finally sought her bed as other faces and names presented themselves.

Maybe Outcast Station could be more than just a posting.

Ravi thought she'd be awake and restless for hours, but she fell into a deep sleep almost instantly and awoke with a start to the *pingpingping* of her statcomm's waking alarm. As the lights in her quarters gradually brightened to station standard, she realized she had rested, despite her confusion.

"Get over it, Ravinisha. It will never go away. *Ever.* Live with it, despite it, like always. And remember," she said to the mirrored reflection of a BVax Scientist, "you really do have friends here."

With those bracing words, she grabbed a nutrition

bar and left her quarters. Cragrral's door was open, indicating he'd departed. Emotion crowded her, but she squared her shoulders.

"He's not here to nursemaid you, Ravi," she reminded herself. "He's your colleague, not your bodyguard."

Despite her earlier self-lecture about going it alone, Ravi was relieved to meet Marshal Trendte as she navigated the many turns her statcomm indicated she should take to arrive at the on-station BVax Research Sector.

"Good station day to you, BVax Trentham."

"And to you, Marshal."

"Everything all right with you?"

She glanced at him as they made the turn to the BVax research area. "Yes, I'm fine."

"Good. Marshal Carruthers and StatAdmin Bashink want to be sure you're not troubled further."

"Thank you," she said, feeling her spirits rise.

"Oh," he said, reaching into a pocket of his khaki, multipocketed uniform pants. "StatAdmin asked me to give you these. It's RealInk copies of your stat orders, and a backup of all your codes and quals."

They'd arrived at the research doors, and Trendte gave her a vague salute. "Have a good one."

"You too," she replied, a bit baffled. She watched him walk away as she clutched the packet of transfer and stat docs. When Trendte disappeared around the corner, she opened the envelope.

Everything was in order. She stacked them against her hand and returned them to the envelope before putting her hand out to the identiplate.

She gasped and jumped back.

There was an info/message dot on the wall next to the identiplate. It was McKeonite red and had her initials on its jellied surface.

Ravi scanned the corridor—as if she hadn't just watched Marshal Trendte walk away—but no one was there. How had the message gotten there?

Shaking and afraid, she hesitated.

"Stop it, Ravi. It's a message, nothing more. If it's ugly, that's nothing new."

She drew in a bracing breath, then pointed her statcomm at it, clicking *download message*. She got a notification of *Marked Private, Recipient Only* and a request for identification. She braced herself, then put her thumb on the dot.

Words scrolled onto her statcomm, lingering long enough for her to read them, then repeating twice before they faded away.

We don't accept bigots in our ranks.

Whether you assist us or not, I won't allow our people, or anyone else, to harass you.

My apologies. The Company Manager.

The dot dissolved as soon as the text was delivered. There would be no way to trace it, or the message.

Ravi hastily scribbled the gist of the communication down in her statcomm notes, then stood paralyzed, her thoughts scrabbling to make sense of everything. She nearly ducked as a drone sailed down the hallway, passing her with a brisk whoosh of air as it flew by.

"Definitely talk to Cragrral and to Brad," she said aloud, making her decision. She didn't want someone killing on her behalf. Ever. She'd tell Brad and Cragrral everything. Tonight.

Decision made, she slapped her hand on the identiplate and got to work.

To her relief, the BVax Hydroponics Sectorhead was an ImaPrinta, with nine appendages and her BVax insignia on a harness that wrapped around her various limbs. ImaPrintas didn't care about race. Or, better said, they regarded any race but their own as inferior. Ravi's status as a non-ImaPrinta was the lone negative strike as far as the Sectorhead was concerned.

Ravi managed to keep her amusement from showing. Her first encounter with an ImaPrinta, in graduate school, had started with the typical ImaPrinta statement that greeted every humanoid: *Why, imagine, only four limbs! And no claws? How do you cope?*

This one wasn't as vocal, but she still saw the typical "oh my goodness" eye-roll across the ImaPrinta's multiple eyes. The glance took in both her two-legged status, and that of Cragrral, as he walked up. At least Cragrral had claws and fangs, the eye-roll seemed to say.

"Be showing BVax Trentham the facilities, I will. Continuing very promising research on Carpathian worm slime, she will be." He told the Sectorhead as he smiled at Ravi. "Predict, I do, great success with that study." Turning back to the ImaPrinta, he said, "Please to be accessing all needed materials for BVax Trentham."

With a nod and a guttural sound of agreement, the ImaPrinta took up a stylus and pad. "Materials list, Scientist Trentham?"

Ravi rattled off the various items she needed to continue her project. Talking about it with Cragrral that first day had rekindled the fire in her heart to pursue the exciting and promising research.

When she was done, the ImaPrinta looked impressed. "For what proposed result is your research Scientist Trentham?"

"Burn treatment, skin replacement, and wound regeneration," Ravi replied.

"Fascinating." The ImaPrinta seemed to ponder for a moment. "I am TurrTerrEel. I look forward to working with you and hearing of the results of this study as it progresses." She tapped the stylus on the pad in a rapid series of clicks. "Supplies will be here for you within three station-standard blocks. Worms, I can get. Trays and other materials we have." TurrTerrEel tapped her stylus on a growing tray now, more like a thinking pattern than a necessary motion. Two of her other limbs were testing the soil in various other trays for moisture. Yet another limb lifted a watering globe. "Maintaining habitat will be interesting. Dry sand soil, with a medium static charge. Hmmm." She closed her eyelids in the ImaPrinta one-two-three pattern of deep thought. "Hmmm. An interesting challenge." She bowed her head a little toward Ravi. "Challenges are good things. Thank you."

"You're welcome." Bemused, Ravi didn't know what else to say. She'd never been thanked for ordering supplies before.

"Good," Cragrral said. "Starting you will be, soon, with your research."

Cragrral turned to TurrTerrEel. "Going we will be to the inner lab. Problems, any, of which I should be aware?"

"None here. All is well. BVax Tech Ruggersha

reports issues in hydroponics on decks two and twenty. There is wilting. The plants have been isolated. Reports will be to you by evening shift." TurrTerrEel resumed the serene expression she'd had when they arrived, and she continued to hold their gazes even as all of her limbs began other tasks.

"Thank you. Good work, then, to you." Cragrral looked satisfied as he turned away, and he and Ravi moved through the growing trays to the inner labs. "She is one who is good to be working with," Cragrral said, striding toward the clear doors of the other lab. Ravi trotted to keep up and nearly ran into him when he stopped abruptly. "Organized and effective, she is. No trouble will you have, working with TurrTerrEel. Or Ruggersha either."

He pointed to a set of covered trays two rows to the left. "There, my research is. Fruitful, in that it has created fruit." He chuffed the words out on an embarrassed laugh. "The juice of the fruit, when crushed, cures the sores formed with Nachina falling sickness." Ravi made an appreciative noise and started to speak, but another chuffing laugh stopped her. "The foul stench of it is, however, an issue."

Ravi choked back a laugh at his self-deprecating humor. "If it works, it works, even if it stinks."

"Yes, but much better it will be if the fragrance altogether I can breed out," Cragrral stated. "As you know, healing patients object, most loudly, to stinking things."

"What is your crossbreeding mech—"

"ALL HANDS!! STATION EMERGENCY!! CODE RED!!" A blasting, piercing siren accompanied the words. "CODE RED! THIS IS NOT A DRILL!" The siren ceased momentarily so the blaring voiceover was clear. "All non-essential personnel report to quarters immediately."

The siren shrieked anew and a second alert sounded. "RED ALERT! BVAX SENIOR PERSONNEL TO CENTRACOMM IMMEDIATELY! SITUATION PROTOCOL ONE!"

The siren and the alerts began to repeat in different languages and trade tongues, but Ravi and Cragrral were already moving.

"Go, go, go!" Cragrral pointed toward a wall cabinet and they raced toward it. TurrTerrEel's rolling gait and proximity meant she reached it before they'd crossed half the distance. She flung open the doors and whipped out full respirator masks. The humanoid-type masks were airborne and in their hands before Ravi managed to process the lighting-fast movement of TurrTerrEel's limbs making the toss.

With a Code Red, there wouldn't be any chance to get their personally designed suits from their quarters. For the stationmaster to call a Code Red, Protocol One, it meant an illness was already moving quickly through the station.

For a Situation Protocol One Alert—possible plague—they would don the strongest protection gear. Faces covered, they pulled on containment garb, snapped on the locking sensi-gloves and the over-gloves, and jammed their feet into the hip-high boots that then sealed to the overhanging top, and air-sealed to form-fitting closeness. Ravi didn't even try to figure out where all of TurrTerrEel's limbs were fitting in her garb. She focused instead on sealing her own suit, grabbed one of the two Lead Situation Packs from the cabinet, and bolted for the door.

Thankfully, all the stations followed the same basic layout. Even the stations in Xttll and Nine Planet League sectors followed the more humanoid layout for the perimeter warning stations. CentraComm was on deck fourteen. They hit the personnel carrier and bolted through the doors. Seeing them—and their suits and insignia—people made way for them as the klaxons continued to shriek the alert and direct personnel to quarters.

Despite a head start, Ravi and Cragrral arrived mere moments before TurrTerrEel. Other BVax personnel, including the few lab techs she'd met, streamed into CentraComm's situation room and pooled in the center of the space. Most were continuing to fasten situation suits as they waited.

"Thank Pleuron you're fast," Stationmaster Shupe exclaimed as she burst through the doors from main command. She came straight to Ravi, Cragrral and TurrTerrEel. Marshals ma'Gonese, Trendte, and Brad Carruthers were right behind her. Two other marshals Ravi hadn't met came in through other doors and hurried to where they stood. All the marshals were in protective gear.

"Good too that you brought your plague-packs," Shupe said, motioning to their stocked Situation Packs.

"Gather up," Shupe snapped, waving the other marshals closer as she popped open a wall cabinet to reveal her own SitOne gear. "We've got medstaff calling from all over the station to report statcits collapsing where they stand. I've quarantined six deck sectors already, and it isn't helping. Whatever it is, it's spreading."

"Latest docking, planets of origin?" Cragrral's demand was terse but calm, his statcomm at the ready. There was no time to snarl about the fact that BVax hadn't been notified sooner. Shupe was competent, and had handled the earlier E-Rep notification with ease. Why the delay now?

Shupe rattled off the names of ten planets. Most were common trade partners, either mining or other non-agro goods, and had frequent docking status at the station. It wasn't impossible that the current disease came from one of them, but it wasn't likely.

"Previous to that? Any of unknown or unusual origins?"

"Amperal," Shupe stated, her words muffled by the mask. "Switching to ECommOne."

Within her suit, Ravi keyed the retinal display and switched to Emergency Communications Station Circuit One.

"Amperal's an agro planet. It isn't swampy, or a common brew spot of disease or trade sickness, seldom get a mutation from there," one of the techs said with an anxious glance at Shupe and the marshals.

"True," Cragrral agreed. "Others? What is due in?"

"No others. Busiest is tomorrow. We're due seven inbound freighters and four passenger ships." Shupe finished sealing her suit as she spoke. Inbounds could be held for several days, but the freighters carried very little extra in terms of fuel. They would be in trouble if they had to wait too long to dock. "No idea of point of origin," Shupe continued. "Medstaff called in initial simultaneous reports from four locations, and it magnified from four to twenty within minutes. ChiefMed PurrlTeeLaa and Stat Admin Bashink called for Protocol One when it hit seventeen. I'm patching him in."

PurrlTeeLa was the Chief Medical Officer. Like TurrTerrEel, he was an ImaPrinta. "Medstaff originally considered it a CO_2 leak for deck two," Shupe continued.

Surprised, Ravi blurted out, "Why?

It was PurrlTeeLaa who answered as his image came up on the visible comm panel. "Rapid onset of nausea, weakness, fainting, sweating, difficulty breathing in multiple patients and across species. That suggested air quality issues to medstaff. There have also been three CO_2 leaks there within the last week with similarly affected statcits, though not so many."

Shupe's voice cut in. "I backed PurrlTeeLaa on considering this a possible maintenance issue instead of plague, because of the multiple CO_2 issues. Medstaff handled it previously, and all statcits and visitors were cleared to return to duty or to go on to their destinations within four hours."

Ravi's heart sank. Air quality issues dramatically affected airborne germs-transfer. Excess CO_2 or NO_2 changed the way in which diseases or molds grew onstation. A significant change in air factors, combined with an unknown pathogen, could drop the whole station into a plague situation within hours.

Apparently, it was happening as they spoke.

"Given that, we waited. Now we're in the shitter."

Shupe turned to Cragrral. "Senior BVax Cragrral, we are officially on Stations Situation Protocol One, BVax. You are in command." She lifted her hands up and out, as if releasing controls. MedStaff PurrlTeeLaa seconded that, and within a few seconds, StatAdmin Bashink popped into the comm conversation to release authority to Cragrral as well.

"We are at your disposal, Cragrral. Let's get this handled," Bashink said next. His face, behind his statsuit shield, looked ill and tired.

"Station Marshals are at your service," Brad said, adding his weight to the exchange. He too raised his hands in the releasing gesture.

"Station Master, Medstaff, StatAdmin, Chief Marshal, I accept command," he replied, as formally. "As BVax, authorize, I do, the high-oxy medscrub blowers. Go online immediately they should. MedStats on every ring and level, opening should be, immediately."

PurrlTeeLaa nodded. "Already underway, Cragrral."

Cragrral smoothly pivoted to TurrTerrEel. "E-Comm1 here in CentraComm will be your priority. Medstaff and BVax reports, you will coordinate. Patterns to be looking for. All non-infected medstaff personnel should go into sitsuits without delay.

"Marshals, seconded you are, to BVax Trentham and to me," Cragrral continued, turning to Brad and the others. The marshals nodded as one.

"Ravi, go you and I will, to first call point and follow the track."

Shupe handed him a pin-file and Cragrral inserted it into his statcomm.

"First to deck two." He frowned. "A stores and retail level, that is. Some warehousing," he noted, bringing up the station map, now showing the red of disease progression in multiple areas.

"Observation is deck one and two," Marshal Trendte interjected. "Tourists go there the minute they get to the station. They want to see the planet, get a meal and watch the viewports change. They also stop on deck two for supplies, and companionship of various varieties."

"Good," Cragrral hissed his approval. "Ruggersha, Po'Ten," he called the names of two of the BVax techs. "Checking deck two with swabs and aerocollectors now, then follow to deck fourteen."

"Yes, sir." They snapped a salute and ran out.

"Ggrglra, Jones and Pshaxt, go through this area of CentraComm, then continue to offices here on deck fourteen. I will be monitoring as will TurrTerrEel. When done there, go to the next data point."

"Yessir."

"Trentham and I go." Cragrral suited words to action and headed for the doors, with Ravi running to match his longer stride. Two marshals ran behind them. She identified Brad and Trendte.

Ravi was already sorting data through her statcomm. She had three vector programs running simultaneously. TurrTerrEel was cross-feeding them information from medstaff.

"Respiration is slowing dramatically on first affected. They are going into coma states. All species affected."

That was bad. Very, very bad.

There was a whoosh of sound and a distant roaring

noise, much like the sound a high, full waterfall makes as the water hits the rocks below.

"Medscrubbers online and at forty-nine percent efficiency. Scrubbers number four, eight, ten, seventeen and twenty-three are in failure mode. Stattech is on it."

The air in her statsuit was flat, but Ravi knew the station air would have a distinct fullness to it. It held a richer mix of oxygen, since most of the statcits were oxy breathers. It would hold a crisp scent as well. An antibacterial agent and an astringent were, hopefully, clearing out the vast ductwork of the station's air handling system, preventing the spread of whatever disease had been brought onboard.

"BVax Trentham, what is first protocol in airborne situation?"

"Get critical personnel into statsuits, and begin to clear the air for all breathers."

"What is second?"

"Vector the pathogen through aerofiltration, utilize the collected sample to test for antigens in the humanoids. Test for high cillipher production in the insectivores. Test for reactivids in the Clunch, if any are present. Determine recoloration in the Pertards, if coloration has been affected by the airborne pathogen." She rattled off more benchmarks in various species.

"Good." He shot her a glance as they slowed to make the turn to the down access for deck two. He lowered his voice. "Good it is for me to have you here to help, Ravi Trentham. Bad feeling, I have about this," he confided. "Too long, they waited to call All Hands to Quarters, I fear."

"It's going to increase the spread," Ravi agreed. The

stationmaster should have called for BVax, to put them on alert, when the second episode occurred on deck fourteen. There had been ten people affected on deck two, and three statcits on deck fourteen. Given the small initial numbers, Ravi wasn't going to criticize Shupe for her decision after the fact, especially given the previous CO_2 issues she'd mentioned…but… "The disbursement puzzles me," she told Cragrral. "There's something odd about it."

From deck two to deck fourteen. The third episode, oddly enough, was the StatAdmin level on deck nineteen, with six people compromised.

Something about that nagged at her. What was it about that distribution? Two, fourteen, nineteen? She checked the display that TurrTerrEel was updating. Calls for decks five, ten and twenty had followed hard on the heels of the others.

Deck two to fourteen to nineteen.

Deck five to ten to twenty.

She looked at the next sequences. If the onset followed a pattern, she couldn't catch it yet. She tucked that into the back of her mind to let it stew. It meant something. She didn't yet know what.

Red lights blazed at the heavy, clear doors of the quarantine seal for deck two. She and Cragrral hurried to the command port, slapping their gloved hands down onto the scanners and leaning in simultaneously for a retinal scan. To read through the gloves, the scanner had changed to a different format, one Ravi had never experienced before. Her bones ached as the scanner assessed DNA through an illumilight bone marrow scan rather than simple palm print and DNA.

"Medscrubbers at fifty-two percent," TurrTerrEel reported. "Ten more reported locations for the outbreak. Individual medstaff calls from quarters and pods rising by twenty-two…make that twenty-eight percent."

Cragrral cursed fluently. "Twenty-eight percent and rising. Means, that does, that we will have casualties in crew quarters, unknown to us. Full-on, epidemic onset, we have now."

Ravi cursed as well. He was right. Crew members would be unable to get rapid help and would succumb to the pathogen, creating secondary issues with decomposition-based diseases.

The quarantine seal pinged acceptance of their identification and began the process of venting the antechamber with inert gas before refilling it with the oxy mix from the scrubbers. The light turned green and they entered the chamber, sealing the door and waiting for the scrubbed air to recirculate and the microbe scan to decontaminate them.

They waited out the quarantine warnings, impatient to get in and assess. Protocol allowed for them both to enter to assess if they were in sitsuits prior to entering the contaminated area.

The doors hissed air as the locks processed and Cragrral tugged open the entry seal.

Inside, equipment beeped, but nothing moved.

CHAPTER FIVE

Ravi ran to the downed personnel at the medstation while Cragrral started checking statcits. The situation had devolved from bad to horrible. When they'd left CentraComm, there had been fifteen affected personnel in this area. Now everyone was down.

"Dead I have," Cragrral stated, "Three so far."

"Medstaff, five down, one fatality here so far."

They counted off the dead and stricken. Ravi's heart sank with each listed fatality. Twenty so far, from a group of seventy-five. Terrible percentages in such a short time.

"Bad, this is."

"It is." She glanced at Cragrral. His face bore a stricken expression at odds with his overall fierceness. She continued checking pulses and observing symptoms, but she spoke. "Cragrral, are you okay?"

"Hoped I had, never to see this."

Ravi's stomach clenched, and she took a moment to look around. "None of the training prepares you."

Their comms crackled faintly and TurrTerrEel had them sound off their location and physical status.

"Confer!" TurrTerrEel called the conference, as per protocol. Ravi set aside the incipient panic and focused on reporting. She spared a moment to be glad she wasn't doing this alone.

"Bad, conditions are. Fatalities to report, we have," Cragrral began.

"Yes. But first the conference," came TurrTerrEel's terse reply . "Symptoms?"

Cragrral responded immediately to her tone, snapping back to BVax mode. "Fever, pallor, profuse sweating, vomiting in three species, muscle tremors in humanoids."

"Diarrhea in four patients, three of whom are deceased." Ravi reported and moved to another group.

"Final stage symptom, that may be," Cragrral said, making a note on his statcomm.

"Possibly, but they were all Blandix, so that may not convey to other species."

"A family?"

"Yes." Ravi knew she had to harden her heart to deal with this, but the small family of Blandix, all but one dead, hurt her heart.

"Protocol," TurrTerrEel reinforced, firmly. "Already we know it is multi-species. Any immunes?"

"None." Cragrral, too, moved to another grouping.

"Marks, hives, pustules, itching, rash?" TurrTerrEel continued the run-down.

"Rash on three of the five Pertards I checked, with loss of color in the neck frill," Ravi said and Cragrral made a note. Something about this was very wrong. Something kept pricking at her instincts, telling her to pay attention to…something…but what?

"Mucous membranes?" TurrTerrEel continued the list.

"Pale, with minimal blood return upon palpating, even in the Pertards. It's slowing the circulatory system."

"Secretions or excretions?"

Cragrral went first with his list. "Excessive perspiration in humanoids and avians. Extreme heat in Xltans, and oo-palateans. Six of the dead are overheated Xltans."

Ravi was glad she was sealed in a sitsuit. Xltans weren't pleasant smelling when they were cool and dry, much less when they were cooked.

"Canthans appear to be in a suspended state and perMankins are shriveled," Cragrral continued. "Extreme dehydration, I am thinking. Trentham?"

"I noted the same issues in the species mentioned. Medstaff are in better shape, but still exhibiting unconsciousness, tremors and sweating. Several medstaff have a faint rash on their faces, from what I can see through their medsuits."

Cragrral hurried to check them as she stated this, hurrying back before she continued.

"Confirmed," he offered, motioning for her to continue.

"Chills, convulsions, seizures?" TurrTerrEel questioned.

"None yet visible. Profuse perspiration may be preventing any fever-related convulsions or seizures."

"Dehydration, an issue will be, potential chloride, ribidnium and potassium loss, for all species." Cragrral paused to count the stricken who still breathed. "TurrTerrEel, seventy-two units of initial fluid needed, on this level alone, species list incoming to you now." His claws tick-tick-ticked on the statcomm as he sent the list. "Order this, with medstaff suited, to be administering immediately." He turned to Ravi, swiveling fully in order to see through his face shield. "Going, we must be, to the second outbreak site."

"Deck fourteen."

They cycled through the airlock, meeting the medstaff team arriving with hydration units. They didn't stop to speak, running for the personnel lifts and heading for their next destination. The same scene greeted them, except that while four medstaff were down, two newly arrived medstaff personnel were already administering fluids to those on the floor.

Ravi and Cragrral observed the same symptoms on deck nineteen.

Cragrral's statcomm pinged. "TurrTerrEel, go ahead."

"MedStaff Chief PurrlTeeLaa is down, as are a significant number of his staff. Maintenance is still working on the scrubbers. We are up to sixty-eight percent."

Cragrral's growl was his answer as he cut off the transmission. Ravi's heart sank, hearing that PurrlTeeLaa and other medstaffers were down. They were the mainstay of any defense when it came to disease. PurrlTeeLaa had been steadily feeding them patient data.

Tremors, profuse sweating, weakness in the limbs, collapse, then a coma-like state or death. Only the humans exhibited the rash.

In several other species, violent sneezing, with aural and visual hallucinations, preceded the collapse, but the sweating, tremors and coma were still the result.

"Aerocollectors, to the lab have been taken," Cragrral said as they finished their counts and observations on deck nineteen. "Same, I think, will be the conditions on all the decks. To be finding causation and cure, we must be going."

"I agree," Ravi said, her mind whirling with data points. A constant list ran in her head, and on her statcomm. As they went, she added more information and input possibilities of what this might be a variant of, with each new patient they encountered. Very few plagues were new. Most were strains or mutations of something else.

Something was still bothering her about the way the virus had progressed through the station, but she had to set it aside as she and Cragrral raced down the corridor to the research lab.

"Medium, set up, has been handled," he said. "Growing cultures we must be, and quickly."

They separated to different workstations, each of them pulling a labeled aerocollector as they went. Ravi separated out the layers of collection and drew swabs from each layer to swipe into the medium. She marked everything and set it into the collator unit. She hit *Analyze* as Cragrral slammed the door on his collator.

They each took another collector, starting on additional batches as if they were racing. They reviewed medstaff reports as they came in. Fatalities were rising.

"Some characteristics of the IL-23," Cragrral said, as the silence grew uncomfortable.

"Not enough. Regena's Syndrome would explain the sweating."

"But explain, it does not, the vomiting and diarrhea in the other patients. No expulsion of other fluids is there with Regena's, which part of its danger, is."

"True." Ravi wracked her memory. "Paralax?"

"Possible," Cragrral agreed, sounding surprised. "Forgot that one, I did. Falling sickness, it offers. Paleness. Not fatal, usually."

"Stronger strain, perhaps. But since no one's responding to fluids yet, I think it isn't true Paralax. A mutation or variant."

"Could be." His collator pinged ahead of hers, even though she'd started sooner. "Info we are getting."

He accessed the results as the collator hummed, sending the samples to a secondary holding bin.

"Unknown configuration of elements." He sent the results to her statcomm as her collator pinged. Cragrral pulled her data, running down the configurations. "Look at this, Ravi," he said, excitement in his voice. "A variant of Xltna-perfa One."

She frowned at the results. "But only on decks twenty and nineteen." She compared both results. "We have Manginid spores on here too, but that's typical where there are Pertards on a station." The readings indicated a high level of various fungi growing throughout the station. "They're all dead though. The spores."

There were some unknown elements too, however.

"What do you think this is?" Ravi pointed to a spike on the collator's data page. Zooming in on it, they stared at the reading. "Lead/magnesium composite? What has those concentrations? And what is this unknown vector next to it?" The concentration chart looked like a particularly jagged mountain range, with the unknown element peaking highest.

"A new element, that is," Cragrral said, frowning. "From what deck is that data?"

"Two, our first outbreak site."

"Checking the others for that element signature, we must be."

They began feeding data into the system and kept on well into the station's night rotation. TurrTerrEel continued to monitor the plague's progress. More than fifty percent of station personnel were now reported as downed by the disease. Those not affected were in sitsuits, or in personnel quarters. The marshals had set up a call-in system to continually monitor those in cabins, keeping them apprised of the station conditions and also confirming the statcits remained in quarters and healthy.

"Report we must, to BVax HQ," Cragrral said, his tone sharp and dangerous. "Do it, you must, Ravi. Clearer it will be. Gather the data."

Fear clutched at her, and a bead of sweat rolled down her back in response. She had to deliberately breathe, forcing herself to calm as she loaded all the data into a file.

"Ready?"

At her nod, he turned to the comm. "BVax Lab to CentraComm, Stationmaster Shupe."

"Go ahead, BVax," Shupe replied. Her voice was tired and weak, and her face was drawn and pale.

"BVax, Protocol One, Emergency Report we must activate. Reached fifty percent engagement of station citizens we have. BVax Trentham will record report."

"Acknowledged. Opening channel to emergency pod

recorder in three, two, one…Go."

As concisely as possible, Ravi detailed the incident report and hit the transmit button to download all the files to the pod. The Emergency Report would go out to BVax Central HQ via interstellar burst and via a micropod. One or the other would reach BVax should everyone on the station succumb.

"Thank you, Stationmaster."

"Find something, Cragrral."

Cragrral nodded and disconnected, but said nothing to Ravi as they got back to work. The hours ticked by, and the data—from blood and fluid samples to air contaminants—continued to roll in, but nothing showed in any database that would direct them to a cause, or a cure. Blood gasses in various species and nutrient levels were all off, but so far that was their sole clue. Every species showed the high oxygenation lent by the medscrubbers, despite three units still being offline.

The medscrubbers continued to improve the air, but the weight of the plague was outstripping the scrubbers. With no improvement as the scrubbers came online, they were forced to assume that the disease wasn't airborne.

With every data byte, they suggested treatments to medstaff poised in bays throughout the station, but so far, very little was working. Medstaff offered ideas too as they worked to stop the flood of those succumbing to the disease. The death toll had slowed with the infusion of mineral-charged fluids and potassium, but no one was coming out of the coma the plague caused.

"This, no sense, makes," Cragrral snarled. He banged on the console where he worked. "Nothing is connecting. Germs, none are replicating. Foreign bodies, none appear. A silent killer this is, with no cause."

"BVax One, this is Chief Marshal Carruthers, actual."

"BVax Cragrral, responding, actual," Cragrral replied.

"Shupe is down. Not dead, but non-responsive. Medstaff administering fluids."

"BVax Cragrral and BVax Trentham." TurrTerrEel's voice broke the tense silence that had reigned in the lab. Collector after collector noted the spike on the readouts. Each showed the bodily fluids of different species, all with excess with lead and magnesium adjunct, an unknown variable. The problem was, the unknown variable wasn't showing up in the patients. There was no apparent connection between the unknown and the afflicted.

"BVax Cragrral actual, answering is. Trentham, present," Cragrral replied.

"Per Protocol One, it is at hour twenty. You *must* both take downtime. Two station hours, minimum. I am turning over CentraComm to Marshal Trendte and Marshal Blaze. BVax protocol must stand."

Cragrral looked stricken, but Ravi knew he would do it. If she and Cragrral succumbed, no one would survive. They had to figure it out. To do that, they had to have at least a little sleep.

"Agreed," Cragrral snarled. TurrTerrEel looked as relieved as an ImaPrinta could at Cragrral's compliance. "To the main lab come, adjacent to our quarters," Cragrral continued. "Telling you parameters of variables, I will be."

TurrTerrEel arrived within ten minutes. With no

traffic on any of the levels and no one using the personnel lifts, she had made the best possible time.

"Monitor these for the rising levels." Cragrral pointed at the lead and magnesium, that were spiking high on virtually every level of the station. They were climbing slowly, but steadily.

Ravi had her own parameters to add. "I'm plotting the incidents of aural and visual hallucinations, tracking those patients and their bloodwork. The additional symptoms, both visual, auditory and respiratory, prior to the collapse phase, may indicate a minimal resistance."

Any resistance meant a fight, and a fight left clues as to what the body fought.

"Done. Go. The correct dosage for the sleep spray," she said, holding out two areo-spray injectors that locked into ports in their suits. "Two hours you must sleep."

Nodding wearily, both Ravi and Cragrral left the lab and entered their quarters. In the main area, Cragrral started to crack his suit.

"No!" Ravi flung out a hand to stop him. "This is an airborne disease. The medscrubbers aren't at full and who knows what was brought into our quarters by all the people we've had here, with the break-in, the chemicals, everything. Stay sealed."

"Correct you are," Cragrral said, his features a grimace. "This, the reason is, why we must rest. Not thinking, was I."

"I know. I've almost cracked my suit twice without thinking about it," Ravi admitted, weariness sinking through every pore of her body.

"Ravi." Cragrral hesitated as they stood at the doors to their quarters.

"Yes?"

"We will beat this."

He said it, but it had more the tenor of a question than a bold statement of pending success.

She looked into his face, understanding and sharing his anguish. She heard the fear, as well as the sense of inadequacy. Those feelings crashed through her system too.

"I hope so." It was all she managed to say, and even that, she had to push past the horror clogging her throat. Fifty percent of the statcits were down. Ten percent of those were dead.

"BVax Trentham," Cragrral's return to formal address had her looking up into his face. The clear mask of his suit seemed to magnify his worry. "Confess I must, a need."

"A need?"

"Tildens are families, groups tight knit, are. We—" He stopped. Whatever he was struggling to say was emotional, personal.

"You need contact." Ravi knew beyond a shadow of a doubt that Cragrral was teetering on the edge. Twenty straight stathours of work and worry had taken their toll.

Without thinking anything further, she put her arms around her friend. Even through the suit, she felt the solid connection of his body as his arms locked around her, squeezing her tightly, as if she were an anchor that would provide the strength they needed to find answers.

"We'll find a solution, Cragrral. It's what we do."

He was silent for a long moment, still holding her tightly. His breathing, irregular at first, evened out to a steady rhythm.

"It is," he finally said, the words expelled on a gust of air. He straightened, releasing her. "Thank you for the contact. It was what I needed."

"Me too." For a moment, they stood, close as lovers, their arms still touching. Finally, Ravi moved to her door. Without looking back, she said, "Sleep well."

"And you, too."

Ravi refused to blush, refused to think, even to herself, about how long it had been since someone held her close. She moved to her bunk, linking the aerospray to the port on her chest. The drug would hit her the instant she pressed the button. She needed to be lying down when it deployed.

Two hours later, Ravi's eyelids sprang open like they were on springs. She knew she'd slept. Knew she'd dreamed—she sensed the nightmares lurking in her subconscious. Frowning, she shook her head, locking the dreams away, but the shake obscured her vision with long tendrils of loose hair.

"What the heck?" she exclaimed and her voice sounded loud in the deep silence of the room. Even muffled by the suit, the echo sharpened her nerves.

The aerospray sedative had worn off with its usual abruptness. Now, the back end stim-booster kicked in with a fierce adrenaline rush.

Her mind knew she hadn't had enough rest to be this active, this alert, but her body was already responding to the "*go!go!go!*" of the stim-booster. It was all she could do not to leap to her feet and run to the lab.

With measured breaths, Ravi calmed her pulse and willed herself to stillness. The strands of loose hair from her long braid were sweat-soaked and clinging to her skin. She checked her suit's temperature regulators. Her temperature was elevated. Not much, but enough that her hair was damp, and her clothes were clammy. She pulled her arms into the body of the suit—not an easy move with something so form fitting—but cracking the suit was not an option. Ravi had to twist and contort to achieve it, but she re-plaited her hair into a tighter braid. She let it slide down her back and slipped her hands back down the suit's sleeves and into the gloves.

She came out of her room as Cragrral's door banged open and the Tilden rushed out.

"Go we must, to the lab!"

"Hang on, hang on." She grabbed his arm, slowing him down. "Per protocol, we have to eat. Having something in our systems will slow the booster." Cragrral's muscles vibrated under her hand, his body still telling him to rush from the room.

"Remember, we're on Protocol One."

He nodded, still looking at the door.

She let go of him long enough to open the emergency panel, grab the emergency nutrient pouches. "Fasten this to your suit."

The nutrients would feed directly into the suit's feeding tubes, adding vitamin and mineral boosters to the protein mix already in their suits' stores, along with a slow-release version of the stim. "Now, start eating as we walk."

They were both silent as they trotted to the lab. Ravi had never tasted the protein mix, and found it barely palatable, but her stomach protested when she stopped eating. Evidently, her body wanted whatever was in the tube.

"Tasteless," Cragrral snarled with ill temper. "Making this better, they should be."

The lab was silent as they entered, and TurrTerrEel nowhere to be seen.

As one, they reached for consoles, pulling up charts and statistics and shooting them up onto the lab's enormous glassine monitors.

Ravi gasped. Fatalities had slowed to almost nothing, but the number of residents succumbing to the illness had risen to nearly seventy percent.

"Critical systems may shut down within hours if we cannot stem the tide," Ravi said, her hand to her throat.

"We must," Cragrral began. He cleared his throat. "We must…"

"Cragrral? What is it?"

"Tremors, I feel. In my muscles."

"No." Panic clawed into her throat, her heart pounding in response.

"Yes."

"Sit. Eat more. Now!" she ordered, yanking a chair over and pushing him into it. "Tell me everything happening as it happens." Terror leached the power from the words, but she forced herself to open a new frame, enter the data on subject Cragrral as he detailed them. She connected it to his medstaff files, pulling the two together to look for anomalies.

She opened a channel to CentraComm. TurrTerrEel's face popped on the screen immediately. It was hard to tell visually, but relief suffused the ImaPrinta's tone as she responded.

"Good to see you awake, BVax Trentham and BVax Cragrral. We are at eighty-two percent efficiency on the medscrubbers, but all races continue to succumb. I have notified marshals Trendte and Carruthers that you are awake."

"BVax Cragrral is experiencing muscle tremors."

The same panic gripping Ravi leapt into TurrTerrEel's multi-eyed gaze. "No."

"Transferring, I am, Protocol One Status Response," Cragrral said, his voice stuttering slightly. "BVax Trentham, in charge is, now. All channels open, report same to station."

He lifted his hands, as Quiana Shupe had done the previous day, releasing the power to Ravi. Before he lowered his hands, she saw them tremble.

No, no, no, no, no. The words were a running mantra in her mind. This would not take her friend, her station. Not on her watch. Not while she had breath.

"BVax Trentham taking Protocol One, acknowledged," she said, even as part of her wanted to scream a denial. Her mind fired with so many disparate thoughts, she wanted to grab her head so it didn't fly off her shoulders.

Cragrral didn't slump, but he let the chair take his full weight. A tremor ran through his long frame and, unexpectedly, he sneezed.

"Carruthers here," a voice rasped into the comm as TurrTerrEel's shocked face was replaced by Brad's. "I'm down to seven functioning marshals. Medstaff is running with about thirty people for the whole station."

"Acknowledged," Ravi said, fighting to keep the dread out of her voice. "Marshal, I need one of your people to go back to deck two. TurrTerrEel, I need one of our people on deck nineteen. I need additional samples." Ravi forced herself to be crisp, efficient, and in charge. She had to solve this.

Now.

"I'll send Keeela. What is she looking for?" Brad asked, his voice a tired rasp.

"Send her now. I'll tell her when she gets there. Trentham out."

Ravi shut down the comm and, bracing her hands on the console, let her head drop and her shoulders sag. Vectors and scenarios raced through her head like a vid on hyperspeed. Tantalizing ideas whirled just out of reach, frustrating her into banging her hand on the console as Cragrral had done the previous night.

"Ravi," Cragrral said softly. She heard the tremor in his voice.

"Cragrral, what is it? Is it worsening?" She hurried to his side.

He nodded. "I'm hearing bells." He sneezed again, three times in a row.

"Blessings," she said absently, out of habit. "The disease progress is slow, though. You're not sweating."

"I am, but not profusely," he countered, looking puzzled. "Dizzy, I am. Disorientation, I have. It overtakes me, then recedes."

"Our BVax regimens must somehow be protecting us, slowing the onset." Every BVax Scientist and most of the techs had regular inoculations with as many vaccines as their bodies would tolerate. They were, in essence, the walking immune, as much as that could be achieved.

"Okay, okay," Ravi said, stuffing the worry down. "Think, Ravi," she admonished herself. "What *is* it about those decks?"

"Decks?"

"The order of the progression. Decks two, nineteen, fourteen."

"The schematics, check. What engineering is there? Docking? Offices? Storage of strange goods?" He hummed a little tune, a jaunty thing. Ravi caught him as he swayed and he looked at her blankly for a minute. When sense returned to his eyes, so did fear. "What happened?"

"You drifted off for a minute." She gripped his arm. "Maybe you should lie down."

"No, stay awake I must. Help I must, until I succumb."

"Okay," she said, worried about him becoming agitated. "Okay, I'll check the specs. We're missing something. This isn't acting like a disease, not a regular one. No clear symptoms other than falling down into a frekking coma," she muttered. "Deck two."

Ravi scanned the schematics. There was the deck two med bay, numerous eateries, a central garden and the main deck two hydroponics area. A play space and schooling facilities for several groups. No housing.

She tapped her statcomm. "BVax Trentham to Marshal Keeela on deck two."

"Keeela, actual. Go ahead."

"Where are you on deck two? Where are you standing?"

"At the edge of the green space and tables for the eateries."

"Give me a visual pan of all the businesses."

Keeela started from the right, panning across the front of the now-closed eateries. Gone were the crowds and the bright bustle of people. It looked like a bad student film for an end-of-the-world scenario.

There was the place Cragrral had bought his snack, there was the florist, then another restaurant, this one with tables and chairs for various species. It also featured cloth napkins and an extended array of cutlery. Was there something on that deck, in one of those shops, that could do this?

The schematics were never up to date for retail locations.

Keeeela continued to pan. Repair shops. Provisions. Furniture. The deck two greenspace was backed by that deck's hydroponics unit. The glass windows into hydroponics showed the bamboo, but the bright, colorful wink of the chrysanthemums was obscured by water. The daily irrigation and drenching rain period was in full force. The simulated wind aided pollination. Ravi frowned. The plants looked wilted, despite the refreshing water.

The camera swung back to the darker view of the corridor going around the hub and the marshal asked, "Do you want me to continue down the corridor? There are more restaurants, and other provision shops."

"Yes, please," Ravi said, but something was brewing in her mind. "Send me the vid when you've come back to this point. I have to check in on the other decks."

"Will do. Keeeela out."

Ravi switched the comm channel and called for Marshal ma'Gonese. "Ma'Gonese actual, BVax Trentham. What am I looking for?"

"What's on deck fourteen besides CentraComm?"

Ravi pulled up the schematic for that deck as she

spoke. There would be nothing but doors on an admin level, no reason to video that.

"Mining Regulations offices. Union offices. Stationmaster's office. Accounting. Import/Export Licensing Office." ma'Gonese took a breath to continue the recitation, but Ravi cut her off.

"Mining. Mining. Ores. What am I missing?"

"I don't know. Should I keep listing?"

"No. I need to check deck nineteen. Stay there. I may need you again."

"Roger. Ma'Gonese out."

Ravi switched to Marshal Tucker, but when she tried to tag him, she got a grey-faced Brad Carruthers. "He's down. He managed to call me before he collapsed. I'm taking him to the medbay on this level, but they've got cots in the hall at this point and only two medstaff."

Ravi nodded. "It's bad. I know. Cragrral is fighting the symptoms too."

Brad looked stricken, but nodded. "I'll ping you back as soon as I get Tucker to medbay."

"Good."

"Ravi?" Cragrral's voice was a whisper, and she spun to face him.

"Lie down."

"No. Ravi, my truename is Bayyneee. You should know. Told you, I nearly did, several times already. Now, you must know it. My song you will sing for me, if the worst happens."

"I won't need to." She put her hands together, making the Tilden sign for honor, repeating the words he had said to her. "I will treasure the knowledge of your truename. I will share it with no other. I will keep it in my heart next to the names of my truekin."

Cragrral smiled, his fangs a bristle of white behind his sitsuit mask. "You remembered it. You're really brilliant. Did you know that?"

Hallucinations. Dizziness. Disorientation.

What was she missing? Cragrral sneezed again, then hummed softly as he looked away from her.

Her statcomm pinged an urgent tattoo and she picked opened it to Brad's hail.

"What do you need?" Brad asked, his face looking even more bleak. He didn't ask about Cragrral. He didn't chide her, or tell her to work faster, or remind her of all the things she knew she needed to do. Relief was a brief flash, before dread resettled in her stomach.

What the hell *was* this?

The pressure of knowledge right at the tip of her mind returned. She was almost there. She could nearly taste it. Ravi knew she knew *something* that might solve the riddle, but she couldn't bring it together, couldn't put the pieces in the proper order and sequence to find the key. She was still missing something.

"What's on deck nineteen?" Ravi asked, urgency boiling through her as she brought up the engineering specs. The three decks were now displayed side by side on the big screens in front of her. She was scanning across the renderings, looking for a common denominator even as Brad spoke.

"It's all Admin. Station Administrator, Station Mechanics Administrator, Station Personnel Resources, Station—" He broke off when Cragrral sneezed three more times in quick succession, and collapsed to the floor.

"Cragrral, no!"

Despair hit her as she fell to her knees beside her only friend.

She was too late.

CHAPTER SIX

Cragrral's face was peaceful, his chest rising and falling, but now sweat darkened the short fur on his face.

Dizziness. Hallucinations. Breathing issues… breathing. Breath. Sneezing.

She had it!

"Shut down the scrubbers!" Ravi shouted, knowing Brad was still listening. The view from his comm, which had been panning offices, swung back to show his face.

"What? What the hell?"

Ravi knew now why the pattern of decks had bothered her.

She shifted a padded carryall behind Cragrral's back to ease his breathing, then leapt to the command console. "TurrTerrEel, it's Trentham. Shut down the scrubbers. NOW," she snapped when TurrTerrEel spluttered. "That's a Protocol One order from the BVax Protocol One Commander."

The minutes ticked away as the subtle, steady rumble that had grown exponentially louder as each medscrubber came online softened and faded. The machinery dropped quickly from full power to an uneasy silence.

"Find me a minerals expert, and whatever medstaff you can muster by comm. I need Administrator Bashink, and the owner of the florist on deck two."

"Bashink is down," TurrTerrEel interjected, as all her limbs remained in motion, her eyes turning various ways to different screens. "Though he lives. The florist is owned by a Decar, who is…." TurrTerrEel made a soft keening sound. "Deceased. As are all the staff of the florist."

"Five pertards made a delivery there. They brought plants and soil for those plants. Find those delivery people, and the plants."

She switched comms, hailing Brad. "Marshal Carruthers, do you know a merchant, a Protean? He brought a holo of a plant to StatAdmin Bashink. It seemed as if he were well-known onstation, a big deal."

"Protean?" Brad's weary gaze sharpened. "Huge guy, big rings, ugly hands and a bad attitude?"

"Yes, yes, that's him. Find him."

"He's our zero?" Brad asked, referring to the old-fashioned labeling of a plague starter as Patient Zero.

"I don't know. Maybe. But I need him, fast as you can find him."

"Done. Carruthers out."

Ravi dropped back to her knees by Cragrral. She couldn't lose him. She infused her voice with command.

"You will not leave me, Bayyneee Cragrral! Fight this. Fight it hard. It's the pollen from a plant. That's what was making you sneeze. The coma is lack of CO_2."

"BVax Trentham, I have medstaff!" TurrTerrEel's voice recalled Ravi to the comm. "Open channel to all.

Go ahead."

"Everyone, I need arterial blood gas analysis from as many patients as you can get. Or urinalysis, or whatever is the equivalent. I think this is from a plant that sucks all the CO_2 out of the air. It works *too* well. This is either a fast onset alkalosis due to CO_2 loss, a pollen reaction from that same plant, or a form of lead poisoning, again due to a heavy lead and magnesium loaded pollen. The medscrubbers and our closed air handling system onstation exacerbated the problem." What would have been a gradual sickness onplanet, became rapid-onset in a station setting. "The air handling system spread the pollen throughout the station. The overwhelming number of pollen spores dropped the amount of CO_2 in the system, and the plant effectively sucked most of the rest out of the air."

She drew a breath in her recitation. "We thought we had CO_2 leaks on several decks, but maintenance couldn't ever find them. It was because the plant pulled all the CO_2, which made the plant bloom and pollenate profusely. The pollen caused the rashes and some of the other symptoms, including most of the breathing issues. The medscrubbers drew and spread the pollen through the station."

"Got it," the current head of the medstaff snapped. "Let's get on it, people," the woman ordered. "We're treating for massive alkalosis, CO_2 deficiency." Turning back to Ravi, she said, "I have patients hanging on by a thread. I'm putting them in cocoons and pumping in oxy with a higher CO_2 ratio. I'm not waiting for stationwide effect on these patients. I take full responsibility."

"Go!" Ravi said, knowing time was of the essence.

"TurrTerrEel, leave the comm open to whatever medbay that woman is in," Ravi ordered when the woman dashed away from the comm.

"Done," TurrTerrEel said. "What next?"

"We have to find the plants."

The second comm channel popped up with Brad's still-exhausted face showing signs of his own adrenaline rush. "I've got the merchant. He's locked in Q-Lock, in the waiting area by his ship. He can't board or leave because no one is there to release the docking rings or the refueling hoses or let him out of Q-Lock." Brad seemed to find this ironic, as did Ravi. "His name's Master Merchant Rehgis Lank, from Protean."

"Patch him through."

"BVax," Rehgis Lank said immediately. Then he pointed at Ravi through the screen. "I remember you."

"Forget whatever stupid prejudice you have against BVax. Your plant is the cause of this," Ravi snapped.

"My hybrid? Impossible!"

"No, it isn't. I can prove it, but that isn't the point. I need information," she ordered, "or more people are going to die."

"How can I help?" the master merchant said, his face anxious now.

"The plant. It pulls CO2."

The merchant's face scrunched into a frown, making him even more unpleasant looking. "Yes. That's why we use it in the mines."

"How many did you sell to Decarian florist onstation? How many did you give as gifts?"

"There are one hundred plants total. I delivered ninety-five of them, per our agreement, to Station Petals, owned by Omah Tlkan himself. One went to Stationmaster Shupe, who put it in her break room where there was better light. One, was delivered to Administrator Bashink late yesterday afternoon. One went to the Head of Mining Administration. She is responsible for the growth of erban-ore mining on—"

Ravi cut him off. "I don't care about that. Who else?"

"Lanka Deq on deck twenty-one, a personal gift. And Mrrek Taldanekban on deck nine."

All decks with medscrubbers. All decks where there had been multiple CO2 leaks that maintenance couldn't locate, because not long after the notification alert, the levels had fallen dramatically.

"It works too well," Ravi stated flatly. "It's drained so much CO2 from the air that people have collapsed, and gone into alkalosis."

"Oh, rocks and stars!" the man exclaimed. His face sheened with sweat and he seemed about to collapse. "What can I do?"

"Get to my station," Ravi snapped, sending a locator to his statcomm. "I may need more information. As to what you can do, I don't know yet." She paused. "Wait, yes I do. Send me a picture of the plant. I have to find them and get them off the station. Now."

Ravi flipped back to Brad. "How do I get him out of Q-Lock?"

"I don't know. You'll have to release him from CentraComm, I think. TurrTerrEel should be able to do it."

"Okay. How many of your staff are still standing?"

"Five now."

"Okay, I need you to find these." Ravi shot through a picture of the plant to his statcomm. "They're the problem. Dump them in an airlock or onto a platform or something, but get them off the station."

"Got it."

To TurrTerrEel, she snapped, "Get someone here from medstaff for BVax Cragrral. Have you found the Pertards?"

"Someone is en route for BVax Cragrral. As to the Pertards, not yet. One is listed as having succumbed, the others I cannot identify. I am sending a mechtech to you who is a Pertard. He may be able to help."

"Good, thanks. Marshal Carruthers is finding these plants," Ravi said, shooting a photo of the plant through to TurrTerrEel, listing the decks. "We have to space the damn things or box them or something. Cram them into a sitsuit if we have to, but they must be contained. They're the source of the problem."

"A plant?"

"A plant that sucks all the CO_2 out of the air. Everyone has respiratory alkalosis. The scrubbers made it worse, with the oxygen-rich mix, low in CO_2. The plant leached so much CO_2 out that virtually everyone not in a suit, with a stable air supply and balanced CO_2, collapsed. Some in suits collapsed too, from an allergic reaction to the pollen, which also sucks CO_2." She paused, sucking in a breath of her own suit's air. It was getting stale, but still breathable.

"Medstaff would probably have caught it," Ravi said, her fingers dancing over the keyboards as results began to flow in from the few medstaffers still able to function. "But medstaff all got hit too fast. Cragrral and I were looking for a viral or bacterial cause."

"Why did Cragrral succumb?" TurrTerrEel said, her many limbs flying as well, as she took in the information Ravi sent. "I am running a pattern recognition to find the plants."

"Great. Cragrral got a snootful of the pollen on two different occasions. On the shuttle and when we came onstation. It made him sneeze." Ravi frowned. "It took a long time to affect him, though. I didn't breathe the pollen on either occasion, so I guess our BVax immunity kept us safe, at least for a while."

A worn-looking woman in a medstaff uniform arrived at that moment, with a hovering gravstretcher and an equally weary looking marshal. It was Trendte, but she barely recognized the formerly crisp marshal, he looked so exhausted.

"BVax Trentham, I'm here for BVax Cragrral," Trendte said, as the medstaffer brought the gravstretcher down next to Cragrral.

They'd barely gotten Cragrral's too-still form loaded when Marshal Carruthers arrived with the Protean. Ravi grimaced at the sight of the Protean in his enormous sitsuit.

"Take off your situation suit mask," Ravi ordered.

"What? Are you mad?" Rehgis spluttered. "There's a plague. You are BVax. I don't trust the company but surely—"

"You created this situation, Merchant Rehgis. Take off your suit mask and tell me what you smell."

The merchant hesitated and Brad motioned two of his marshals nearer. "Take his arms."

"What? I protest!"

It was too late for protests, as Brad had already put his marshal seal to the activation button on the suit and flipped the exterior control switch to allow Rehgis to take off the suit hood.

The merchant tried, unsuccessfully, to hold his breath. When he had taken two gasping breaths, Ravi repeated her question.

"What do you smell?"

The merchant looked puzzled. "It smells normal to me."

"Normal?" Ravi insisted, watching him closely. "Normal how? Station normal?"

"No," the merchant said instantly. "More like home…"

Ravi nodded in satisfaction. "Like home. Iron rich and thick, like Protean, right?" She didn't wait for the merchant's nod, but spoke to Brad. "Heavy on the lead. The plant has leeched all the CO_2 that leaked, so the station techs thought they'd solved the problem, but they didn't." She turned back to her console as she continued to advance her theory. "So CO_2 continued to leak, and the plant bloomed profusely, shedding a massive amount of pollen, heavy with lead, cadmium and other metals. Those then spread as the medscrubbers came on. The medicated and heavily oxygenated air spread the pollen. It also increased the air pressure in the station, which increased the CO_2 leaks, which hyper-oxygenated the air as the plants bloomed, synthesized CO_2, and continued to bloom—"

"So the cycle kept repeating as people collapsed from lead exposure or CO_2 loss," Brad concluded.

"Exactly. According to TurrTerrEel's correlations,

races who need more CO_2 were the first to go down, and most of the dead are from planets where CO_2 is higher than on-station."

Ravi's comm beeped, as did Brad's. Ravi threw both calls up on the screen, since it was TurrTerrEel trying to reach both of them.

"We have secured five of the plants in a pod outside the station." She hesitated, then hit a series of commands. "Now. The marshals are still seeking the other plants, but expect to have them soon."

"The medscrubbers have to be sterilized. Are there enough bots and drones on-station to clean all the ducts in the medscrubbers?"

"I am unsure. I will attempt to access that information. The current head of MedStaff, Dr. Mirchan Bis, indicates that the CO_2 and lead-abatement therapy is working and patients are reviving. Cadmium therapy will be last, since the half-life is short in most species. Dr. Bis says it is going slowly, as he does not have enough staff."

TurrTerrEel turned to look at Brad, not so much as twitching a limb at the sight of the marshals holding the merchant, having forcibly removed his sit-suit hood.

"Marshall, three of your men reported finding the rest of the plants, as well as the packaged potting soils and nutrient packages for growers." TurrTerrEel swiveled all her eyes to look at Ravi. "Should these items all be spaced in a pod, BVax Trentham?"

"Yes, as soon as possible," Ravi replied.

TurrTerrEel inclined her head, and her many limbs moved behind and beside her as she continued to speak. Ravi was so tired, she had to look away from the mesmerizing, multi-tasking appendages.

"BVax Trentham, the few maintenance workers still functioning have agreed to direct all drones to cleaning ducts and dur-sealing all the contents of the ducts for BVax inspection. One of the remaining workers would like to speak with you privately."

"Direct the worker here, please," Ravi said. TurrTerrEel cut the contact with a, "Done, sir," and Ravi turned back to the marshals and the merchant.

"You can put your suit back on. I needed to prove the point that it was the plants, it was the air you 'knew' from home and the plants were causing it. Until they get the system rebalanced, you'll need the oxy-CO2 mix in the suit bottles."

"Mine are running thin," Brad said, checking his levels. Ravi did the same, noting she had about 3 stat-hours left before the suit would have begun pulling air from the station and filtering it. It probably would have filtered out the pollens, but she didn't know if it would have re-balanced the air to provide CO2.

The subdued merchant restored his suit with no comment. After a few minutes of them all watching the meter on the screen show an infinitesimal rise in the station's CO2-oxy balance, Brad cleared his throat.

"BVax Trentham, we'll take Merchant Reghis into custody." To the merchant, who spluttered in protest, he said, "Save it. There are several hundred people dead. You've got a license for the plant, yes, but these unforeseen consequences have to be answered for."

Subsiding, and looking frightened, the merchant left docilely with the other two marshals. Brad stayed.

"I hope Cragrral recovers quickly," Ravi said,

without looking at him. Cragrral's collapse had been one of the most frightening moments of her life. She had so few friends. Even as a child on McKeon she'd been alone thanks to her advanced educational placements. Somehow, in one short week, Cragrral had become a friend.

He had to be okay. He just had to.

"I hope he does, too." Brad slumped in a chair. Weariness spoke in every motion of his body. "I've lost two of my marshals, a couple of support staff. Four more are still in medbays around the station."

"I'm so sorry, I should've figured this out sooner," Ravi said, and she had to force herself not to wring her hands. She felt responsible, culpable.

"Stop that," he said brusquely. "You're not to blame for any of it. Hell, Ravi, I don't know how you even figured this out. Who would have thought it was a plant and not a plague?" He looked at her, his eyes like dark pools of pain. "If not for you, this station would have been found floating out here, empty of all life, except for a bunch of big-flowered and very deadly plants."

The visual of that sprang into her mind in brutal, colorful possibility. "Yes, it could have happened," she said, hating the thought. "But BVax Cragrral is as responsible as I am for finding the source."

"I'm not so sure about that, but if you say so." Brad shifted and stretched, as if to erase the weariness. "The two of you will get credit for averting a major disaster, that's for sure." Brad heaved himself out of the chair. "I better get going. I've got a million things to do before I can collapse into my bunk."

"Yes, do get some rest though. As soon as you can.

125

I'm worried about secondary infections and lowered immune system response in all of the statcits who've been affected."

"I'm sure medstaff will get that in hand, now that you've stopped the plague."

"More of an accident than a plague," she corrected. "A biologic accident."

"An accidental plague." Brad managed a weary laugh. "That's what I'm putting on the incident report and the millions of reams of reports I'm going to have to file. *Accidental plague.*"

Ravi swayed a little, reaction setting in. Brad slung his arm around her shoulder, squeezed. "Let's check on Cragrral and get you to CentraComm to supervise the mop-up of all of this insanity."

"Oh, right. I should go there." Ravi looked around, trying to see if there was anything she needed to take with her. Nothing presented itself. "I need a shower," she said absently.

Brad laughed. "Don't we all? I think you can probably persuade Shupe, once she's on her feet again, to let you have a shower every day for your entire stay on Paradise."

Ravi battled the fatigue fogging her brain. "That would be lovely," she admitted.

"I'm gonna tell her that's what you need," Brad said, steering her to the door and to the personnel lift. Part of her recognized how empty the station was, how quiet, just as the door closed.

"I don't want to impose," Ravi said, picking up the dropped thread of the conversation.

"Yeah, not to worry. We'll work it out."

They arrived in CentraComm, and Brad waved at TurrTerrEel before staggering back to the lift with an absent, "Ping me if you need me. I'll be in medbay on deck nine."

He was going to see Cragrral. Ravi stood staring at the door, wishing she too could go. When she swayed where she stood, TurrTerrEel reached out a long arm and pulled a chair close to the emergency comm system where she sat.

"Come, sit down, Scientist Trentham. You are nearly done."

Ravi nodded, plodded to the seat. "Please, call me Ravi."

TurrTerrEel looked vaguely shocked, as if Ravi had said something scandalous, but she nodded, one hand stroking the BVax emblem on her harness as the others switched comm systems and one typed a response on a screen.

"Thank you, Ravi, for that honor."

Ravi nodded, too tired to speak.

"Now I will connect you with Acting Station Manager Bill Farr and Acting MedStaff Chief Dr. Mirchan Bis. After you speak to them, and take their reports, I will connect you with Acting Maintenance Chief Hram Phu, for an update on the cleaning of the scrubbers. Once you have talked to them, having already talked to Chief Marshal Carruthers, you are off duty for twelve hours, barring emergency."

"What about you?" Ravi said, realizing TurrTerrEel had worked as long a shift a she and Cragrral. "You will need rest as well."

"I am fine, Ravi," TurrTerrEel insisted. "ImaPrinta

sleep for one statday out of every five. I came off my restday the day this event took place." TurrTerrEel took a moment to consider. "However, I will requisition extra rations, as I seem to have lost body mass while dealing with this situation. That must be remedied."

With a brisk nod, TurrTerrEel pushed Ravi's chair closer to the console. "First medstaff and operations."

Ravi didn't remember what she said to medstaff or operations, much less maintenance. When she woke twenty hours later, still in her sitsuit, she was disoriented and fell off her bunk, flailing at the imaginary dream monsters who were trying to wrap her up in their vines and choke her to death.

"Aaaaagh," she gasped, sitting on the floor, panting and shuddering in the aftermath of the nightmare. "Terrorized by plant life. Ugh."

Struggling to stand, Ravi made her first call to the medbay where Cragrral had been taken. The medtech on the comm wasn't wearing a sitsuit, just her regular uniform.

"BVax Cragrral is awake and eating, BVax Trentham," the medtech told her, her face slightly green. "He, uh, asked for raw food and the kitchen staff was able to bring him a..." the young woman swallowed several times before continuing. "An unprocessed haunch from a buffle. BVax Cragrral made short work of that and is now eating...liver." The woman paused and swallowed again. "I'd give it an hour or so before visiting," she concluded, still looking vaguely nauseated.

"Good, that's good. Tell him I'll be there after I've checked in with CentraComm. How's everyone else doing?"

"Virtually all beings responded quickly to the rebalancing of the oxy-CO2 mix. Some are slower to come out of the sleep, but most are awake and eating and drinking. Some are already mobile and complaining." The last was said with some asperity, but a smile showed the young woman was more relieved than bothered.

"Okay. Okay," Ravi said, gathering her thoughts. "I'll see you soon."

"Good. Thank you for all you did, BVax Trentham," the tech said sincerely, tears in her eyes now. "You saved all of us."

"Oh, um…you're welcome." Ravi was totally unsure how to take the woman's thanks.

But the tech didn't press it, or comment further, simply wiped at her eyes and nodded. "Medstaff Nine C, out."

Next, Ravi opened a channel to TurrTerrEel in CentraComm. "Ah, BVax Trentham," the ImaPrinta said, her limbs stilling as Ravi made eye contact "You're awake. StationMaster Shupe is also, and StationMaster Bashink is on the mend, although not yet mobile. Chief Marshal Carruthers is still asleep, but he went to bed after you did. Maintenance Chief Phu has notified me that the scrubbers are at seventy-five percent cleaned. He has kept all the material in hazardous containment cubes for later processing, per your orders."

Ravi struggled to remember when she'd ordered that, but gave a mental shrug. They'd need the stuff to see if there were other contributing factors.

"In addition," TurrTerrEel continued, "per your authorization prior to your rest period, most of the station has returned all sitsuits to the property lockers for cleaning. Medstaff are returning them in lots. However, there are not enough transfertechs to process everything. I took the liberty of having all sitsuits delivered to an empty warehousing facility on deck five until they can be processed. Downside planetary communications are all cleared with each agency. They have been apprised of our recovery and have sent additional supplies by drone. Additional marshals will arrive to supplement Chief Marshal Carruthers's staff at the next launch window."

"Thank you, TurrTerrEel. Is there enough staff upright for me to turn control back over to the acting stationmaster? I know we have freighters inbound, as well as passenger liners."

"Not yet, but there should be by the third meal time, which will be timely for the freighters. You've missed the first two meal shifts, Ravi, so you won't have to be Command for too much longer. You are authorized for a thirty minute water-shower and you may break sitsuit discipline."

"I can?"

"Yes." TurrTerrEel gave what passed for a smile in the ImaPrinta—her multiple eyes wheeled wildly in their sockets—before continuing. "As acting Protocol One Commander, you gave the stationwide release order before retiring last night, ergo you too may break your seal."

"I did?"

"You did. Your exact words were, 'You can now take off your stinky sitsuits and get some sleep, people.'"

Mortified, Ravi went to drop her head into her hands, and only then realized she still had her own suit on. She must look like a ten-year castaway. Now that she focused on it, she could feel her clothes—three days old, slept and stressed in—sticking to her body. Some of her hair was clinging to her neck and face, though most of it was still thankfully braided back.

At that moment, TurrTerrEel's words clarified in her overtired brain.

"A thirty-minute *water* shower? Seriously?"

Again, TurrTerrEel's eyes revolved with humor. "Yes. Thirty minutes. I will continue to monitor, and will provide a renewed report when you arrive in CentraComm in—" TurrTerrEel consulted her comm, "—no less than a stathour."

"An hour?"

"Yes, take your time, BVax Ravi Trentham," the sectorhead said kindly. "Restoration is good for the soul and the career. TurrTerrEel out."

The comm closed and Ravi stood staring at it for a long moment before lifting her hands to break the suit's seal. Air whooshed in, crisp and clean. It still held the familiar tang of the medscrubbers, but nothing else.

She set the suit mask and hood aside, then stripped as fast as she could. The suit pants, close-fitting and filled with sensors, were wrapped around her legs like a lover. She managed to peel them off, dropping the whole thing to the floor. She could smell herself, and the suit, so there was no way she wanted that thing on her bunk.

Stripping off her uniform, which was so sweat soaked it might have to be disposed of, Ravi stepped into the sanitation facilities and turned the tap to water, temperate, and hit the activation.

A shower of warm, deliciously sensuous water fell from the ceiling, stripping away every stress. Soap did the rest of the work until she stood, clean, awake and ridiculously happy in the narrow stall, letting the water cascade over her.

She'd survived. She'd figured it out. Cragrral had survived, as had Brad. She grinned wetly as the image of Cragrral tearing into a buffle haunch popped into her head. She laughed at the thought of the tech's nauseated reaction.

The *pingping* signal from the shower metrics let her know her time was almost up. She rinsed one more time and pushed the off button.

"Thank you Marshal Carruthers," she said, turning the controls to dry. When she'd dressed in a fresh uniform, and dried and braided her hair, she took stock.

A lingering weariness that would go away over the next few days. A sense of solidarity with her team. An unfamiliar, but welcome, feeling of belonging. All of them were there, inside her. She marveled at the new-found hope that grew like a k-zu vine in and amongst the pillars of her psyche.

Maybe, just maybe, she had found her place on Outcast Station.

Maybe, just maybe, she'd be able to keep it.

EPILOGUE

"Thank you, BVax Cragrral, for your welcome and your tutelage," Ravi said formally as she stood waiting with Cragrral as his shuttle prepared for boarding. The remainder of the statmonth had passed uneventfully. No more E-Reps, no more threats, no other contact from the smugglers or "The Company."

"Already, I have sent you the beginnings of the paper for our publication, BVax Trentham," Cragrral said, with the same formal dignity. "Expect, I will, your response promptly."

"And get it, you will. Promptly," she replied tartly.

Cragrral laughed and reached out a long arm to pull her into a hug. His arms were long enough to wrap around her completely and he did so, and squeezed tightly. "Miss you, I will, Ravi Trentham."

"And I'll miss you, my friend, Cragrral."

"I heard you, you know," he whispered. "You called my truename, and told me to stay. I could not answer, but I did not refuse."

"I'm so glad."

"Me too."

A chime sounded in the waiting area and they separated. There were any number of people who were watching them, some with approval, others with distaste or indifference.

"Write to you, I will," Cragrral said. "Tell you of my adventures with Degeurro, I will."

"I can't wait. I'll keep you posted on what's going on here."

"You will tell me if they contact you again?" he whispered.

She nodded, and spoke of other things. She'd told both Brad and Cragrral of the message and the contact. Brad had decided she should take the smugglers up on receiving cargo, to try and see if he could ferret out who ran The Company. He still had two murders to solve, after all.

A second chime rang and Cragrral picked up his BVax duffle and the large case that held his research notes, plants and materials. The rest of his gear awaited him on the passenger liner bound for the Clunch Sector.

"Safe travels, my friend," Ravi said, moving in to hug him once more.

"Prosperous work, my friend," Cragrral replied, squeezing tightly once more. "Write me!" he demanded.

"I will."

She watched him board the shuttle, but as soon as he disappeared, she turned away, heading for CentraComm. The last of the statcits had left medbays, which meant she had final reports and after-incident data to prepare for briefings and to file.

Maybe the paperwork would distract her from the loss of her friend. At least he was leaving on two healthy feet, rather than through death. They were writing a joint paper on the incident, so she would still be able to talk with him.

That was good. That was a first.

There had been a lot of those firsts since coming to Outcast Station.

It took Ravi several hours of work in her auxiliary office in CentraComm, but she was able to file the last of the reports before the third meal break. She was tidying her desk when her statcomm pinged.

Dinner, then singing?

Yes. Thank you, Brad. Meet you in deck nine mess?

See you there.

The outcast McKeonite shut her desk and door, and headed for the lift with a light step. In a station of outcasts, she was finally home.

THE NEW BADGE

By

Nancy Northcott

CHAPTER ONE

Paradise Station, my ass. Seated in the one chair in his tiny cabin, Federated Colonies Deputy Marshal Hank Tremaine set his jaw as the arrival announcement droned on. *They should call the place what it really is, Outcast Station, where careers go to die.*

Not his, though. Not if he could help it.

He would keep his nose clean—especially when it came to crossing well-connected idiots—and survive this three-year exile and the blot on his record that came with it. Then he could get a better posting, one closer to Earth and less...tainted.

A faint shudder through the ship's structure signaled the docking array clamping on. The announcement ended. The cabin lights blinked, the signal to get moving. Hank grabbed his duffel and joined the trickle of people heading for the exit portal.

There weren't many travelers. Outcast Station, encompassing the orbital station and the sparsely settled world below it, didn't have a lot to offer anyone who wasn't desperate. Or compelled.

Except for extreme sports enthusiasts and hikers

drawn to either the steep volcanic mountains or the deep oceans and fjords filled with unique life forms. Or so his briefing packet said. But the cost of interstellar travel meant only the seriously dedicated and seriously well-off could make the journey.

Still, there were enough passengers to create a logjam at the exit hatch. His khaki and brown uniform set him apart from the rest of the crowd, who all wore some combination of civilian pants, boots, jackets, and shirts.

After five minutes of mostly polite jostling, he followed a twenty-something guy with a big backpack through the hatch and into the station's docking bay.

The station air had a tang to it, almost…piney. Must be from the hydroponic garden that was part of the air-scrubbing system.

The docking bay doors were open, leading to a corridor painted in cream and blue that had seen better days. The paint on the walls looked dingy and had chipped, not surprising considering that people carting baggage so often banged it into walls. The corridor ended in a small lobby with the Federated Colonies seal, a stylized swirl representing the galaxy with three stars around it to signify FC-controlled areas, on the wall. With a handful of other people, Hank veered left, into the hallway marked "FC Employees." The one on the right was for immigrants, residents, and the smattering of tourists.

One by one, the arriving employees walked through an archway at the end of the hall. As each person stepped in, flashing blue light signaled the emission of a decontaminating radiation burst calibrated to that individual's species and the diseases each might carry. Non-employees, not having been vaccinated regularly against anything a bureaucrat thought they might pass along, would also go through decontamination but then would have to wait half an hour to see if the radiation triggered any illness.

Beyond the archway lay the Customs Department processing station. Aside from the bored-looking guard at a desk to one side, the room held only a dozen waist-high, foot-square counter units of gray metal. Between them were clear plexiglass gates. Each countertop held a foot-square monitor with a retinal scan lens embedded on the left side, and each station's base had an ID-sized slot in the counter below a glass scan plate.

Hank slid the plastic card encoded with his ID and his orders into the nearest slot. The machine whirred, hummed, and clicked. Frowning, he glanced at the other people by the machines. Everybody seemed to be getting that, so no cause for alarm.

A metallic voice came out of the speaker above the slot. "Welcome, Deputy Marshal Henry Davidson Tremaine. Please place your right palm on the scanner in front of you, and bring your left eye to the blue light."

Hank complied. A tiny needle pricked his right middle finger, drawing a bead of blood for DNA analysis.

More whirring, clicking, and humming ensued. Geez. Yeah, this was the ass end of nowhere, but it was also the nearest jump point to the Drachan Empire. You'd think they'd have more up-to-date equipment.

"Identity verified," the voice announced. "Access authorization encoded. Proceed through the gate at your left."

Step one down. He now had clearance to go wherever he needed to on the station or the planet. Marshals service local authorizations would be added at HQ. Only then would the shockstick and stunner attached to his gear belt be charged.

The barrier to his left slid aside, and the machine popped out his card. Hank tugged it free, grabbed his duffel, and strode through the barrier and the swinging door behind it.

The door opened into a lobby about twenty feet square with a glass wall and doors fronting the station hub beyond. Half a dozen people, some in rough pants, boots, and jackets and others in finer fabrics that screamed *city,* waited there to meet new arrivals. They looked up when he entered. His gaze zeroed in on the petite, dark-haired woman in regulation marshal uniform, khaki slacks tucked into brown boots and a dark brown jacket worn over a tan shirt. Her badge gleamed on the jacket's left chest with a name bar under it.

"Tremaine?" she said as he walked up to her. When he nodded, she stuck out her hand. "Barnet. You can call me Dree. Welcome to Paradise Station."

"I'm Hank. Thanks." He couldn't keep a dry note out of his voice, and she grinned, brightening her medium brown complexion, as they shook hands.

"Yeah," she said. "We don't really call it Paradise, but it's the official name for the official greeting. Is that all your stuff?"

"Couple of crates in the cargo hold."

"Those'll be shipped down to the barracks later, with

the supplies. Meanwhile, I'll take you dirtside so you can report in."

He followed her into the hub, where a round garden of stubby trees and bushes in the center softened the blue-and-cream surroundings. Glass-fronted shops, restaurants, and bars lined the circular space. Their neon signs, in a variety of bright colors, added a cheerful note despite the clashing shades.

People of various ethnic and species backgrounds walked through the area. Tall, tan-furred Tildens crossed paths with cream-furred or gold-furred Gallupian felinoids and humanoids of varying colors and shapes. The empty-handed ones walked fast, obviously with someplace to be, and the ones with baggage strolled along, rubbernecking. Lizard-like Pertards with green or orange scales steered a package delivery cart around the perimeter.

No scorpion-like Drachans walking on four of their eight legs, though. The chance to learn more about that reclusive race was one of the few pluses to this assignment.

"I understand you get a lot of sports enthusiasts here," he said. "Any tourists?"

"Not many just to see the sights. Not much to see that would be worth the cost of getting here. Mostly we get scientists studying something here or in transit to Dracha and students on fellowships. And, as you said, the sports enthusiasts—hang gliders, hikers, and tournament-level fishermen looking to land something exotic."

Hank nodded. The volcanic mountains on the planet below hadn't been worn down like the older ranges on

Earth, so the terrain was steep, rocky, and inhospitable. "No one faint of heart would consider this a playground."

"Nope. Our landscape's a magnet to those who like to test both their skills and their nerve."

"You have plenty of backcountry, though, right?"

Most development was on the plateaus or the coastline and around the fjords that slashed through the mountain ranges, and most of that was limited to the temperate zone around the equator. Or so his packet said.

"We call it outback, but yes."

She led him around a corner to a plain door. A swipe of her ID opened it, and they walked down a utilitarian, off-white hallway. A service elevator with plain, gunmetal doors took them down ten levels.

When they exited, Dree led the way into another docking bay. A bar-shaped light above the airlock hatch read "Airlock engaged." On either side of the sign, round lights glowed red, indicating that the airlock leading to the ship was secured.

"This is the marshals service's dedicated docking bay," his guide informed him. She swiped her card in the reader beside the hatch. "It's near the detention area, and our on-station office controls access. We can use the others, of course, but we have to get clearance through the station manager's office."

"My packet said we still have to get launch and docking clearance from traffic control."

"Right." She flashed him an appraising look. "So you read the packet. Not everyone does."

Hank shrugged. "Forewarned, and all that."

The light over the door turned green. Tapping the

control panel, Dree said, "Yeah. Not everyone gets that, though."

Especially here, he'd bet. The people who usually landed here were reputedly sloppy or defeated, mostly past giving a fuck. Dree seemed to be on her game, though. So what was she doing here?

The door slid aside, revealing a plain, gray airlock. Hank followed his companion through it and into a battered, twelve-seat shuttle that had been current in the more accessible systems fifteen years earlier.

"Stow your gear overhead," she said, dropping into one of the two pilot seats. "You know how to fly one of these?"

"Yeah, but nothing bigger." Hank shoved his duffel into the nearest compartment and took the seat beside her.

"Most of us don't." She answered absently, her gaze on the instrument panel and the switches she was flipping.

Hank tracked her sequence. She was proceeding in the right order, checking each gauge before she activated the next system, so he relaxed in his seat.

As he strapped in, she threw him a grin. "Yes, you can trust me with your life."

"What can I say? You caught me." At least she didn't seem pissed about it.

Dree studied him for a moment. "On Outcast Station, a little paranoia is a good thing."

Before he could ask what that meant, she turned back to her board. "Ready?"

"Sure." As much as he'd ever be. Maybe she didn't want to say too much—paranoia being a good thing and all—to somebody she didn't know whether she could trust.

Dree radioed for launch clearance and a heading, but Hank only half heard her. Her warning echoed in his brain. This assignment just kept getting better and better.

#

At the spaceport dirtside, they traded the shuttle for a battered, four-seat hovercar with the Federated Colonies Marshals Service logo, a five-pointed star in circle, like their badges, on its hood. The glass windshield was dusty and marked by a couple of small nicks. "Believe it or not," Dree said, "This is one of the nicer cars."

"If you say so."

An old-style chain link fence reinforced by an energy barrier surrounded the base. She headed for a gate with a sentry hut beside it, and the guard waved them through. Ahead sprawled the town of Micah's Junction, all weathered, one-story or two-story, spray-stucco buildings, dingy brown or dingy gray except for the occasional one with a green or yellow or blue façade, all of them faded.

The paved surface gave way to dark, glittering volcanic gravel. The spaceport had a forty-foot easement all along its rim, with nothing growing in it. Steep, volcanic mountains encircling the town on three sides were a crazy quilt of various green shades from trees bearing summer foliage. On the fourth side would be the ocean, but he couldn't see it from here.

"Is the sea really purple?"

"As a Terran grape," Dree said. "Office is two blocks down this street. Learning your way around isn't hard. By the end of your two settling-in days, you'll—"

A tall, dark-skinned man and a lanky, pale woman, both in spacers' coveralls, ran from a doorway ahead on the left and looked wildly around. Their gazes locked on the marshals' hovercar. Waving frantically, they hurried toward it. Behind them, a man flew backwards from the doorway into the street. Another man dived out and landed on top of him.

Dree pulled over, killed the engine, and hit her red flashers. The sounds of shouting and crashes came out of the building.

"Shit," she muttered, jumping out. Hank leaped out his side.

"Are you hurt?" she asked the people who'd flagged them down.

The pair shook their heads, and the man said, "There's a big fight. Gonna need more'n the two of you."

That was kind of obvious from the loud crashes, grunts, and curses coming through the closed, wooden door, but the duo were trying to help.

Racing toward the sidewalk brawlers, Dree called back to Hank, "You're not read in. Stay here."

When she was going to wade into the fight? It sounded like a serious brawl.

Standing back galled him, but she was right. Until the chief deputy marshal logged Hank's orders, thus *reading him in* to the post, and authorized charging his weapons, he had no official standing here.

He couldn't help following her, though. Sounded

like they needed a riot squad inside.

Dree snatched something off her belt. A flick of her wrist extended the stubby cylinder a couple of feet, and Hank relaxed, recognizing it. She tapped the shockstick against the thigh of the guy on top. He yelped, clutched his leg, and rolled clear.

"Freeze," Dree snapped. "Both of you."

Hank knelt and helped her restrain the men's hands, linking them together back to back. "I got this," he told her with a nod at the doorway. "Go."

She clapped him on the shoulder and ran into the loud bar. A moment later, the shrill blast of a whistle sounded inside.

A whistle? Wha—Oh, right. Some of the species that passed through here couldn't tolerate the safe-for-humans jolt of a shockstick.

He stepped up to the door. When it slid aside, he couldn't see her though the place was brightly lit. Had she called for backup? If not, all she had was him.

Hank scowled. Official or not, he could at least watch her back. He pulled his personal comm unit out of his jacket pocket and snapped a photo of the two men on the ground. "Stay here, or this goes to your bosses and we add charges of fleeing the scene."

He edged inside the door. Bodies parted, giving him a view across the room. A few feet farther in, Dree was exchanging blows with a four-foot, rotund, blue humanoid. Judging by the way it took a punch, a lot of that roundness was muscle. The space beyond her was full of brawling beings cussing and grunting in multiple languages.

The room was strewn with overturned chairs and

tables. Spilled food and drinks created muck and puddles on the floor. Five people were down, not moving, that he could see. They'd be lucky if no one trampled them.

A heavyset woman staggered backward into him. When he reached to steady her, she swung a haymaker at him.

Hank ducked, caught her swinging arm, and used her momentum to spin her face-first into the wall. "Marshals service," he shouted in her ear, kicking her feet apart. "Freeze."

"Bastard," she muttered. He used zip ties to restrain her hands behind her back, patted her down, and ordered, "Sit here and don't move. Except to dodge bodies."

The *crack* of breaking wood came from his right. He pivoted toward it. A burly, green-skinned humanoid grabbed the leg of a smashed chair, straightened, and whirled toward Dree. Engaged with her opponent, she had her back to the new threat.

"Fuck it," Hank muttered.

Snatching the shockstick off his belt and snapping it out, he lunged forward. Even with no charge, the stick could serve as a baton. He grabbed Chair Leg Guy's upraised arm and whacked the baton against the back of his knee. The leg crumpled. Hank shifted his grip to twist the arm behind the guy, pushing so he fell forward. The guy landed hard, and Hank dropped a knee into his back.

The guy bucked but couldn't throw him off, so he was enough like a Terran for standard restraint methods to work. For good measure, Hank zip-tied the guy's ankles as well as his wrists.

"Thanks," Dree said. "But—"

"Watch it." Hank pulled her aside as a pair of brawlers staggered toward her. If backup was coming, they were taking their sweet time about it. "Let's get this settled."

"But you shouldn't be here."

He shrugged. "I'm in it now. Pick a pair, and let's get this done."

Procedure dictated that two marshals breaking up a brawl worked together to take down the combatants one pair or clump at a time. Working in tandem, they had most of a dozen pairs of combatants restrained and down in a few minutes.

A group near the bar, though, still traded punches and shoves.

Over there, somebody yelped. Straightening, Hank shifted to see why. A scowling brunette stood behind the wooden counter with an empty pitcher in each hand. The small group in front of her were sopping wet. Exchanging a glance, Hank and Dree hurried over the sloppy floor to help her.

"You don't bust up my place," the woman announced. Her clear voice carried over the muttering around the room. She set the right-hand pitcher down behind the bar. When her hand rose again, it held a machete, and the look in her eye said she wouldn't hesitate to use it.

Damn, but she had guts.

Sputtering, the wet brawlers glared at her. One big guy stepped forward.

"Stand down," Dree called, her voice don't-push-it hard.

The guy hesitated, and the two marshals took stances in front of the bar, confronting the indignant, wet group. Five of them, all human except for one tall, pink-skinned humanoid.

"Stand down," Hank and Dree ordered together.

From the doorway came the shrill blasts of numerous whistles. Marshals in brown, batons deployed, flooded into the room. Everyone turned to look, and groaned curses came from various people still on their feet.

"Cavalry's here." Hank grinned at Dree.

She shook her head. "I appreciate the backup, Hank. I'm grateful not to have my head bashed in, but you shouldn't have done it."

"I'm glad I was here to have your back." Diving in before he was authorized was an infraction, yeah, but a minor one when it was done to save a comrade under attack.

"No. You don't understand." Her eyes grim, she touched his arm briefly. "I mean you really should not have done that."

The flood of marshals into the room and the routine of dealing with prisoners stopped him from asking her what she meant. What the hell was wrong with backing up an outnumbered comrade?

CHAPTER TWO

With two prisoners to transport in the back of their car, Hank couldn't ask Dree to explain her comment. They stopped behind the marshals service HQ, a four-story structure that took up an entire block. Its cream, stucco walls were dusty and weathered, but the door the marshals herded the prisoners through was well-maintained, two-inch steel.

Inside, the corridor was the same institutional beige Hank had seen everywhere he'd been stationed.

They hustled their prisoners into a lift, up to the second floor, and into an already-crowded holding cell that faced the heavy glass window of the booking office. As the gold-furred, feline guard reactivated the cell's force screen barrier, Dree said, "I have to handle the booking, but you should go report in. Elevator's halfway down this hall. Take it down to the ground floor and turn—"

"Marshal Tremaine," said a metallic voice over the intercom. "Marshal Tremaine. Report to the chief deputy marshal immediately."

"Guess I better go." Time to get started building that

clean record. "Thanks for meeting me."

"Sure. He's in 103, two doors down to your left from the elevator. And Hank…"

"Yeah?"

Lowering her voice, she added, "Don't sit unless you're invited to, and always call him sir."

"Barnet," the man behind the booking screen called, "you got charges to list or not?"

"Coming." With a last warning look she hurried away.

#

Finding the chief deputy's office took only a couple of minutes, but the setup was odd. No chief Hank had worked with before had an outer office or a reception area. But maybe this guy was formal. Hank could live with that. He stepped in and gave the middle-aged man at the reception desk, who wore civvies, his name.

The man spoke into a headset, listened for a minute, and said, "Chief Winslow will be with you shortly."

Hank nodded his thanks. The reception area was not painted but paneled in gleaming, dark brown wood. Four blue leather chairs sat against the wall in front of the desk. Behind the desk was a closed, eight-paneled door with brass fittings and a nameplate that read CHIEF DEPUTY MARSHAL ARLEN WINSLOW. It had to lead to the inner sanctum.

Okay, then. Not just formal but maybe a little pompous. But a guy determined to keep his nose clean could handle pompous. Unfortunately, Hank hadn't been able to pick up any scuttlebutt on the guy. If he'd been here long enough to fall off radar, that was a bad sign.

Despite the *Report immediately* summons, Winslow didn't emerge to call Hank in. Hmm. Did the *No sitting unless invited* prohibition apply to the reception area?

Best not to risk it.

He had time to check out all four of the pictures on the walls, scenes from around Paradise Station, including an interesting beach resort, before the receptionist said, "Chief Winslow will see you now."

He led Hank to the door, opened it, and stepped aside. "Deputy Marshal Tremaine, sir," he said. Once Hank was inside the room, the receptionist closed the door.

The man behind the desk, either studying or pretending to study a tablet, had a stocky build, a gray buzz cut, and a bit of a gut that might or might not have been muscle. His stony expression didn't change as Hank crossed the surprisingly large expanse of dark green carpet.

Carpet? In a marshal's office? Yeah, definitely pompous.

Hank advanced until he was even with the two chairs across from the desk. Standing casually between them, he waited.

Winslow leaned back in his chair, clasped his hands across his stomach, and studied Hank. The silence stretched, but Hank refused to blink. He could speak up, take charge of this interview, but if he wasn't supposed to sit uninvited, speaking first would likely not start things off well.

"Did I miss something?" Winslow asked in a smooth, deep voice worthy of a vid star.

"About what, sir?"

The chief deputy shrugged. "About you. Like maybe the part where you were read into the post roll before you charged into a bar and started banging heads. Did I miss that?"

"No, sir." Hank kept his voice even and his face bland. *Asshole.*

Yeah, he'd acted prematurely, but the circumstances made that a forgivable breach. Which Winslow had to know as well as he did.

Yet the guy was baiting him.

"I've read your file, Tremaine. Asked around, too." The chief deputy paused, and the gleam in his eye had Hank bracing.

Winslow continued, "Chief Deputy Johannson and I were at the academy together. So I know all about you being a hotshot."

Being a hotshot was what Johannson and his nephew, the nominal on-scene commander, called Hank's decision to go in alone and rescue a hostage while the nephew dithered. The fugitive who'd kidnapped the woman was about to shoot her, and everyone else in the strike force had backed up that assessment. They'd said he should get a medal.

Instead, he'd gotten sent here. With an asshat of a CO who was out to get him before he'd even reached the station. Shit.

"Nothing to say?" Winslow raised a steel-gray eyebrow.

"No, sir."

Something that might have been disappointment flickered over Winslow's face before his expression became assessing. "I don't tolerate insubordination, Tremaine. Remember it."

"Yes, sir."

Definitely disappointment that time. The chief deputy stood. "Let's get you read in and charge your weapons. We'll do that by the book."

What a shock. Winslow would get one if he thought Hank didn't know the regs. This looked to be a posting that would give him plenty more practice pretending to stoic calm.

In the doorway, the chief deputy stopped. "Good thing they got working cams in that bar," he said. "Otherwise, we might have to delay reading you in."

Again, he paused. Again, Hank refused to be drawn.

Winslow smirked at him. "You're a witness, and without cams showing you were nowhere near the victim, you'd be a murder suspect. One of the men on the floor of that bar turned up dead."

#

Finally, the orientation app directed Hank to a place he actually wanted to stop into, Addison's, the bar where he'd gotten himself in trouble earlier. Where the bartender had demonstrated surprising grit at the end of the melee.

Hank took a deep breath of fresh air, so much better than the stifling atmosphere in HQ. But maybe that was due to the warm camaraderie of his meeting with his boss.

Before going into Addison's, he checked the orientation app to be sure he'd covered the route accurately in the two hours he'd been walking around. If he missed a site, Winslow would rag him about it.

Nope, he was on track. Most posts didn't issue comm unit apps with prescribed routes. He'd rather find his way on his own, but orders were orders.

The wooden door slid aside in time for him to walk through it. It *shushed* closed behind him, the sound faint under the buzz of conversation and the clink of utensils.

Hank stood still and waited for his eyes to adjust. Yesterday's bright lighting had been dimmed. Maybe the manager had turned the lights up when the fighting started. The tables and chairs had been restored to order, with about half of them now occupied. The smells of meat, bread, and something like beer wafted through the air. Under them lay faint hints of sweat, human and metallic other.

His mouth watered, a reminder that he'd missed lunch and was heading toward dinner. Nothing on the annoying app dictated a time limit for covering the route. He strolled toward the bar. His uniform drew a few glances but no comments.

At a table near the bar's far end sat four deputies in uniform, and thus on duty. Three looked seriously overweight, and all had what looked like beer. Hank grimaced. Those guys were closer to his expectations of Outcast Station than the brisk friendliness Dree had demonstrated.

The brunette from yesterday and a seven-foot, gray, avian being moved back and forth behind the counter.

"Aw, come on, Addie," a thin man in gray ship coveralls said. Perched on the edge of his stool, he smiled at the brunette. "I'd show you a good time."

She grinned at him. "I have a good time in my own place, Jed. Besides, I wouldn't want to disappoint the other women in Micah's Junction. You'd have a better time with one of them."

His companion, a stocky woman, nudged him with her elbow. "Told ya, Jed."

"Aw, Addie." He shook his head and sighed.

The avian bustled over to Hank. Its round, black eyes focused on him. Up close, its gray feathers showed as a blend of gray, black and white. They covered its face, neck, upper body--visible except where a green vest covered it—and four-fingered hands. What first appeared to be six-inch beak looked, up close, more like a nose, albeit one with a sharp, pointed hook at the end. Like a raptor's beak. A slit below the nose moved, and a metallic voice issued from the amulet at the being's throat.

"What will you have, marshal?"

"Dinner. What's good?"

"The special is buffle stew and root vegetable salad for 8.57 credits."

Buffle—? Oh, the local buffalo equivalent. "Sounds good. With ginger beer."

The bartender strode away, and Hank's memory finally supplied the species name. The being was a Grog, natives of the planet Grahglax in the Five Star Consortium and kin to the predatory rocs that roamed the upper reaches of the mountains here.

He watched the room via the mirror above the bar. The marshals in the corner mostly ate and drank, ignoring their surroundings. The other tables held people in shipsuits interspersed with others in casual civilian garb. The two groups didn't mix, as usual in a port city. The spacers often found the townies unwelcoming, while the townies considered the spacers to be reckless, loud, and arrogant.

The brunette bartender set his ginger beer in front of him. "Not having regular beer?"

"On duty." Hank shrugged.

"Doesn't bother some," she noted, studying him out of hazel eyes.

"Some aren't me."

"Guess not. Where you in from, marshal?" When he raised his eyebrows, her grin flashed again. "I know all the local faces, so it's easy to spot the new badges."

"Figures." He nodded. "My last post was Granville Station." Close to the Nine Planet League, Granville's bustling station and world had a heavy flow of commerce and a lot of things to do in off hours.

She patted the bar in front of him. "That ginger beer goes to your head, the local coffee'll fix you right up."

"I'll bear that in mind," he said, his voice wry.

She chuckled, extending her hand. "Grace Addison. This is my place. Everyone calls me Addie."

"Hank Tremaine. Good to meet you." Her firm, brisk handshake suited her manner.

"Certainly a better meeting than yesterday's. Thanks for what you did, you and your mates."

"You're welcome, but we just did our job."

"Really?" she drawled. A speculative look lit her eyes. "Not quite the way I heard it."

Damn if he would ask what she'd heard. "You were impressive this morning, by the way, and you've gotten the place back in order fast. I'm glad no one on your staff was hurt."

"Thanks for that. They know to take cover if trouble starts." She cocked her head, as though something he'd said puzzled her. But she replied only with, "You settled in okay?"

"Mostly. Doesn't take long to unpack a duffel and a couple of crates." Nor were there many choices about where to put the contents in quarters consisting of a small living room/kitchenette combo and one small bedroom and bath.

"Guess not." Again, she patted the bar. "Food should be up in a minute. Signal if you want that coffee."

He nodded. The pager on his comm unit buzzed. What the hell? He wasn't on the call rotation for another two days.

But he tapped the mike stud at his throat. "Tremaine."

"Dispatch here. Report to the Officer of the Day immediately."

Hank grimaced, but an order was an order. "On my way."

Maybe Winslow had found some way to nitpick Hank's use of the idiotic orientation app. Regardless, he was going to have to get that meal to go. He signaled the avian.

#

"We have a murder in the outback," the sturdy, grim woman behind the OD desk informed Hank. She did not invite him to sit. What was it with these people?

She stared at him, waiting.

"I don't guess that's unusual," he ventured. Surely that had nothing to do with him, the newest badge on the post. But uneasiness crept up his back.

"No, unfortunately," she agreed. "The information we have and the crime scene photos are on the main server under Lothian, where the crime was committed, and today's date."

"Okay." This was not going in a good direction. She wouldn't tell him that unless—

"You fly out in two hours. Deputy Corker will take you out there and return. We don't have enough runabouts for you to take one and keep it there."

Hank's face felt frozen. His first day, and he was actually being assigned to a murder case in a remote area he knew next to nothing about.

"Well?" the OD frowned at him. "Is something wrong?"

"You're assigning me this case." He kept his voice carefully neutral.

Her frown deepened. "Obviously. Unless you're not up to it."

Up to it? Seriously? He hadn't been here long enough to learn the ground, the customs, or the people, and he was being sent out on a Grade 1 felony.

But he could see the trap yawning in front of his feet.

Hank shrugged. "A murder's a murder." Per his orientation materials, Lothian was a demesne, or vast colonial landholding.

"Am I solo, lead, or backup?" he asked.
"Solo."

Another bad sign. Custom dictated that deputy

marshals have six months to ease into a new post before being handed a major investigation to lead, let alone handle solo. Because, of course, knowing the area made inadvertently screwing up less likely.

The OD wouldn't have assigned him without Winslow's express order.

She continued, "Grange Tarpon, the marshal posted there, will help you in a pinch, but he has his own duties to see to."

Recognizing dismissal, Hank nodded and left. At least he wouldn't be completely on his own, but the deck was stacking nicely against his solving this case. With Winslow's hand doing the backdoor stacking. Still, Hank had earned his former good reputation. He would apply all his training and experience to this case. Solving it would not only make him look good but have the added dividend of thwarting Winslow.

If he could do it.

CHAPTER THREE

Maybe Winslow's plan wasn't actually to brand him with a spectacular failure, Hank decided after an hour in the air with Deputy Marshal Corker. Maybe the plan was for this drunken idiot of a pilot to kill them both outright. That would probably remove two irritants from Winslow's sandbox in one stroke.

Corker flew above a seasonal thunderstorm, just not far enough above it to avoid buffeting winds. Hank gripped the edge of his seat with one hand and willed his stomach to stay put. The buffle stew had been great, but seeing it again wouldn't be.

"You know," he commented in what he hoped was a relaxed tone, "the autopilot would beef up the stabilizers." It would also correct the meandering course the other man was flying. Its light on the console showed blue, meaning it was ready but not engaged.

"Busted," the other man muttered. "Besides, autopilot's for sissies."

There was the real answer.

Hank gritted his teeth and eyed his companion askance. Most posts wouldn't put a guy who slouched in his seat and couldn't fly a straight line anywhere near a pilot's chair. They certainly wouldn't trust one who'd been in the bar only a few hours earlier to fly anything. Hank had seen him in Addison's, and his bloodshot eyes and the faint odor of beer about him confirmed that he'd been drinking. His attention seemed focused on the big viewport above the controls instead of on the console screen showing course and heading.

"Been a while since I flew anything," Hank noted. "I wouldn't mind trying out this baby."

"You're the passenger." Corker grunted. "Orders."

Or possibly another excuse, like the *busted* autopilot.

Rapid beeping erupted from the console, and red lights flashed around the altimeter. A dark shape loomed out of the twilight in the front viewport. A fucking mountain.

This is it. We're done.

Corker yanked back on the altitude stick. Hank's stomach dropped away with the ground, but the runabout, a six-seater with a holding cell in the back, cleared the crest of the mountain.

"Damn fog," Corker muttered.

Fog of drink, more like. Shit. They really would be lucky to reach Lothian alive.

Confronting a drunk was seldom a good idea, but crashing was a worse one. Better to be thought lacking in nerve than to be dead.

"Look," Hank said, pointing. "The autopilot shows ready. Let's test it."

Before Corker could refuse, Hank punched the button under the blue light. The light turned green. A metallic, gender-neutral voice said, "Maintaining current course and speed. Enter any desired change."

Corker scowled. "I got this."

"The mountain nearly had this. I'm the new guy, Corker. Humor me. Besides, if the autopilot takes over, you can kick back instead of babysitting me the whole way."

"That's a point." The other marshal's bloodshot eyes narrowed on Hank's face. "Not a word to the boss."

"Not one."

Corker blinked at the navigation screen. "We're on course. I'm gonna take a break in the back."

"Sure. I'll keep an eye on this."

Corker shuffled aft, likely for a nap, a drink, or both. Hank checked the navigation screen. They were more or less on course for Lothian City, where the marshals service office was, but the altitude could use a boost. He muted the verbal function and entered the necessary correction. The ship's rise left the bumpy air behind. The autopilot would adapt for any obstacles, so they'd clear any more mountains in their flight path.

As minutes ticked by, Hank gradually relaxed. Snoring came from the rear of the runabout. A glance back confirmed that Corker was out.

The guy was more what Hank had expected from an Outcast Station marshal than Dree Barnet was, with her brisk efficiency. Which left him wondering, again, how she'd landed here.

Well, he could worry about that later. Right now, he would do better to look over the info on Lothian City. And hope the marshal who was his backup was more like Dree than Corker.

#

Not knowing the ground was going to be a disadvantage. Hank frowned at the information on the screen. The victim, Abner Brek-Hathra, part human and part Glotrelan from the Nine Planet Guild, had been a warehouse supervisor. He'd overseen the packaging and shipping of kova, the local coffee, in an outlying community, Cartwright's Creek. The place had a couple of bars and restaurants and a handful of shops. Knowing how the workers usually related to each other, which hangouts were unsavory or not, and how the workers interacted could be important in tracking down leads and evaluating what witnesses said.

Well, maybe the Lothian City marshal, Tarpon, would be at least decent. Anyone posted here should know such basic info. Even if—maybe especially if—he liked the sauce as much as Corker did. He'd moved back to the pilot's seat while Hank read. Despite Hank's misgivings, Corker brought the runabout down smoothly behind the marshals service office.

Hank shrugged into his insulated jacket, grabbed his duffel, and followed Corker out. Lothian's higher altitude meant cooler nights than in Micah's Junction. He would meet Tarpon and check his preliminary plan against the local marshal's info. Tomorrow, he'd head up to Cartwright's Creek and dig into the case.

Unlike the buildings in Micah's Junction and the ones visible above the ten-foot, stone wall around the landing area, the marshals service outpost was made of stone, two stories with what looked like a slate roof, maybe 20 by 40 feet. A similar but much smaller outbuilding, probably 10 by 10, sat on the opposite side of the landing pad. Next to it, a covered parking area held a runabout and two hovercars marked with the marshals service badge logo.

On the hillside high above the town, lights showed in a sprawling structure. That must be the demesne headquarters, or keep. Lothian, his info said, was governed by a woman known as the Lady. Geez, the things people carried over from Earth! This wasn't the Middle Ages. Regardless, he would have to pay a duty call on her, but that could be useful. He might need info from her staff.

Heading toward the outpost's rear door, Corker spoke over his shoulder. "You can dump your stuff and head up to the keep. The Lady wants to meet you."

"Tonight?"

"So I'm told. The DPSO on duty'll meet you at the keep."

Demesne public safety officer, that would be. Lothian City should have four of them, with one in each of the outlying agricultural communities as well. They would do the day-to-day policing of minor incidents and leave major issues to the marshal.

"This person have a name?" Hank asked.

"They wear nameplates, same as us. Like it matters." Corker snorted. "They're all alike. Think they're supercops 'cause they get to carry a shockstick. Woo-fuckin'-hoo." He swiped his card in the reader beside the door. "Keyed to yours, too," he said. "All of us."

If the local officers were merely competent, that would be fine. The last thing any investigation needed was shoddy backup. But Corker's attitude didn't bode well for a good working relationship between the marshals and the local cops.

Hank followed Corker into the outpost and a narrow, institutional green hallway. "Cells back here on the right," the older deputy announced. "Three of 'em. With bars, not force screens. Latrine and storage on the left."

Pausing by a wooden staircase on the left, Corker said, "Quarters up there. Bullpen ahead."

Hank stepped through an open doorway to take a look. Beyond it lay a wide room with two battered, metal desks and chairs on each side of the steel front door. Narrow, horizontal windows high in each of the room's three exterior walls admitted the faint glow of the streetlights. Each desk held a computer monitor. Holocubes sat on two of the desks, but only the one in the rear corner also held work tools. A stylus and tablet lay on it.

It looked efficient enough as a work space, but having such worn equipment was unusual, even on remote posts. Was it from budget shortages? Or did the Lady just not like the marshals service?

"Where's Marshal Tarpon?" Hank asked.

"Probably down at the Singing Hornet."

Great. Another bad sign. Per regs, Tarpon should've been here to see Hank settled in.

Corker continued, "I'm going down there after I drop you off. DPSO Whoever'll bring you back. Don't let the bastard hang around here. They got their own office a couple blocks down, and they're supposed to work out of it. Unless we need their help—what a joke —on something big."

"Okay. Why the empty desks?"

"One's set aside for them." Corner shook his head. "C'mon. You can put your stuff in the spare room, then we gotta go. You don't keep the Lady waiting."

"What's she like?" Hank asked as they mounted the stairs.

"Snooty. Like most of the demesne bosses. Thinks everybody needs to lick her boots."

If most of the marshals posted here were like Corker or the absent-when-he-shouldn't-be Tarpon, there might be a reason—

"Not a bad rack on her, though," Corker continued.

And there it probably was.

"Get her alone for ten minutes, she'd loosen right up. That kind always does."

Hank clamped his mouth shut. Calling Corker a pig wouldn't qualify as keeping his nose clean.

"Not that she'd look at a working man like me or you," Corker added. "Can't run over a man like us the way she can those sissy lords in her *la-di-dah* set."

With an oink, oink *here and an* oink, oink *there,* Hank thought. Just as well Corker wasn't going up to the keep with him. The guy wasn't subtle enough to keep the chip on his shoulder from showing. Besides, if a demesne's lady decided to make life rough for a marshal, she could. Money talked as loudly here as anywhere else. Maybe louder in a place so remote.

They reached the top of the stairs and a wide landing. The paneled door to their left was closed. The one straight ahead stood open, revealing four shadowy bunk beds. Next to it, a small kitchen was visible through an archway. Corker gestured to the open door on the right. "Spare quarters. Dump your stuff and let's go."

Hank complied. Unlike his quarters in Micah's Junction, this door had no lock plate. Just as well that he hadn't brought anything personal with him.

They went back outside and climbed into one of the hovercars. As Corker backed it out of the shed, Hank revised his to-do list. First, make nice with the DPSO in hopes of gaining at least one assistant he could rely on. Second, try to convince the Lady of Lothian he wasn't a buffoon and actually did know what he was doing. Otherwise, she might decide to put up roadblocks that would kill his slim chance of solving this case.

#

When a guard ushered Hank through the keep's massive steel doors—painted with a faux wood finish—a middle-aged, blond woman in the DPSO uniform of green trousers and shirt with black jacket and lace-up boots already stood in the vaulted entry hall. Her wary expression confirmed his misgivings about the working relationship between marshals and the locals. He had ground to make up unless he wanted to work this case virtually alone. Marshal Tarpon's actions so far didn't imply that he'd be much help.

With a quick glance at her nametag, Hank smiled and stuck out his right hand. "Hank Tremaine. Thanks for meeting me, Officer Ballard."

"Uh, sure." Despite the surprised look that flashed over her face, she took his hand in a firm grip.

"Have a seat," the guard said. "Someone will be with you momentarily."

The man walked out, but that didn't mean no one

was observing. Or listening. Hank glanced around at the high stone walls and the staircases that started up each side, took a sharp turn, and rose further to meet in the middle, at the hall's rear. No sign of any spyware, but he'd bet money it was there.

"I'm new on Out—er, Paradise Station," he said. "I'm hoping you and your colleagues will fill in the local knowledge I lack."

"Okay."

She still looked uncertain, though. Why?

A stocky man in blue trousers and jacket of fine wool walked into the entry hall. "The Lady will see you now. Please come with me."

He led them up the stairs, along a carpeted hallway lined with landscape paintings, and to a door halfway down the corridor. Tapping on the door, he said, "Marshal Tremaine and Officer Ballard, my lady."

He stood aside so they could enter and then closed the door behind them.

The fortyish woman behind the desk rose. She eyed them coolly, her expression giving nothing away. "Come in, please."

They crossed lush carpet figured in gray, blue, and dark red, but the distance to the two gray chairs in front of the desk was about a third of the gap from door to desk in the chief deputy marshal's office.

The woman offered her hand. "Welcome to Lothian, Marshal Tremaine."

"Thank you, ma'am." Oops. Should that've been *my lady*?

The woman didn't seem to care. They shook, her grip firm and her palm calloused. Whatever Corker said, this woman was no stranger to working with her hands. The plain, gray trousers and tunic she wore, the level look in her gray eyes, and the sleek, chin-length auburn hair gave her an overall take-no-crap appearance.

Yet she didn't supply her name, which his records said was Moira McQueen. Why?

She offered a handshake to Ballard, too. "Good to see you again, officer."

"Thank you, my lady."

"Please be seated." As they settled, she added, "I take my responsibility for my employees and the other residents of my lands seriously. I want you to find the person responsible for Abner Brek-Hathra's murder. To that end, I've directed my security chief to make available any records or other materials you need. He has already compiled video showing Brek-Hathra's public movements in Lothian City during the hours before he died and has a list of his coworkers for you. The vid covers only the main business district, but it may help. He'll send the file to your email if you'll write it down."

She pushed a pad and a stylus across the table. Hank jotted down his contact info as she added, "If you need to question any personnel, you will inform him, and he will make those persons available."

While monitoring the interviews, maybe? Hank shook his head. "That's kind of you, my lady, but I prefer to manage my own investigations." Especially since some bosses didn't hesitate to eliminate employees with inconvenient knowledge.

"You'll manage this one. But none of my personnel will talk to you without my approval, which Chief

Mortimer is authorized to give." Raising an eyebrow, she added, "You can conduct your interviews wherever and however you wish. But meetings with my personnel will go through my office."

Or else, plainly, there would be roadblocks. Hank nodded. "Fair enough." But not exactly a point in her favor.

"Officer Ballard," Lady Lothian said, "Please tell the marshal and me what you've learned so far."

The request jolted Hank. Were the local marshals so inept or so lazy that a DPSO needed to investigate? Or was the Lady letting him know she had more than one finger in his pie?

"Of course, my lady," Ballard replied. "As you probably noticed from the crime scene reports, the deceased had taken a blow to the back of the head that caused considerable bleeding. We didn't find anything onsite that looked like it had caused that injury. There was a short blood trail, as though…"

Half listening to a description of the crime scene he'd already read, Hank watched the woman behind the desk. She seemed to listen attentively, but he would bet she'd already read all of this, too. So why was she having Ballard run through it all again?

"There were three-finger marks in various locations on the furniture that left no prints," Ballard was saying. "They appear to be Rorlan, but I swabbed them and sent them for genetic analysis to be sure."

Many species didn't have the distinguishing whorls on their fingers, and Ballard had followed procedure. But the crime scene should've been processed by a marshal, not a local officer.

Had the Lady's gaze sharpened, or did he imagine it?

Ballard finished, "Results are pending, as are blood toxicity tests and autopsy results. That's all the information I have to date."

"Excuse me," Hank said, keeping his voice bland. "I gather that you processed the scene, Officer Ballard. Alone. Is that correct?"

"Yes, sir. On Marshal Tarpon's orders."

"I see." Hank nodded. The records hadn't reflected that, but of course they wouldn't, not with Tarpon doing the database upload. A marshal who sloughed off the work wouldn't dare admit it. Even out at the ass end of nowhere. "Is that usual?"

Ballard's face tensed. "Sometimes, sir. Not that we have much serious crime."

"Let's ditch the *sir*," Hank suggested. "We're working together, so I'm Hank." Though a good nickname might be *disgusted*. Marshals were the elite of law enforcement because they had, and deserved, a rep for dogged efficiency and a high rate of closing cases. Tarpon's negligence would smear the rest of them, too.

As would Hank's failure if he couldn't close this.

"I'm Krista," the startled local officer said.

The Lady was definitely watching him now. She knew. And she was judging.

Blast it, Tarpon.

Hank said only, "I noticed the three-fingered contacts, with no fingerprints or distinctive skin textures showing, on several surfaces at the crime scene DPSO Ballard mentioned. Since those are typical of Rorlans, I'd like a list of those working or living in your demesne."

"That's already prepared. I'll have that sent to you."

Yet she hadn't offered it initially. Was she testing him?

"I'd appreciate that. And, of course, anything else Chief Mortimer thinks might be helpful."

His flat tone drew a quick sideways glance from Ballard, but Hank ignored it. Breaking eye contact with the Lady would be like a concession.

"Thank you, Officer Ballard," she said. "I'd like a private word with the marshal. My secretary will escort you back to the foyer."

"Yes, my lady. I'll wait for you there, Marsh—ah, Hank. Good night, my lady."

"Good night."

Hank and Lady Lothian eyed each other in tense silence until the door closed behind Ballard. If she was waiting for him to apologize for Marshal Slackass, she would have to say so. Tarpon's negligence wasn't Hank's fault, and even if it were, no apology could make up for unforgivable dereliction of duty. And there was probably worse. A marshal who would fob off processing a crime scene had to be fucking up in assorted other ways.

Holding eye contact, she said, "I would like you to process that scene again. Officer Ballard is diligent but not as highly trained as a marshal."

"Is that a request or an order?" No matter how bad the marshals here had been, she couldn't be allowed to consider herself the boss of them.

"Take it either way you like, so long as you do it. I want my foreman's killer found."

"As do I, my lady."

The look between them held for a long moment before she nodded. "We understand each other, then," she commented.

"I hope so. If there's nothing else…?"

"One thing, which I'll deny—with recordings to support my denial—if you repeat it. Most of the marshals who rotate through here are idiots. If I ran this demesne the way they conduct their business, we would be bankrupt in under a year."

She was probably right, but he couldn't admit that. "And?"

"You don't seem like an idiot, but everyone has hidden depths. Until I know you're competent, I'll have eyes on you. Don't screw this up."

CHAPTER FOUR

This morning's to-do list was plenty long enough. Head to Cartwright's Creek. Find out who the victim's friends were. Question same. Ask around town about anyone he was on the outs with. Find anyone who had left town, then track down and question him/her/it. Pin down who'd seen him the night he died, what he'd done or said, and what those individuals had observed. Check with the demesne security chief about why there were static-filled gaps in the video of Brek-Hathra in town.

And, yes, process the scene again to placate the Lady.

Seated at the desk he'd claimed in the bullpen, Hank scowled at the computer screen. At least he had one competent DPSO to help tackle it all. If two of them happened to be competent, this might be doable.

Security Chief Mortimer had sent addresses and shift schedules for the victim's girlfriend and a couple of workers known to be his friends. That at least provided a place to start interviews, which Mortimer's office already had approved.

Hank sent back a request for a list of all of the

victim's direct coworkers and a question about the gaps on the video, then pulled up the crime scene photos. Ballard had tagged all the places she'd swabbed. When he clicked on them, the lab reports from those locations came up. The five DNA runs for the sites that lacked fingerprint whorls were still pending. Looked like she'd done a thorough job, though.

Footsteps came down the wooden stairs in the back, audible only because the connecting door was open. A man in a marshal's uniform strolled into the bullpen.

"Morning," Hank said without looking up. If collegiality wasn't a priority here, he could go with the flow. It was too bad, though, as effective teamwork always produced better results than running solo.

The other man grunted, crossed his arms, and surveyed Hank. He looked to be in his early fifties, lean, with thinning brown hair and a confident stance. Too bad the bleary eyes and the whiff of alcohol around him undercut the image.

"You're the new guy," he said at last in a gravelly voice. "Trent or something like that."

"Tremaine. You must be Tarpon."

"I must be." He strolled to the kova pot in the corner and poured a cup. Seated at the desk across from Hank's, he blew on the steaming liquid. "Thanks. Whoever takes the last cup—or wants the first—makes it."

"Roger." And unnecessary to point out since that was customary at marshals service installations everywhere.

Tarpon's chair squeaked. "The chief must really have it in for you. Outback murder's tough enough when you know the ground. The people are clannish. Protect their own."

"I figured. Good thing it's rare."

"Read up on us, did you?" Tarpon did not sound pleased.

Hank shrugged. "Standard prep." Which thus should've been expected. So far, Tarpon and Corker were living down to his expectations of those stationed here.

He flagged a few places on the photos to check again. Tarpon watched him over his coffee.

"Don't talk much, do you?" the older marshal asked.

"When I have something to say." What he would absolutely not say was, *How about lending a hand with this?* Tarpon would've offered if he had any intention of assisting, and if he was a habitual drunk, as seemed likely from what Hank had seen so far, the investigation was better off without him.

The hum of running water came through the walls. On the outer worlds, water was abundant and chem showers costly, so water was the rule rather than the exception for bathing on the planet. Corker must be up.

The front door opened, admitting the rumble of people and vehicles on the street and a whiff of cool, eucalyptus-scented air. A short, stocky man in the green uniform of a demesne cop walked inside. Lines lightly marked his dark tan face below graying, brown hair, and his blue eyes held keen intelligence. He and Tarpon exchanged nods.

Marching up to Hank's desk, he stuck out his hand. "Joe Nahz, head public safety officer."

Ignoring Tarpon's eye roll, Hank stood to shake the offered hand. "Hank Tremaine. I take it you're on duty today."

"Ballard was, but since the Lady wanted her to come with you last night, we reworked the schedule. Besides, we thought a second pair of fresh eyes wouldn't hurt when you go back over the crime scene."

"Agreed."

"Where do you want to start?"

"Might as well get the crime scene done. Hang on while I transfer this data to my pad, and we'll roll."

Nahz grabbed a thermal cup from a drawer in one of the vacant desks. By the time Hank had his jacket on, the local officer had kova in his cup and was ready to go.

"Tarpon, does that runabout in the shed work?" Hank asked.

"So far. I need it for patrol, though." Tarpon scanned something on his tablet. "Maybe Corker'll let you take his if you hurry. He'll be expected back at Micah's Junction by midday."

A jerk of Hank's head signaled Nahz to go on out. When the rear door thudded closed behind him, Hank said, "The crime scene and initial witnesses are up in the hills. Hiking up there would be a waste of time." Like three hours or more to cover the rough terrain, even on the dirt road that led up to Cartwright Creek, the small community where Brek-Hathra had lived, then the same to return. A runabout could make the trip in forty to fifty minutes, depending on wind conditions.

"I might need it. You can rent a flitter over at the Depot."

A two-seater but with no room for gear or passengers. Uh-huh. Hank studied the other man, who had yet to look up. Wanting to keep the runabout because he *might* need it was pretty blatant obstruction, but the reasons for that could wait.

Hank kept his voice relaxed. "I'm taking Nahz with me, and we need room for gear. A flitter's sufficient for solo patrol." Which was supposed to be conducted on foot anyway. "So is the hovercar out back. Since we're on a homicide, that gives me priority."

He pivoted and headed for the door.

"You can't take the runabout," Tarpon snapped.

"Regs say I can." Hank kept walking, but his shoulders tensed. Would the other marshal make an issue of it?

He reached the door without further argument, so that would be no.

Nahz waited by the door. The look he shot Hank was concerned.

Hank said only, "Let's get going."

In daylight, he could see that the trees on the mountainside showed spotty gold or orange. Fall approached earlier in the high altitudes.

They crossed the landing pad to the open garage and its two runabouts. Corker would use the one they'd come in to return to Micah's Junction. When Hank headed for the other, Nahz paused.

Hesitantly, the local officer said, "Sir, Marshal Tarpon isn't one you want to cross."

"He's not the first difficult colleague I've had." Hank entered the standard access code on the keypad and leaned in so the sensor could pick up the signal from his badge. A moment later, the hatch slid open.

Nahz followed slowly. "Yes, sir, but…"

"You have a runabout we could use instead?" Hank

asked, dropping into the pilot's seat. "Because we're not hiking up there. And it's Hank, by the way."

"Okay. Then I'm Joe." Nahz still looked uneasy but strapped into the copilot's seat.

Hank started pre-flight. "I requested a full list of those who worked with Brek-Hathra, but it hasn't come through yet. Any Glotrelans here in town who might know him?"

Joe shook his head. "The purebreds don't travel much, and they don't mix much. Not many hybrids."

"Okay, then. We'll do it by the numbers. Crime scene first, then we'll start with the victim's girlfriend. By the time we finish with her, more info may have come in."

#

"Tell me more about Cartwright's Creek," Hank said as they locked the local DPS office behind them two hours later. The crime scene kit would be safe in there while they questioned Alice Margs. He'd read about worker housing, but Joe probably knew more than whoever compiled the briefing materials.

"Sure. Workers in harvesting and packaging live in the areas where they work. A shuttle goes down to Lothian City a couple of times a day and in the evening. Workers can have flitters. A lot do, but many don't bother."

Hank nodded acknowledgment. They were crossing a wide, grassy area that seemed to be a town square. At each corner stood an apartment block. Between and behind them, bungalows filled in the spaces. One low building boasted "Thrall's Eats" in orange neon. Cartwright's Creek looked a lot like every other remote community on any of the four other worlds where he'd been posted. The terrain might be more dramatic, but the settlement itself had a familiar feel.

The addresses he'd requested from Chief Mortimer had come in, along with the unhelpful news that the gaps in the video must've come from jamming. That implied furtive intent on the part of Brek-Hathra, whoever he'd encountered, or both, but it was no help solving the case.

"Joe, do we need to inform the local officer of what we're doing, as a courtesy?"

"Not necessary. Officer Latham spends her day making rounds. She wouldn't want to be interrupted."

"That's fine." The town sat on a plateau carved out of the steep mountainside. Terraced levels rose above it and led downward about half a mile, all full of pale green bacca plants in various stages of production. Some were mere seedlings while others, fully grown, stood four feet tall and had oval, platter-sized leaves growing off a three-inch, round stalk.

As the base for a number of medications, the plant was a linchpin of the planetary economy. It was no wonder that this demesne devoted so much land to it.

At the foot of the lower terraces stood a row of greenhouses, each about the size of a large family home. The community likely housed about a hundred workers, which was the norm for three shifts running the machinery, plus families. The processing plant, according to his map, was over the ridge beyond the greenhouses.

A patrol route covering all that would keep an

officer busy, even without a problem to handle.

Hank glanced at his pocket tablet. "Margs is at 17 Tulip Terrace. Works in the admin office for this growing zone, but she's off today. Personal time, probably because of Brek-Hathra."

"This way, then." Joe set off to the right, and Hank fell into step with him. They walked around one of the apartment blocks and toward the one-story houses scattered behind it. The road wasn't paved, but it was heavy gravel that would withstand weather. A long, narrow plot with grass, trees, and a swing set stood between it and the apartment block.

"Is all the housing in clusters like this?" Hank nodded at the neighborhood ahead. On Earth, it would've been called a cul-de-sac, with eight houses around the end and half a dozen more on each side leading from the main road.

"Mostly. Terrain restricts the options." Joe turned left. "Here we are."

The house looked tidy, the natural area in front of it neatly raked, the gray paint fresh, and some kind of red and yellow flowers in beds around the front stoop.

Hank pressed the buzzer. "Creds out," he reminded Joe, reaching for his own.

The village officer spoke softly. "Does she know we're coming?"

"Not unless Mortimer or one of his staff tipped her."

Shuffling footsteps approached from inside. Three distinct buzzes signaled locks being disengaged. Did she really need that much security?

The door swung open. A human woman who looked to be in her midforties clutched the edges of a dressing gown together. Puffy redness around her gray eyes implied that she'd cried a lot lately.

If her grief was genuine, disturbing her just sucked. There was no help for it, though.

Hank said, "Ms. Margs, I'm Deputy Marshal Tremaine. This is DPSO Nahz. We're sorry for your loss and sorry to intrude, but we need to ask you some questions.

Annoyance lit her eyes. "Can't this wait?" She ran a hand through already-disheveled, graying brown hair.

"I'm afraid not, no. We need to move quickly to find whoever killed Abner."

She bit her lip, as though considering that, but she didn't actually have a choice. Shoulders slumping, she stepped back. The two men tucked their creds away and followed her into a square sitting area furnished with a sofa and a couple of chairs in inexpensive fabrics and dark colors. A counter separated it from a kitchen.

Margs slumped on the sofa. "What do you want to know?"

Hank and Joe took the two chairs. Being a marshal made Hank senior officer, so he would take the lead. "I need to record this," he said, engaging the recorder at his belt. She nodded, and he read off the case info. "When did you last see Abner?"

"The night before he died. He was here when I got home. We had—had dinner." She took a shaky breath. "He should've been here the night he died. I waited up, thinking maybe he'd missed the regular shuttle and would hire one, but he never called or nothing. I didn't think nothing of it. He—If I had…"

"It likely wouldn't have made a difference," Hank

said as she wiped her eyes. "A mentally competent adult isn't classified as missing until 24 hours have passed. What did you do that evening?"

"Talked to a friend, Leela Bates. We had wine about eight at her place and watched a vid. Then I came home, about 2100."

"You were alone after that?" At her nod, he added, "Did you comm anyone?"

"No." With a heavy sigh, she shook her head. "Just waited for Abner."

"Did he say anything about expecting trouble?"

"No, but...he did say something weird. Said he had to meet Otis Ransom in a few days." Frowning, she added, "He kinda made a point of it. I asked him who that was, and he said just a friend. But I know his friends. There's no Otis."

"Did he say where he was meeting Otis? Or what day, exactly?"

"No. Except...he was talking about Micah's Junction. So he must've meant on his days off. If it wasn't a poker night, I'd go with him down to Lothian City a lot. That wasn't something to make a point about. So I'm thinking it was Micah's Junction. Maybe in, oh... five days from now? I've kinda lost track. Y'know?"

"Yes, ma'am." A check of the planetary residents would reveal where Otis Ransom lived, but only if he actually lived on Outcast Station and wasn't simply passing through. Though there were few places that going through here was a logical way to reach.

"Do you know where he went the night he died?"

"He said he had a poker game down in Lothian City. At the...um...yeah, the Piper's Roost. He was coming back here after." Her lip trembled, and she bit it.

"Did he say who was in the game?" The comm at Hank's waist vibrated. Without looking away from Margs, he silenced it. An emergency call would actually make the unit beep, not just vibrate.

A headshake answered him, but she added, "It was probably the usual bunch. Five or six of 'em play together regular on Wednesdays. Not always the same bars." She rattled off a series of names.

Hank glanced at Joe, who nodded imperceptibly. He knew some of these people. Good.

"All of them called me," Margs noted, sniffing. "Said how sorry they were. Didn't talk about the game, though. Except Jolt Peters—I mean Dray, but his nickname's Jolt—said as how Abner won a bunch off him."

"Any of those Rorlans?" His info said there were three in the demesne.

"No. There's one what lives up here, but Abner didn't have much to do with him. Said the gills creeped him out."

He wouldn't be the first, but most people got over that. Members of the amphibious race were generally low-key and law-abiding, with a planetary religion that called for humility, tolerance, and charity. Easy to get along with.

"Did he leave anything here?" Hank asked. "Boxes or envelopes? Clothes?"

"Some clothes in the bedroom closet. You can go look."

Hank and Joe exchanged another look, and Joe headed back to the bedroom.

"Did anything unusual happen in the last few days? Anything that made you stop and think?"

Margs shook her head. "Just the Otis thing."

"You work in the shipping office up here?" When she nodded, he asked, "What do you do there?"

"I'm the traffic clerk. I log shipments going out and supplies coming in."

Hank ran back through some of the same questions from different angles. As he was finishing, Joe came back out of the bedroom. His quick headshake confirmed that he'd found nothing there.

Hank stood. "Thank you for your time, Ms. Margs." He drew a card from his back pocket and passed it over. "If you think of anything else or find anything else, please let me know immediately."

He and Joe took their leave. When they reached the street, Joe said, "She seems distraught, but you never know."

"Yeah. Her place isn't that far from his. She could get over there, argue with him, kill him, and be back in under half an hour. With time of death being between 2200 and 0200, she has no alibi." Hank pulled his comm off his belt and glanced at it. "Autopsy results are in. Let's take a look at those before we talk to his friends. You know some of them?"

"Jolt Peters, Lon Besek, and Doral Mars live in Lothian City. I think Merida Keane and Torv B'Lare live up here. Don't know the other one she mentioned."

"What are they like?"

"Best I remember, Keane and Peters took a couple of runs through court for being drunk and disorderly. Besek, Mars, and B'Lare haven't been in trouble. Peters has a rep for being sleazy in general, with one rap for importing porn without a license to back it up."

"A nice assortment. Let's see what the records have for us."

Now that Hank thought about autopsies, he should also check the report on the guy who'd died in the bar fight without a mark on him. Just to know what the deal was, since Winslow had thrown it in his face. But that could wait.

"Then we'll interview the two poker players who live up here," Hank decided. "I'll send a message to notify Mortimer."

#

"That's a fat lot of nothing so far," Hank commented an hour later. He and Joe sat in the town public safety office's tiny interview room. The two local poker players were off work and not at home.

"So we go back to Lothian City?"

"No, first let's interview the Rorlan who lives up here, Dex Allarth. The lab chemical got a weak chemical trace off those three-digit prints, enough to confirm that they were made by a Rorlan, though possibly not enough for a match. So some Rorlan was in Brek-Hathra's place fairly recently. Maybe Allarth and our victim didn't know each other, or maybe they just didn't let on that they did. Despite claiming to be creeped out by the Rorlan gills, the victim let at least one Rorlan wander around his place."

"Too bad it takes so long to match that chemical compound to an individual. If it's not in the database, getting a warrant can be tough."

"It always is." Hank shrugged. "Speaking of chemicals, though, look at the tox screen." He called up the report on his tablet and passed it to Joe. "See that flagged substance. It reads as a mild hallucinogen. Has elements in common with bacca, this says."

Joe frowned at the screen. "That's a new one on me. Bacca isn't a hallucinogen. They must've mixed it with something else. But why do that with a medicinal crop?"

"Maybe the combination boosts the buzz?" Hank tucked the tablet into his jacket. "Let's go see the local Rorlan."

They headed out, and Joe locked the door as they left.

A few people strolled across the green or toward Thrall's. "The food there good?" Hank asked.

"Nothing that would stand out in a place as big as Micah's Junction, but good enough."

"Okay, then. We'll take this interview and then eat before we head down the mountain." The protein bar he'd snagged from kitchen supplies this morning hadn't been very filling.

They walked to Dex Allarth's apartment. Along the way, the people they met gave them nods of greeting. Not exactly friendly but not hostile either. No one asked if they'd caught Abner's killer yet.

The apartment entry hall had four doors opening off it with a lift at the end.

Hank knocked on Allarth's door but got no response.

He pulled out his tablet and consulted the file on Rorlans. "He's second shift. He should be here."

"I'll check with the neighbors." Joe knocked on the

door across the corridor.

A stocky man with a weathered, tan face answered it. Hank hung back to observe. Joe spoke courteously when he asked about the guy's neighbor.

"Is he in trouble?" The man's gravelly baritone rumbled into the hallway.

"We need to ask him some questions about an investigation," Joe said.

The man rubbed his stubbled chin. "If he's not here, I 'spect he's down at Thrall's. Might've gone to the city on an errand, but I'd bet on Thrall's."

Joe thanked him. The man shut the door, and the two law enforcement officers walked out into the sunlight.

Thrall's was busy, but Allarth was not among the customers. "We'll get him later," Hank said. "For now, let's eat."

They squeezed into a corner table. Most of the customers, humanoid men and women with a few others mixed in, wore brown Lothian Bacca Fields coveralls and work boots.

The automated menu had about a dozen choices. Not bad for such a small place. Hank and Joe made their selections.

A few minutes later, a five-foot droid wearing a neon orange Thrall's tee over its round, one-foot-diameter, pillar-shaped body rolled over to the table on two narrow wheels. Some wit had painted a face onto the upper end of its body. "Gentlesirs," its androgynous voice said, "a guest is asking about you." It gestured toward the entrance with one of its two bifold, steel arms. Each ended in a clamp suitable for carrying a tray.

Joe turned in his seat, and Hank leaned out to look

beyond him. A Rorlan male, familiar from his ID shot in the planetary records, stood near the front door. About five feet tall, stocky where most of the species were thin, he frowned into the room.

"Allarth," Joe said.

Hank turned to the droid. "Sorry, but we need to cancel our order."

"We deliver if that makes a difference."

"To the public safety office?" Hank asked.

"If you wish."

"Bring it there, then." He and Joe paid before pushing away from the table and making their way to the door to meet Allarth. As the only Rorlan in the community, Allarth was the most likely being to have left those prints in the victim's apartment. If he hadn't, he might know who would've.

#

"I didn't know the man," Allarth insisted half an hour later. "My neighbor said you were looking for me. I have nothing to hide, so I came to see what is the matter." His *s* pronunciation carried a faint hiss, likely from the interplay of air coming into his gills at his jawline and out of his mouth.

Hank glanced at Joe. Those who announced, unprompted, that they were hiding nothing were almost always lying.

"Your place is about ten minutes' walk from his," Hank observed. "Did you see anyone between the two?"

"It was a windy night. I stayed in."

The comm console buzzed. Joe walked over to

answer it.

"Anyone with you?" Hank asked Allarth.

"I was alone. Marshal, am I suspected of something?"

"Not yet," Hank said easily, "but there are chemical impressions of Rorlan digits in Mr. Brek-Hathra's apartment. You're the local Rorlan, so we need to ask. If you weren't there, do you know of any other Rorlans who were here that night?"

"No. It was not a good night for travel."

"Yet Mr. Brek-Hathra and some friends went down to Lothian City to a bar," Hank noted as Joe came back and sat down. Though he had to admit the chilly weather that night wouldn't invite travel. Or the walking around the victim had done in Lothian City.

Allarth's mouth twisted. A flatulent sound—his species' equivalent of a snort—issued from his gills. "The folly of others is not my concern. I watched a vid alone, then meditated. I know nothing else."

"What do you do for the demesne, Mr. Allarth?"

"I'm a pedologist." At their blank looks, he added with a touch of impatience, "I study soil. I also monitor the health of the plants in the fields."

Hank kept asking, but the Rorlan insisted he had seen nothing, heard nothing, and known nothing of what transpired that night. At last, Hank told him he could go.

"Was the call that came in important?" Hank asked.

"Unfortunately." Joe shook his head. "The lab got a very weak chemical trace off those three-finger impressions. Enough to say they're Rorlan, possibly not enough to identify with certainty. Regardless, they're not in the database."

"So much for the easy jobs." Hank pulled a wry grin. "Let's go talk to the poker players in Lothian City. By the time we finish, you'll be off shift."

"I'll work over if I need to. The Lady pays well."

They strapped in and lifted off.

With the weather clear, they had a view of the steep terrain through the front windscreen. Hank banked into a turn around a mountain, and they swooped over a plateau full of big, brown, chunky animals that resembled North American Earth's buffalos.

"Let me guess," Hank said. "Buffles."

"You read your file."

This again? Was it *that* rare for a new badge actually to prepare?

Joe continued, "They're mild enough 'til you get 'em riled. Then watch out."

"I'll remember that."

The ground fell toward a wide valley where more buffles grazed. A forest of twisted, stumpy trees covered the slopes.

"What are those trees?" Hank asked.

"Kova. It and a sort of cherry grow well at this altitude. Both are close to the Terran strains."

Hank put the runabout on autopilot so he could gawk. In the distance, swatches of bright yellow, orange and blue swooping off a ridge had to be hang gliders. He'd never been able to decide whether that pastime was brave or incredibly foolish, but the gliders in flight had an undeniable grace.

Something big, brown, and avian flashed by, dangerously close to the viewport. Hank's jaw dropped. "What—?"

"That's a roc," Joe said. "Predatory bird named for the one in Earth mythology. I'd say one of those buffles back there is doomed."

"Damn, it's big." Hank craned his neck to see the creature wheeling over the woods. "My file didn't do them justice. It did say they don't go after people. That right?"

"Usually. They're rare and tend to avoid towns. A shockstick will drive one off, as will certain sound frequencies we can't hear. Still, I'd better notify those hang gliders' guide to be sure they have audio repellent in place."

He radioed the guide and handled that. Then he and Hank cruised along in silence.

Hank mulled over what they'd done. He'd studied Lothian before coming up here. Knew they exported buffle meat and leather, fine goat wool, kova, wine, and pricey, handmade furniture. They even had mining farther up in the mountains, which was rare for the northern continents. He could ace a civics test on the place. But none of that told him how the different species got along, where people went to get into trouble, or how they liked to kick back and relax. It was a good thing that he had competent local help.

The dashboard comm buzzed. He flipped the switch. "Tremaine."

Tarpon's gravelly voice said, "Got a relay for you. Patching it through."

"Marshal?" A woman's voice came from the speakers.

"Yes. Who's this?"

"It's Alice Margs. We talked this morning?" Her

tentative tone implied that he might not remember.

Hank frowned at Joe. "Yes, ma'am, I recall. How can I help you?"

"Well, it's the strangest thing. After you left, I thought I'd maybe do some clearing out to keep busy. Sorting, you know. Haven't done that in a coupla years."

"Yes, ma'am." Why did people always have to relay the leadup to the info that mattered? Joe's headshake implied that he shared that thought as Hank asked, "Did something happen while you were cleaning?"

"Well, no. Not exactly. But I found a box in my storage room. It had Abner's handwriting on it, and it was full of the strangest things."

"What kinds of things?" *Please, not stuffed animal corpses.* He'd had a case involving those, and they hadn't been properly preserved. Despite vigorous cleaning, his uniform had reeked faintly for two weeks.

"More boxes, but they got things like off-planet food, cigarettes. Even some fancy chronos. One box had jewelry. And there were some weird little statues. You know, knickknack things."

Many brands of the items she described were priced out of the market here. Had old Abner been doing some smuggling? "You didn't know it was there?"

"Well, no. I said, didn't I? Anyways, it was way in the back, behind some old clothes. I found it when I went to sort those out."

"Yes, ma'am. We'll come take a look. We're about halfway to Lothian City, so it'll take us a while. Until we get there, don't talk to anyone else about this and don't handle the things you found."

"All right. Sure. I'll just put them back in the box

until you get here."

As Joe rolled his eyes, Hank said, "No, ma'am. Don't trouble yourself." *Or mess up any latent prints you haven't already smudged.* "We'd just have to pull them out again anyway."

"Oh. Um. Fine."

"Thanks for letting us know. We'll see you shortly."

They signed off, and Hank toggled over to the marshals service frequency to let Tarpon know where they were going. The guy seemed about as likely to care as one of the buffles they'd flown over, but procedure was procedure.

Hank swung the runabout into a wide turn and retraced their path.

#

Ninety minutes later, they were headed down the mountain again. Hank looked over at Joe. "So what do you think?"

Joe leaned back in his seat. "Smuggling widens the range of motives."

"And possibly of suspects. You get much smuggling out here?"

"Not so as we actually know." Joe's wry tone conveyed a lot. "We suspect there's a good bit more than we uncover. Word came out last winter about some group called The Company, but nothing's ever turned up about them, far as I know. Most smuggling here's somebody bringing in contraband plants or knockoffs of fancy electronics. Most folks out here don't have the money for the black-market goods, and those that do can bring them in legally."

"There are always those who resent paying duty on something."

"True enough. Coupla years ago, we caught a bunch of spacers bringing in what they said was Drachan brandy. But it was really a cheap version cut with the Drachan stuff that they were charging a fortune for. Still, the bastards made a crapload of money before we caught them."

Hank grinned. "My dad loves wine. He likes to say those who pretend to have a good nose or a discerning palate deserve to get rooked."

"You can't officially agree, of course."

"Of course."

The runabout shuddered. The cabin lights flashed as a loud honking sound erupted on the console. Hank sat up and grabbed the stick as the little ship bucked.

"Stabilizers," he said, fighting to steady their course. "The backups should kick in."

Except they didn't. The ship bucked again, then started to roll.

At least the viewport showed the terraced bacca fields again, not the forest. The fields would be a pricey place to set down, but less likely fatal than—

The ship rolled. Wind buffeted it to the side. Stabilizers were fucking gone. Hank clamped both hands around the stick. "Joe, hit the autopilot," he snapped.

Joe's hands flashed onto the console, stabbing the autopilot, but he ground out, "No joy." He clung to the arms of his seat.

They were losing altitude. Marshals trained for being spun around, but that didn't help with an unresponsive ship.

The bacca fields were growing larger. Filling the viewpoint. If the runabout went in headfirst, Hank and Joe were dead.

"Grab your stick and pull back on it," Hank ground out.

He yanked back on the stick on his side with both hands and all his weight. Beside him, Joe did the same. The nose came up a little. Then a little more.

Just a little more...

The ground surged up to meet them. *No more time.* Hank let go of the stick and flung his arms up to shield his head. With an ear-splitting crash and the scream of tearing metal, the ship slammed into the field.

CHAPTER FIVE

Deep in Hank's skull, drums pounded. His right shoulder and left leg throbbed. Breathing wasn't a lot of fun either. *Cracked ribs. Great.*

Now someone was calling him. He forced his eyes open. A young, brunette woman wearing a white coat stood by his bed. Which had guardrails and was in a room with bland, gray-blue walls. Typical hospital ambience.

The woman smiled. "I'm Dr. Porter. Can you tell me your name?"

"Hank Tremaine."

"And your job?"

"Federated Colonies Deputy Marshal."

"What about today's day and date?"

"Tuesday, the…sixteenth."

"And the president of the Terran planets federation?"

"M'Artin Maxwell."

Smiling, she patted his shoulder. "Very good. You have a bit of a concussion, but it appears to be resolving. You couldn't answer all of those questions when you came in."

"When was that, where are we, and which ones did I miss?"

"You're in Lothian Hospital and have been for about three hours. As for which questions you missed, that would be telling. We'll ask you again later."

Frowning, he rubbed his jaw. He remembered going in and out as he and Joe were pulled—

"How's Joe? DPSO Nahz."

"He's doing well in a room just down the hall."

"So what's all this for, besides the concussion?" He had no memory of anyone strapping his right shoulder. There was a vague something about someone using a vibro-wand on his right arm, but he couldn't bring it clear.

"When the runabout crashed, some of the storage compartments popped open. The vehicle rolled, and things flew through the air. You were hit in the right shoulder, left thigh, left ribs, and the back of your head. That last, by the way, seems to have been the first-aid kit."

You had to love irony. He nodded, then winced at the movement. Crappy runabouts. Still, for both systems to fail...But he'd best focus on the doc, who was still talking.

"Your right shoulder was bruised and dislocated. Your left knee is swollen and bruised from the crumpled front end jamming the console into you, and your left ankle sustained a hairline fracture. We've treated all of those and expect to release you tomorrow unless there are complications. You'll be on medical leave through day after tomorrow, then on restricted duty for five days."

Jerking up in the bed made his head pound harder. Damn it. Hank settled back reluctantly. "I have a murder to solve." A career riding on it.

"That'll be someone else's job for the next few days."

"I need to call the office." Alerting HQ would be smart, given Tarpon's slackass tendencies. So would getting back to work, even with restrictions. Maybe DPSO Ballard could step up for a few days.

"I've notified them." Now the doctor's voice held hints of steel. "Patients on bedrest do not comm their workplaces. Besides, Chief Deputy Winslow is on his way. You can discuss whatever's on your mind with him. Then you put this case and any others aside until your body—and your head especially—are fit to deal with them."

Her stern look warned him not to argue, so he muttered, "Got it."

"See that you do. And don't even think about not taking your pain meds. They contain agents that'll help your fracture heal and will keep your muscles relaxed so the healing radiation we applied will continue working." She marched out, back straight and pace brisk.

Winslow was coming here. Great. Just fucking great. Somehow, Hank bet, this would all turn out to be his fault.

#

An hour later, Winslow knocked on the doorjamb as he strode into the room. "Bad luck, Tremaine," he announced, studying Hank.

"Yes, sir." That didn't sound too bad, but Hank braced as a precaution.

"At least one good thing happened. Your case is solved."

"What? How?"

"A tip came into the Lothian City office. Found what appears to be the murder weapon in the potting shed of that Rorlan you interviewed."

That seemed a little too easy, but Winslow continued. "He has no alibi, and the likely murder weapon, a cricket bat, was in a shed on his property. It has impressions consistent with Rorlan fingers on it, as well as blood that matches the victim's. On top of that, one of the victim's neighbors says he saw a Rorlan leaving that night in the right time frame."

"I'd still like to follow up, sir."

"Tarpon will do that."

Hank managed not to wince. "Is there a motive?"

"Smuggling, most likely. Allarth has a fat bank account squirreled away that he can't explain. Claims it's not his, but his name and signature are on it. So that's that."

"So it seems." Yet it felt wrong. Or was that the drugs fuzzing his head?

Winslow scowled down at him. "What's the matter, Tremaine? The case is solved. You should be happy. Unless you were looking for another chance to play hotshot."

"No, sir." Saying he'd never played hotshot would get him nowhere.

"Good. Glad I didn't come all the way up here to take a body back."

"Thank you, sir." His coming at all was a shock, but maybe he had some redeeming qualities as a commander.

Hank looked up at Winslow. Might as well get the coming tirade over with. "Sorry about the runabout, sir. Stabilizers went out."

"They're pieces of crap. We never get the new stuff out here, but any replacement they send us has to be better than that one was. Maintenance will figure out what went wrong."

"Uh, okay." Maybe Winslow wasn't ragging on the crash because he'd decided it was useful. "Anything on that box of contraband Alice Margs found in her house?"

"Looks like Brek-Hathra was trying to set up a sideline. We'll keep an ear to the ground, but nothing has turned up so far. How're you feeling, anyway? Doc says you're out for two days and on restricted duty for five after your release."

"Since I expected to be dead," Hank replied, his voice dry, "I feel pretty good. Considering."

Winslow nodded. "Right, then. I have to get back. Do what they tell you, get yourself discharged, and I'll send someone up here to get you." Waving away Hank's thanks, he bustled out.

Hank stared at the ceiling. Allarth had a high-tech job. Which meant he was smart. Would he really put a murder weapon in his own shed and keep it there for two days? Without wiping any prints off? His job took him out into the bacca fields daily. He could've dumped the thing out there, where dozens of people had access.

And wasn't it convenient that the mysterious tipster had acted just after Hank and Joe were asking their questions? Even more convenient, the accident—if it was one—took them out of the equation and left the case to Tarpon and his ilk.

Come to that, how could the stabilizers and the secondary system go out at once if not by sabotage? Nothing on a marshals service vehicle, though, was supposed to open except for someone with a badge.

Was it sabotage? Or just a long history of crappy maintenance coming home to roost?

One thing for sure was that none of the answers would come dancing by this bed. He had to get out of it, get back to work, and be sure the case, his case, was closed properly.

#

By the next evening, back in Micah's Junction, Hank was heartily sick of his quarters. He'd already spoken to Nahz, who had a broken leg, a black eye, and various bumps and bruises. His friends were on distant posts, meaning any personal communications would suffer a time lag he didn't have the patience to tolerate now. None of the many books on his tablet appealed, and the couple of vid series he followed hadn't yet made it to the ass end of beyond.

He sat in front of his terminal and hit the news channel. There might be something of interest.

The colonial governing board had proposed a new tax to support increased customs enforcement. No one liked the idea. Big surprise.

Despite still being on pain meds, he could read over the case file on Brek-Hathra. Maybe convince himself everything was as it should be.

Except it wasn't. The anonymous tip, the neighbor who happened to hear raised voices. The way they'd come in so quickly after the start of the investigation was...off.

And Allarth had no alibi. The town surveillance cameras showed no movement into or out of Allarth's place during the relevant time. So he'd been alone.

But where was his motive? This all looked good on the surface, but it didn't feel right. Too bad those Rorlan chemical traces weren't strong enough to identify.

Hank couldn't shake the feeling that this just wasn't right. And he knew someone who was a genius at identifying weird substances. Sending her the scans on the bacca hallucinogen would truly delight her.

Poking around won't keep your nose clean, a little voice in the back of his head said.

Shit. Yeah. But...he'd think about it overnight. See what else he could turn up without doing something a martinet like Winslow would jump all over. See if this would be worth taking flak over it and setting back his campaign to get out of here.

He was about to shut off the terminal when he realized he'd forgotten to check on the guy who'd died in the bar fight his first day.

Finding the case when he didn't know the number or the victim's name took a few minutes, but he finally located it. The video from the bar showed a stocky woman bump the guy—not hard enough to knock him over—and move on. No one else touched him, as he backed clear of the fight, but the time stamp showed fifteen seconds passing before he swayed, crumpled, convulsed for about half a minute, and then lay still.

Weird. Damn weird.

Frowning, Hank pulled up the autopsy report and scanned down to the cause of death. Anaphylactic shock? But from what? The guy hadn't yet eaten or drunk anything.

The medical examiner didn't know from what, either. But there was a mysterious chemical in his blood. Hank clicked on the link to the lab report and paged down. *Sonofabitch!* The substance, which the Micah's Junction toxicity screen had been unable to pin down exactly, was a derivative of bacca and a probable hallucinogen.

The chemical diagram looked identical to the substance in Brek-Hathra's blood, but he called up that autopsy to be sure. Yep. Point by point, they were the same.

The report had gone to the central lab at the HQ for this region of space, Xerxes Station. It wasn't flagged as urgent, though. They might not look at it for weeks. If Allarth pled to Brek-Hathra's murder, it would become low priority.

But it couldn't be just coincidence that two murder victims in two days had died with the same hallucinogenic substance in their blood. At minimum, it meant someone around here was dealing illegal drugs, maybe one person both victims had known. Maybe someone who was making them on-planet.

Since he had so much time on his hands, he might as well look into the dead guy in the bar. No rules against reading the files on closed cases. Especially if you suspected they warranted more digging.

But then what? Winslow obviously wasn't interested in pursuing this. He'd issued a memo to keep alert for beings who appeared to be under the influence of hallucinogens, but that was it. It didn't take much to figure out that he wouldn't like someone going over his head.

Yeah. Like that was news. But if there was any chance to nip something in the bud, they should take it.

So was it better to ask forgiveness or permission?

CHAPTER SIX

When Hank came off the mess hall line with his breakfast tray, nobody in the big dining room made eye contact. No shock, really. He was not only the new guy but on the boss's shit list. People got along at posts like this by keeping their heads down. No one would want to get too chummy until they saw whether he survived.

There was an empty table near the back. Holding the tray in his right hand and his cane in his left, he limped toward it. At least he was getting used to the medical boot on his left foot and ankle.

A blond woman in uniform paused beside him. "There's room at our table. If you don't mind eating with the spooks."

The telepaths, she meant. Every marshals service HQ had at least one.

Okay. He had nothing much to hide, and they could be very informative. The Spook Brigade, as the psi services were known, liked rotating into all sorts of situations. Alone among the personnel here, they retained their group rep for competence.

Unfortunately, there were so many legal restrictions

on using them that it was rarely worth the trouble, but they were great for search and rescue operations or verifying info for deals with offenders.

He followed her to a table occupied by a man with traces of gray in his dark hair. Introductions took only a minute.

"So where was your last post, Hank?" the woman, Jodie Lang, asked.

"Granville Station. You?" The breakfast steak wasn't bad.

"Lucifer's, also known as Hades. Ryerson, here, had the cushy slot, Valhalla."

That was the first station to go into service. And still one of the best.

Lang continued, "Next month, he rotates back to civilization."

"I wish," the man said, forking up eggs. "I'm headed to that new station, McAvoy's. Consortium of Scots, Irish, and Poles put it together. There's always a lot of stuff to settle when a new station opens."

"You could retire, Brad," Lang said. Her grin across her kova mug implied that they'd discussed this before.

Ryerson shook his head. "Yeah, when I'm ready to plant petunias and play with the grandkids. Got places to go before I slot into that."

"How many in the psi unit here?" Hank asked.

"Six," Ryerson answered. "Two on call for case work, including out in the demesnes, and two on station duty. Two off at any time."

"Twelve-hour shifts." Lang grimaced. "But I do like those two days off every week. Hank, I heard you were assigned to that murder up in Lothian. How was it going before you got hurt?"

"Slowly at first. Then we had that little surprise on the way back." A surprise he should check with vehicle maintenance about, now that he thought of it. "There were other surprises waiting when I woke up."

He told them about the tip, Allarth's arrest, the mystery substance, and Winslow's insistence on closing the case. Not a flicker of expression betrayed their reactions. That was telling. He'd bet real money they were communicating telepathically.

"So what's your issue?" Ryerson asked.

Best to keep it casual, so Hank shrugged, wincing when his shoulder protested. "It just seems too pat."

"And there's no motive," Lang added. "Pesky things, motives."

"Exactly." She'd just confirmed that his suspicions weren't only in his slightly-drug-fuzzed head.

Eating his now-cold eggs, Hank considered. He didn't know either of them, but they knew the ropes here. He didn't, so he had to reach out to someone, however indirectly. Might as well be members of a group had a rep for being conscientious.

"Something on your mind?" Ryerson asked.

"We move around in this job," Hank commented idly. "Get to know people in different fields."

The other man nodded. "Like biochemistry."

Had he read Hank's mind? No, that most likely came from logic. Or so Hank hoped. "Yeah. What's the policy around here about reaching out to people elsewhere? If, say, a person was curious about something."

This time, the other two did look at each other. Lang turned back to Hank. "There's no rule against satisfying idle curiosity. Without spreading info outside law enforcement circles, of course."

"And if that curiosity turned up something interesting?"

"Anything that makes this post look good," Ryerson replied, "is always welcome."

"Gotcha." The post and the chief deputy, he meant. "Thanks."

Reaching out on the bacca derivative should be okay, then, if Hank was discreet. Getting Brek-Hathra's murder reopened was probably another story. But he had to try.

#

"No," Winslow snapped. "Absolutely no. I am not reopening an investigation because a marshal whose brain is fogged on meds sees phantom connections."

Hank held onto his temper, though barely. Great way to start the morning, trying to convince this asshat to pursue leads he'd dismissed. At least Hank had been invited to sit this time.

"Sir, Allarth doesn't have a motive. No one knows what he supposedly fought with Brek-Hathra about, and the identification is dicey at best." Hank had been over the file several times. Had even looked at the guy who'd died in the bar fight to see if he could find a link. Unfortunately, he hadn't. But he had found that two neighbors, not one, as the initial record said, had reported seeing a cloaked Rorlan leave Brek-Hathra's building during the pertinent time. One had identified the Rorlan as Allarth, but that didn't ease Hank's misgivings. The info in the file was too sketchy to rely on her statement.

"Don't try to tell me my job, showboat."

Bastard. "Sir, all I'm saying is that I'd like to look a little deeper."

"I'm satisfied, Tremaine. The prosecutor is satisfied."

Likely because the prosecutor was as big a screwup as most other government employees out here, but saying so would be a truly stupid move.

"Leave this case alone," Winslow said. "If you need work to fill your time, try the shooting range."

Blasting holes in outlines that could stand in for assholes. Great idea. But it did nothing to further the cause of justice.

Still, Hank couldn't resist saying, "I'm not cleared for weapon use until I'm off meds, sir. That's day after tomorrow."

Winslow's glare could've peeled the fancy paneling off the walls. "Get out of my office, marshal. I'm cutting you a break because you got hit on the head. And because your lousy flying will force Central to send us a more modern runabout. That's as far as it goes, though. If I hear of you talking about this, we'll have another little chat that will be far less pleasant for you. Understand?"

"Yes, sir." Hank marched across the pompous-as-shit carpeting and out of the office.

Now what? He'd already sent a comm to Dr. Becca Starne on Calliope about the mystery hallucinogen. It would intrigue her. When they'd dated all those years ago, she'd been unable to resist a mystery, and her holiday cards always mentioned some whodunit she'd read. She'd never quite gotten that living whodunits made them less attractive for downtime reading.

But she would need time to get back to him.

Standing in the corridor, he glanced toward the lift. Being really, truly sick of his quarters killed any potential appeal of holing up and reading case files. He wasn't cleared for PT yet.

But nothing said he couldn't take a walk. Explore a little. And he was no longer tied to that idiotic orientation app.

The front door was closer to the street than the back, so he headed toward the lobby.

#

As a marshal, Hank could get a tour of the port facility just by asking for it. But requests had to be made in advance.

He headed that way anyway, more or less at random. There was still enough kid in him to enjoy watching the ships land and take off.

Hovercars tooled down the aptly named Port Street. Residents were going about their business. The closer he got to the port, the more spacers in one-piece shipsuits crossed his path. Of course, some of those in civvies could be spacers, too. Not everyone walked around in clothes that identified their jobs.

Case in point, himself. Until he was cleared for duty, he was stuck with civvies, heavy denim pants, tee, synth-suede jacket, and a single boot on his right foot. Plus the orthopedic boot on his left.

A bookshop, A Page Turner, oddly named since turning pages had given way to swiping screens centuries ago, stood on the left. Outside it, a couple of women chatted and laughed. Beyond it, a restaurant whose multi-consonant name he couldn't pronounce offered lunch specials.

His left knee and ankle weren't thrilled about the walking bit, but at least his shoulder and ribs were almost normal. He could make it a little farther. He soldiered on, passing a clothing store, a souvenir shop—amazingly, the only one in sight—an outdoor gear store, and a florist.

By the time he reached Addison's, his ankle was throbbing and his hand protesting from leaning on the cane. Time to take a break.

He made his way into the bar, which was sparsely peopled so early in the day, and to a corner table near the door.

A short, wiry woman bustled over. "What'll you have, sir?"

"Lunch. What do you recommend?"

"The two specials today are roasted roc with a side of tubers for 9.4 credits and a root vegetable ragout over crice—that's rice to Terrans—for 7.8."

"Really? You can eat rocs?"

"If you can shoot one down. Nest hunting's forbidden."

"Good to know." Not that he had time to go ferreting out predator nests. "What do you like today?"

"Can't go wrong with the fish sandwich. Mild whitefish with a spicy batter we make here, on three-grain bread, and a side of fried yams or fruit."

"I'll have that with the fruit. And ginger beer." Too bad real beer was off-limits because of the meds. After the interview with Winslow, he could use one to unwind.

The server brought his ginger beer and left him in peace. The Grog wasn't working now, but there was no sign of droid fill-ins. Even the bus girl clearing the table two over was human. Droid servers cut costs, and they were undeniably efficient. Lacked something in the way of customer relations, though.

Three beings, two dark-skinned human and one humanoid with mottled orange and white fur, sat at the bar, plenty of space between them. Seven tables were occupied. Even the music, some kind of technopop, was low enough not to be intrusive.

Addie moved around the room, picking up dirty glasses or plates here, having a few words there, taking orders for refills. She was keeping an eye on things without seeming to do more than greet her customers.

She had a way about her, for sure.

A way a guy who didn't intend to stay on this planet long should ignore.

Hank pulled out his tablet and scanned the Brek-Hathra file. There were hardly any interviews in here. Everything was taken at face value. As a whole, the file could serve as a perfect illustration of sloppy casework. Geez. No wonder the Lady of Lothian had such a low opinion of the marshals service.

His sandwich came, and he set the tablet aside. The food was as good as promised. The bread had some texture to it and tasted faintly of nuts. The fish was spicy, and the fruit, something yellow he couldn't identify, tasted sweet with a tang. Maybe the food, rather than proximity to the spaceport, was what drew people in here.

Frowning, Addie stopped beside him. "Not to pry, but you don't look so great."

"A crash'll do that to you. I'm good, thanks." He forced his mouth into a grin.

Her frown deepened. The grin hadn't done its job, and now his head hurt.

"Look," she said, "my dad had to take a lot of pain meds his last years. He had a special tea that cleared the brain fuzz without making him hyper. Seeing as people are always getting banged up, either in accidents or from drunken falls, I keep it on hand. You want a cup?"

That sounded great, but... "What's in it?"

She rolled her eyes. "Various herbs. All legal, I promise."

"Then sure. Thanks." Turning down a friendly offering was never smart, and if the rest of her food was as good as this, he'd be eating a lot of off-post meals here. At least until he could escape back to civilization.

"Be right back."

In a couple of minutes, she set a steaming mug by his ginger beer bottle. "Let it steep for a few more minutes, until it's a deep blue."

"Thanks." He wrapped his fingers around the mug to peer into it, and the heat seeped pleasantly into his hand.

"You're welcome. It's on the house."

He looked up quickly, but nothing in her face implied anything beyond a desire to be helpful. Still, regs were regs.

"Appreciate it, but it needs to go on my bill."

"Okay." She seemed to hesitate, then said, "Enjoy

your lunch. I hope you feel better." She strolled toward the bar before he could thank her.

Thinking about the case, Hank munched his sandwich. The tea might or might not cut the fog, but the fruity taste was pleasant enough, and the heat soothed his throat. He finished, paid his bill, and started back to HQ.

Halfway there, he blinked. The brain fog had eased up. Despite his skepticism, the tea had done its job.

He made his way back to HQ and up to his quarters. Maybe going over the files on the murder and the guy in the bar fight again, with a less fuzzy brain, would yield some insights.

The light on his desk console flashed green, indicating a message. Hank sat down and logged into the message center.

A male felinoid's cream-furred face appeared on the screen. "Marshal Tremaine, I'm Vic da'Gorez, the head of vehicle maintenance. We've been over your crashed runabout." Looking grim, he added, "An acid bomb took out your gyroscope. Without that, none of the stabilization systems can work. They have nothing to orient them."

So it was sabotage. But why? Hank had just arrived on-planet, and the investigation had scarcely begun.

"I've informed Chief Winslow's office," da'Gorez continued. "The acid was in a chemical bomb triggered by remote. You'd know better than I would whether this was a malicious prank or aimed at you in particular. Until we figure it out, you might want to watch your back."

The message ended. Hank returned the call. How

had someone gotten into a marshals service vehicle to sabotage it? Had they checked that?

Da'Gorez didn't pick up, so Hank left a message. Then he leaned back in his chair. Sabotage. He'd suspected it, but the ramifications of someone gaining access to a marshals service runabout when it was parked in town were disturbing.

The comm at his hip buzzed. He pressed the stud to answer it. "Tremaine."

"Dispatch here. Report to the chief deputy marshal's office at once."

"Roger. On my way." Had Winslow reconsidered? Or had he learned of, and been pissed off by, Hank's contact with Becca? Regardless, dallying would only irritate him. Hank picked up his pace as best he could.

#

Winslow kept him waiting in the outer office, as usual. After informing the boss that Hank was here, the receptionist ignored him.

His leg throbbed, so he sat in one of the visitor chairs. Protocol be damned. He wasn't standing on a bum foot to gratify Winslow's ego.

Minutes dragged by before the receptionist ushered him into the inner office. Seated behind his desk, Winslow glared at Hank. "What the fucking hells do you think you're pulling, Tremaine? I warned you about insubordination."

Was this about his request to Becca? Hank kept his gaze locked on Winslow's. "I don't know what you're talking about, sir."

"That snooty bitch up in Lothian. Did you whine to her before you came back? Try to make this case more than it is so you could impress her?"

"No, sir." Had the Lady intervened? She'd said she was watching—

"Bullshit. If you're thinking to get in her pants, forget it. Better men than you have tried. And if you're thinking you can make this office look bad, you'll regret the day you were whelped."

Hank gritted his teeth. Breathed through his nose. Looked over Winslow's head at the fancy seascape on the wall. A good commander didn't make unfounded accusations. A bad one, like Winslow, would be unlikely to listen to any defense.

The chief deputy finally ran down. "Well? What were you trying to prove, hotdog?"

"Sir." Hank turned his glare on the older man, who looked startled. "I have not communicated with the Lady of Lothian or with anyone else in her demesne except medical personnel since Officer Nahz and I crashed. I have no idea what you're talking about. You're welcome to have one of the psi squad in here to verify that."

Winslow continued to glare, but the offer seemed to deflate him. No one volunteered for psi monitoring. Even in criminal cases, it could be used only with a suspect's consent. After a moment, he sank back in his chair. "You didn't call her?"

"No, sir." But now maybe the case would get the hard look its so-convenient solution deserved. "Sir, she said she would monitor the Brek-Hathra investigation. I can only assume something about it set her off."

"Likes to throw her weight around," Winslow

muttered. He rubbed a hand over his chin. "Okay, Tremaine. You wanted another look at this case. Now you got it. You're going back up tomorrow, if the doc clears you for limited duty, as expected. Nothing strenuous about talking to witnesses. The woman said she'd send someone to get you, which is good since we're short a runabout."

"Yes, sir." Restricted duty or not, he'd do what needed doing if he had to limp all over the demesne to ensure that justice was done.

"You go up there," Winslow ordered. "You jump through whatever fancy-ass hoops she sets out. But you be sure your actions are a credit to this office."

In other words, don't make the chief deputy look bad. Yeah. Great. "Sir, do we have any word on how someone accessed the runabout to plant an acid bomb it?"

"Not so far. Hackers can figure out any damn thing, though, so I'm betting it's something like that. The security codes on all the vehicles are being changed, and so are the badges' signal frequencies. Be sure you get yours done before you leave. Now get out of here. I have work to do."

Hank walked carefully back to his room. He had his chance to be sure the right being paid for Brek-Hathra's murder, but if he found anything that cast doubt on Allarth's guilt, his nose would be officially not clean and his chances of getting out of this lousy post, torpedoed.

CHAPTER SEVEN

Hank used the rest of the day to study everything about the Brek-Hathra case file. Unfortunately, no Otis Ransom turned up in the roll of planetary residents or the list of licensed traders. No new insights popped up either, but by the time the Lothian demesne security chief and his pilot arrived the next morning, Hank had a plan forming.

The runabout, a new six-seater far more luxurious than anything the marshals service had, lifted smoothly off and banked into a turn over Port Street before wheeling north. Seated in a middle row, Hank peered out the round window on the side at the spaceport. A ship was coming in to land, the lettering on her hull pegging her as the *Susan Constant,* and he froze. That was a name. Like Otis Ransom, but not for a person.

Why hadn't he thought of that sooner? Yeah, the pain meds fuzzed his head a little, but he'd been around spaceports for the entirety of his ten-plus years as a marshal. He should've thought of it.

But he shouldn't access the HQ database from an unsecured, civilian vehicle. He would have to wait until he reached the office in Lothian City.

Meanwhile, he could sit back and enjoy the view. More forests flew by below the little ship. Evergreens mixed with trees whose broad, green leaves ranged in color from almost black to nearly white, with flashes of fall color interspersed.

A flash of golden brown in a clearing below might have been a lynx, one of the pony-sized, predatory cats that roamed the upper mountains. Named for the Terran lynx because of similar tufted ears, the big cats could take anything else that walked the planet.

Mortimer strolled back and sat opposite him. "You need anything, marshal?"

"Thanks, no. Except to know why the Lady insisted this case be reopened."

"The easy answer isn't always the right one. Allarth seemed a questionable prospect for the killer. She wants to be sure whoever murdered her manager pays for it."

"Can't argue with that."

The chief's brown face gave nothing away as he studied Hank. "We looked at all the security vids but couldn't see who damaged your runabout. Someone did, though, so we're assuming you have a target on your back."

"Maybe it's Head DPSO Nahz's back that's targeted. I've only been here a few days."

"Maybe, but we can't know. The Lady'd like you to bunk at the keep. Your data would be secure there, as would you."

He would also be directly under her thumb, and anyone who wanted to control an investigation could not be fully trusted. "Thanks, but I'll be fine at the marshals service office."

"If the doors are locked when they should be," Mortimer grumbled.

"I'll see they are." Hank grinned at him. "Don't get me wrong. The Lady's hospitality would be a lot more comfortable than a barren room and only Marshal Tarpon for company. But I have a duty not to appear compromised."

The chief's dark brows drew together. "You implying the Lady's mixed up in this?"

"Of course not." Though he hadn't definitely ruled that out. "But I have to act as an agent of the federated government, not an individual."

"I guess." Mortimer looked stern. "She means to provide a flitter for your use. When it's in its hangar, our people will guard it. If a problem occurs, responsibility will be clear."

Though not if the problem arose after he'd been out somewhere. Still, with marshals service vehicles apparently hackable, this wasn't a bad idea. "I appreciate it."

"Yell if you need anything."

Hank thanked him, and the chief went back to the front. The Lady of Lothian had tried to push in from the beginning, wanting interviews cleared by her staff. That might've been only a high-level official wanting to be sure the investigation met her standards, which he would bet were as exacting as his own.

Or she might have had a more sinister reason. Smuggling would be a lot easier with the demesne government helping it along.

Hank slid down in his seat. The Lady of Lothian

would bear watching.

#

Tarpon was about as glad to see Hank as he'd expected, which was to say not at all. "Dunno why she needed to drag you back up here," he said when Hank limped into the office. "Case is closed."

"It never hurts to look again. Besides, you know some people throw their weight around just because they can." Not that the Lady seemed to be one of them, but Hank needed not to have an outright enemy in Tarpon, especially after the earlier disagreement over the runabout.

"Huh. What're you gonna do first?"

"Stow my gear. Then look at video."

Without the boot on his leg, climbing the stairs was easier than it'd been at HQ, but he'd been told to rest his leg periodically for the next few days. Hank dropped his bag in the same room he'd used before. He wouldn't be surprised if no one had checked the vids for the area around Allarth's building, so that was step one.

He closed the door, sat at the corner console, and pulled up the feeds. Good thing he was used to watching vids at accelerated speeds, or he'd be sitting here for hours. People came and went, all of them tagged by the system. Most lived in the building. Some visited.

Hank took a break and got more kova. Even this undoubtedly cheap brand tasted better than what they'd had on Granville Station. But this, of course, was a strain of actual coffee.

The feed resumed. The timestamp advanced quickly

on video of empty streets. At roughly 0420, the building's door opened. A cloaked figure emerged, face obscured by a hood. No identifying tag accompanied the figure as it crossed the green and passed out of camera range. He zoomed in on the face, and the delicate lips implied that the figure was female. But that wasn't necessarily reliable. Many species had delicate lips.

He couldn't tell whether there was a nose, but the gloved hand holding the figure's cloak at the throat came clear. It had three fingers. Like a Rorlan's. The one Rorlan in that community was male. The demesne's other Rorlans lived in Lothian City. If this was a woman, as he would assume for now that she was, she wasn't a resident.

When had she arrived?

Backing up the video, he found that she'd crossed the green toward the building about 2050 the previous night. But she'd gone behind it. Maybe to go in the back door?

Hank toggled over to the case notes. Tarpon hadn't interviewed any of Allarth's neighbors. Of course not. That would be work, and he'd doubtless followed Winslow's lead in accepting that the case was all tied up with a pretty ribbon. Lazy bastards.

A search for Rorlans residing on-planet produced a list of two dozen individuals, nine of them women. The figure wasn't necessarily a resident, but coming in from another world via the station and port, or even via a small interplanetary ship, would be a long trip.

He started to place a call to Joe Nahz, then reconsidered. It would be just like Tarpon to spy on him for Winslow. The console was easy to tap into, but his individual comm would be harder to monitor. He set it on the desk so he could have visual as well as audio contact.

Joe picked up almost immediately. "Hank. How are you?"

"You hadn't heard?" When the local officer shook his head, Hank filled him in. He concluded by saying, "The Lady isn't buying it, and neither am I. I need an officer for backup and someone to do the scut work of looking through hours of video to track down a Rorlan. And see about getting a facial match on a piss-poor image from a public camera."

"I'm still on leave. Anything's better than sitting around watching dust collect and trying to keep out of Tinya's, my wife's, way. Send me the video. I'll do that and get you someone to help with interviews."

They exchanged medical updates and signed off. Hank sat back to think. Maybe Allarth would have some ideas as to who might want this murder hooked on him.

#

Tarpon was absent when Hank went back downstairs. Before heading to the cells, Hank checked to be sure the alarm would chime if anyone came in.

He also left the door to the back area open so he could hear the chime if it sounded.

Allarth sprawled on his bunk, his expression glum.

Hank leaned on the wall by the bars that made up the cell's front. "Let's talk, Allarth. Want me to call your lawyer?"

The Rorlan sighed and sat up. "I've told you

225

everything."

"Do you want your attorney here?"

A headshake was the only answer.

Hank waited a moment before saying, "Not a lot of Rorlans in this demesne. Hard to mistake one for another."

"Not that hard." Bitterness flashed in the solid black eyes. "To humans, we all look alike."

"That's a point," Hank said easily. "I've heard we humans all look alike to some species, too. Who do you think might've been confused for you?"

"How would I know? One of my fellows in Lothian is quite old, so his skin is very dark blue. The other is my age, but with lighter hair." He sighed.

"That's all the Rorlans around here?" When Allarth nodded, confirming Hank's info, Hank asked, "You got any ideas about who would set you up?"

The prisoner's head jerked around. "You believe me?"

"I haven't made up my mind yet. So who?"

"I do not know. I have had no serious disputes with anyone." Allarth shrugged, a very human-looking gesture. "There is work friction, as at any job, but always minor."

"So who would've had the ability or opportunity to do it?"

"Anyone. I was meditating and…quite absorbed." He rubbed absently at the center of his face.

The gesture called attention to his lack of a nose. Made Hank feel antsy where just looking at Rorlans never did. Hank cleared his throat. "Are you sure no one saw you?"

"I was home alone," Allarth said simply.

Hank nodded. "Y'know, I hear Rorlans don't mix much with other species. That you tend to keep to yourselves." Their strict religious observances rarely appealed to other species longterm.

"That is not a crime."

"No, sure isn't. Makes me kinda curious, though."

Allarth sighed. "About what, marshal?"

"About this." Hank opened his folder and took out the print he'd made of the mystery woman on video.

When he showed it to Allarth, the Rorlan's eyes widened. His shoulders stiffened. He closed his eyes and visibly relaxed. "That has nothing to do with me."

"A Rorlan woman came out of your building. You're the only Rorlan who lives there, and she was there during the time of the murder. Want to rethink your statement?"

Allarth wrenched his gaze away from the photo. "No," he choked.

"Suit yourself." Hank put the photo back in its folder. "But there aren't very many Rorlans around. I will find her. And when I do, I'll have to question her."

"That's not a Rorlan." Allarth's voice rasped. "Many species have only three digits."

"But very few humanoids lack noses." The photo wasn't definitive about the nose thing. Allarth's averted gaze was. Hank studied the man in the cell. The most common reason someone denied an alibi was to protect the person who could provide it. Was that the case here?

"I'll have to question her in detail," Hank said. "If she's been coming up here a lot, she might know about some things we're interested in. Might even be involved."

As he spoke, Allarth's shoulders grew tense again. His soft jaw seemed to set.

Hank added, "Word will probably get out. It always does."

Allarth licked his lips.

Straightening, Hank said, "I'm not looking to blow up anybody's private life. If I knew where to find her, we could talk discreetly. Keep it quiet."

Allarth opened his mouth, then shut it.

Hank swallowed a grin. Definitely something there. "Think about it, huh?"

The something might not be an alibi. Might be something worse. But he had to eliminate the possibilities.

He shut the corridor door and walked back to the main office in time to see Officer Krista Ballard open the door. The alarm set up its steady—and piercing—beep. She deactivated it quickly.

"I heard about your crash," she said, scanning him. "Glad you're okay."

"That's two of us. Are you my backup?"

"Yep. Chief Nahz called and asked me to help you out. He's getting one of the newbies to take over office and patrol duties. What do you need me to do?"

"Leg work. We have two witnesses who reported a cloaked figure coming out of Brek-Hathra's building in the relevant time. One didn't see any details but thought the figure was Rorlan. We'll interview him later. Now we're going to interview the witness who lives in the building and identified that figure as Allarth."

#

Kendra Jarel was working in the fields. By the time Hank and Ballard reached the outlying community, the demesne's security personnel had her in the DPS office. Chief Mortimer had stayed with her, either just to observe or so he could report to the Lady. Either way, there would be no getting rid of him.

Ballard went to interview Allarth's neighbors while Hank talked to the witness. Dirt from the fields crusted her boots. The gloves laid over the knee of her brown coverall were a little cleaner, looking as though someone had tried to brush the soil off of them. She looked to be about midforties, though the official report of her interview said midthirties. Her hair, a deep, rusty shade of brown, belied her age. A scattering of freckles dotted her nose and cheekbones.

"Look," the woman said, "It was dark. I thought it was the Rorlan. Heard that funny hiss noise their gills make when they get agitated. And that one is frequently agitated. Bit of a prig, actually."

"How well do you know Allarth?" Hank asked. Mortimer hovered in the background but stayed out of the way.

"Not well. I see him in the fields at work, but he doesn't usually stop to speak. Too busy." She rolled her eyes. "I told the other marshal that already."

"Thanks. Now we're going over it again." Hank deliberately kept his voice pleasant. No point in antagonizing her further. "Where had you been that evening?"

"Thrall's. I go over there most every night."

"Were you there all evening?"

"Until I went home, around 2330. Before you ask, I had supper there."

"All right. So you met Allarth when you came home?" When she nodded, he continued, "The report I have doesn't say what he was wearing when you saw him."

"A cloak, o'course. Like anybody would on a cold night."

"Was it hooded?"

"Yes, and the hood was up. It. Was. Cold."

Hank nodded. She could enjoy her irritation, even the hint of contempt in her tone, but she would still sit here until she answered all his questions. "But you saw his face."

"No. Like I said. I saw his weird hands. And his lower face, you know, with no nose showing."

"Were you indoors or outdoors?"

Jarel looked beyond Hank. "Chief, I got work to do. I already told those other marshals this."

"The Lady wants us all to cooperate," Mortimer answered, "so she'll understand about the work. Now, please answer Marshal Tremaine."

"Like. I. Said." An eye roll accompanied the emphatically spaced reply. "I was coming into the building and met the Rorlan coming out."

The foyer had a glass door. Hank raised an eyebrow. "Where was he when you met him?"

"Out. Side. Like I—"

"Was he on the walk, on the steps, coming through the door, on the street?"

"Coming down the steps. I was going up. We

passed." She shot him a sullen glare.

"So the light was behind him? Or was there a porch light?"

"The porch lights are by the door. The hall light was behind him."

Which also meant it had been in her eyes. "Had you ever seen any Rorlans with Abner Brek-Hathra?"

"No. He didn't much care for them. Or them for the rest of us."

"Did you see anyone, or did anyone see you?" The other witness had seen the cloaked Rorlan a few seconds before he—or she—reached the street. The man might not've looked until after Jarel was inside.

"No. It was a crappy night."

"That's all for now," Hank told her. "Thank you for your time."

"Not like I had a choice," she muttered.

Chief Mortimer stepped forward. "I'll have someone take you back to the fields, Ms. Jarel. You can wait outside if you like."

With muttered thanks, she stalked outside.

Mortimer turned to Hank. "So, marshal, did you get from that what I did?"

"Depends." Hank slid off the edge of the desk and into the chair Jarel had used. Getting his weight off his leg was a relief. "What did you get?"

"That her identification is anything but solid."

Rubbing his chin, Hank asked, "How hard would it be for someone to come up here from Lothian City in the late evening, go visit someone unobserved, and then get back before morning?"

"Not hard at all for anyone with a flitter. Or someone

who rented one at the local Depot. Those have the Lady's franchise for landing fields and vehicle rentals. You have to pay extra for an overnight, but it's not exorbitant."

"Good to know. Is there video?"

"Should be."

"Great." Joe could get that video easily enough. It would keep him busy while his leg healed. If Hank had a twinge of guilt over dumping the scut work, it wasn't a big one. Joe could always pass it off to a deputy. Otherwise known as a minion. At least Joe had minions.

Hank's comm buzzed. He touched the speaking stud at his throat. "Tremaine. Go ahead."

"Ballard, marshal. I've talked to the people who were home at Allarth's building. No luck there, but his neighbors are on first shift. They'll be off in a couple of hours, and I'll try again."

"Sounds good. Meet me at Brek-Hathra's building. We'll see who's home there." The witness who'd reported raised voices should be. The notes said she was on maternity leave with a new baby, which was why she'd been up so late at night. If she wasn't home, she'd likely be somewhere close or return soon.

Hank walked across the green toward the crime scene. A glance to the right showed him the Depot at the end of the developed area. A flat, paved, landing surface beside it held a boxy vehicle labeled "Lothian Shuttle" on the side. But there was room to land three or four small flitters beside it. The shed at the far edge of the paved area held four two-seat flitters, with empty slots for three more.

No, getting up here unobserved wouldn't be hard at

all. Especially with the cold nights keeping most people inside.

Ballard stood on the steps to Brek-Hathra's building. When he walked up to her, she said, "The witness lives upstairs. The unit above the victim's."

"Okay. We'll talk to her first, then see who else is home."

CHAPTER EIGHT

Brek-Hathra's upstairs neighbor confirmed hearing raised voices but couldn't confirm gender, language or even any distinctive accent. She'd been too occupied with her crying baby.

"Still," Hank pointed out to Krista Ballard as they left, "she confirms that someone was there."

"Now we just figure out who." The local officer zipped her jacket up higher. The wind had a bite this morning. "Before I forget, Hank, my wife and I would like you to join us for dinner tonight if you're free. My idea of cooking is opening packages and nuking them, but she's amazing in the kitchen."

"I'd like that. Thanks." A home-cooked meal would be a great change. "Two of Brek-Hathra's regular poker buddies are off today. Let's go see what they can tell us."

They walked across the public green, past Thrall's, and into another area of housing blocks, these smaller. "You take Merida Keane," Hank said. "I'll check Torv B'Lare."

He would much prefer to be in on every interview, but that wasn't feasible. With so much ground to cover and so many people to see, operating in tandem would take too much time.

Torv B'Lare answered his door with his hair rumpled and the tan robe covering most of his wiry frame gaping open. "Sorry. Slept in." Scratching his rear, he swung the door wide and ambled into the sitting area, where he plopped onto a worn, blue couch.

"I guess this is about Abner," he said, "but I thought you arrested that Rorlan for the murder."

"We're still investigating." Hank read the case info into his recorder and started with preliminary questions about how B'Lare and the victim knew each other. As expected, B'Lare said they worked together.

"Tell me about this weekly poker game," Hank said.

"Not much to tell," B'Lare answered around a yawn. "We meet up in Lothian Major, usually at the Piper's Roost, sometimes other places. It's mostly just us, but sometimes somebody'll wander by and want in. If we know 'em, we're good with that."

"What stakes do you play for?"

"Small ones." The man grimaced. "On our salary, that's all we can afford."

"Define small, please."

"Buy-in is ten credits. Cap is forty. Except once a month, we go down to Micah's Junction, get rooms at Jory's, and play all night. Buy-in's the same, but the cap is sixty."

Micah's Junction. Where the spaceport was. "When's the next time you're going down there?"

B'Lare rubbed a hand over his face. "Ah...three days."

With Brek-Hathra supposedly meeting Otis Ransom

in three days. "Jory's again?"

"Yup. He gives us a repeat business discount."

"Good of him. Mr. B'Lare, do you know an Otis Ransom?"

"Nuh-uh. Should I? Who is that, anyhow?"

"Just a name that's come up. Take me through your last poker game. Did anything unusual happen?"

"No, but…Well, maybe." Frowning, he stared into the distance. "Abner always sits out a couple hands. Leaves his money in the pot, so that's fine. This is our off time. Nobody wants to feel tied to the table. He was gone longer'n usual, though. Jolt—that'd be Dray Peters —went to look for him."

"Did he find him?"

"They both said not. Jolt was gone longer'n Abner, so that made sense." Yet he continued frowning.

"What else?" Hank prodded.

"Well, mebbe it's nothing. Just…they both seemed a little miffed. Didn't look at each other or shoot the shit like usual. Not for a while, anyway."

"Do you think they actually did meet up?" If so, why had they hidden that?

"Got no reason to think so, but it was odd, that's all."

Hank made a mental note to check on that with the other players. He and B'Lare discussed the game a little longer, but B'Lare continued insisting that nothing else unusual had happened. At last, Hank decided he'd gotten all he could.

When he reached the sidewalk, he commed Krista. "You still with Keane?"

"Affirmative."

"Ask about Peters and the victim leaving the game and how they were when they came back."

"Roger. Almost done here. Where do you want me to meet you?"

"Thrall's. We'll have lunch. By the time we finish, Peters will be off-shift. We'll tackle him about what Keane and the others say."

#

"Sure, I left the game," Peters said. "Went out to look for Abner, then smoked an herbal. You want one?"

"No, thanks," Hank answered for himself and Krista. "Why did you go look for him if his leaving the game wasn't odd?"

Peters shrugged. "He was gone longer than usual. I thought he might've run into trouble. Lothian City's pretty safe, but we got our share of crime, right, officer?"

Krista nodded. "Did you find Abner, sir?" Her eyes widened, and she shot Hank a guilty look. Maybe DPSOs didn't usually participate in the questioning when working with marshals, but there was no sense in wasting brainpower. He gave her a nod to say what she'd done was okay.

"Well, I…" Peters ran a hand through his hair. "Look, if I happened to know something, who'd hear about what I said?"

Hank replied, "It'll be in the case notes, but even the press usually reads just the highlights."

Peters blew out a sigh. He picked up a pack of herbal cigarettes from the side table and lit one. A sweet, grassy aroma wafted through the air.

"Okay. Thing is, I did find Abner. He was with a street whore. You both know that's a bad idea."

"Risky, at least," Hank commented. There was a reason every city had at least one licensed brothel.

"I didn't say anything. His business if he wants to be stupid, except I like Alice. Everybody does. Him cheating on her, especially like that, it didn't sit well."

All that was logical, but the part about the whore didn't quite ring true. Street whores were rare because brothels offered job security and regular medical monitoring.

"Did you ever see this whore before?" None of that showed up on the video Chief Mortimer had compiled. Maybe the jamming accounted for that. Or not. No way to know, damn it.

Peters shook his head. "Hell, for all I know she was just some woman he picked up. I just thought she was a whore, maybe because I didn't like him doing Alice that way. Made me wonder if she was why he always left the table."

"Don't players regularly sit out a few hands?"

"Yeah. But only Abner did it every game. I saw him with that woman, and I just thought...well, you know. I confronted him after they finished, and he admitted he had her on the side. Insisted it was nothing, but Alice sure wouldn't've bought that."

They ran through a few more questions, then Hank thanked him for his time.

When he and Krista reached the street, she asked, "Can I say something?"

"Sure."

"The bit about the whore...that's a stretch, Hank. I

haven't heard about anybody arresting a street whore in a couple or three years."

"Could've been a one-time deal. Or, as Peters said, a regular hookup."

"Yeah, but…Did he seem a little too cooperative to you? He spilled goodies like a piñata on Cinco de Mayo."

"You have that holiday here, huh? Good to know." Terran humans had carried their holidays into space with them, but few planets celebrated all of them. "And yeah, he seemed unusually forthcoming. But that doesn't mean he was lying. Maybe it only means he doesn't want us to look too closely at what he does when he leaves the game."

"Like smuggling, maybe?" Krista grinned.

"Or a hookup of his own." Hank shook his head. "We need more info. Let's see what Joe has turned up on the videos and do some checking of our own." In particular, he wanted to find out whether Otis Ransom was a person or a ship.

#

A couple of hours later, a call from Joe came in. Hank and Krista leaned over his comm unit at the desk in his Lothian City quarters.

"Not much luck so far," Joe reported. "A Rorlan female came in at the Cartwright's Creek Depot at 2038. They're closed then, but visitors can log in on a pad to pay for landing slots. The female is on video walking toward Brek-Hathra's building about 2038 and coming back around 0400, but she used a false name, Zandra

Vlax. Paid with a prepaid card. The flyer had a Depot rental decal on it, but it doesn't say which Depot. There are more than a dozen, in Lothian and a couple of other demesnes, that she could've come from if she didn't mind flying a long time. I'm working on whittling that down."

Hank rubbed his chin. "Since she was careful to leave before dawn, let's assume that she had to be back by the start of the business day and so couldn't have had that far to go. And yeah, I'm not keen on assumptions either, but we have to start somewhere."

"Fair enough. I'll do that."

"Of course," Krista added, "if she rented the flyer under a different alias, that's another complication."

"Let's hope not," Hank muttered.

They signed off with Joe, and Hank leaned back in his chair. "You know, Cartwright's Creek isn't a very big community. If I wanted to bend the law and not be noticed, it's not where I'd pick."

"Micah's Junction would be better," Krista agreed.

"It would. And Brek-Hathra was going down there in a couple of days. If he was up to something shady down there, odds are, he would've gone regularly. Let's try feeding his facial recognition into the Micah's Junction surveillance feed and see what we get. I'll log you into the system."

She looked about as thrilled as he would've been but nodded. "What are you going to work on?"

"Tracking down Otis Ransom."

With Krista at his desk, Hank settled in one of the two armchairs with his tablet. It could access the government databases, but he probably wouldn't need them for the first stages of this.

Or maybe he did, he decided half an hour later. There were three Ransom families living on the planet, none of them named Otis. There was no *Otis Ransom* registered with the Federated Colonies Merchant Marine. No military vessel by that name in the FC or among their allies, most of whom wouldn't have used such a mundanely Terran-sounding name anyway. Naming conventions varied widely among the known worlds.

He switched to the restricted databases and reset the search for Ransom or Otis. While the computer searched, he made kova for himself and Krista. Finally, a ding heralded his search results.

Four people named Otis, three on-planet and one on the station. Ok but not what he needed.

Same three families named Ransom.

No ships with *Otis* in the name. But...a freighter named *Blake's Ransom* stopped by Outcast Station every six to eight weeks. That had to be it. He switched to the schedule for the port at Micah's Junction. The *Blake's Ransom* was due to make planetfall in three days. No Otis on the crew list, but the freighter had to be involved somehow.

"Gotcha," he breathed, setting an alert to let him know if that schedule changed.

"Hank?" Krista said. "If that's good news, please share. I've seen Brek-Hathra and his buddies, occasionally with Alice or other women, having a great time on Port Street and on Ocean Drive. Nothing helpful, though. I tried to follow him when he left the poker games, but he went off-camera. Very few places to do that."

Frowning, she added, "Of course, it could be that he jammed or fooled the street cams. Which we don't know are jammed unless we look at the relevant times, so it could be we've got all but the important stuff, which we'll never get."

"Strangely, I follow that. Try a 48-hour window around..." Hank turned back to the freighter schedule. "...Tuesday, six weeks back."

He drifted over with his kova and watched the screen over her shoulder. "How far back does the Cartwright's Creek security footage last?" he asked.

"Four weeks active, then another four archi—Hey! Nailed it."

Sure enough, the video showed Brek-Hathra walking down Port Street in Micah's Junction. He and his buddies turned left and walked into The Smorgasbord. A brothel, according to the orientation app. But *geez*, what a name.

"Huh," Krista said. "I guess Peters isn't so very disapproving of Abner cheating on Alice. Not if they went to a brothel together."

"Yeah. Strike one against him."

They sped up the vid. The men left, all looking satisfied, walking close together and laughing. If Peters disapproved of Brek-Hathra's behavior, he hid it well.

The computer patched different camera feeds together, staying with Brek-Hathra and his buddies as they turned onto Ocean Drive and strolled away from the beach.

"If Jory's is on Ocean," Hank said, "it's not cheap."

"Everything costs more in Micah's Junction," Krista

responded. "But yeah, I've heard of that place. It's popular with the demesne's miners."

"I'd forgotten you had miners. Didn't see any mining."

"It's farther up in the mountains. Not as bad as it used to be but still dirty, claustrophobic work. Those crews like to cut loose when they can."

"So Brek-Hathra could've been meeting a local as easily as a spacer."

Locals...some locals on some planets had home security video. "Krista, does anybody up in Cartwright's Creek have home security with cams?"

"About a third, the ones who get paid better. Chief Nahz had the feeds near Brek-Hathra's place checked. Turned up nothing. There should've been a note in the summary Chief Mortimer sent you."

There was, but he'd forgotten. "Nothing? Or jammed?"

Her brows drew together. "Good question. Some jamming creates internal loops. What we've seen so far, with the static, has been the clumsier kind."

"The more sophisticated the jammer, the more power it needs—"

"And the shorter its range!" Krista bounced in her seat. "We asked the near neighbors directly. Didn't put out a wide appeal. We could check with others."

"How long is video stored on those systems?" Could this really be a break?

"Most home systems, about ten days."

She looked excited and hopeful, and this was her bailiwick. Hank asked, "Do you want to call Chief Nahz and get the officer up in Cartwright's Creek to check those?"

"Love to!"

Hank's personal comm buzzed with a message from Nahz. "Hold on, Krista," he said. When he answered, Nahz said, "You owe me big, Tremaine."

"What have you found?"

"I got your Rorlan female. ID isn't the best, but it's a 73 percent probability. She kept her hood on until she got in the flitter at the Depot in Harkett Town. Shot through the privacy glass, the image is distorted, but the computer cleaned it up some. Sending you the info."

"Great. Thanks." Armed with this, he could take another pass at Allarth. "Krista had a great idea. She wants to talk to you."

He transferred the call to the console and scanned the info. If he could get Allarth to admit to knowing this female and she gave him an alibi, that would bust the arrest. It would vindicate the Lady's demand for another look and confirm that Hank's hunches were still working. At least some of the time. Unless she didn't give him an alibi, but Hank would swim that river when he reached it.

Of course, Winslow wasn't the type to enjoy being proved wrong. But there was no help for it. Hank glanced around the spartan quarters. Maybe he'd better get used to this place.

CHAPTER NINE

Holding a printout of the mystery female, whose name turned out to be Azra Velarth, Hank walked down to the cells. Tarpon, as usual, was nowhere in sight.

He found Allarth slouched on a corner of his bunk. The Rorlan glanced at him and then away.

Hank leaned on the wall by the bars. "Azra Velarth," he said.

Allarth's body tensed, but he kept his gaze on the ceiling.

"Rented a flitter in Harkett Town," Hank continued. "Married. Husband's a circuit judge. He was out on circuit the night Brek-Hathra died. Returned home the next day. Funny, but she rents a flitter—under an assumed name, which is a Class 6 misdemeanor, carrying up to three years in prison, every time she does it—at the Harkett Town Depot every Thursday night that he's gone." That was fudging since he had no video old enough to back up such a generalization, but that was fair when questioning a suspect.

"I'm going to have to go talk to her," Hank added. "Whether or not the judge is home."

Allarth still said nothing.

Hank waited a few seconds before pushing off the wall. "Okay, then. I'll let you know how that goes."

He headed for the back door and the landing pads. Not until he'd stepped out did Allarth call, "Wait!"

Hank strolled back to the cell. "What is it?"

"If I…" Allarth's throat worked, and he wiped his palms on his gray trousers. "If I explain to you, could you…keep her out of it?"

"There's no way to do that if she's your alibi." The Rorlan looked so anxious, though, that Hank said, "What I can do is give you a chance to get her up here. I can talk to her here, in an interview room. Her name'll go in the report, but if we break this case, I might be able to protect her anonymity."

The rules on anonymous sources were tight, and Winslow didn't seem the sort to let go of his settled arrest without names. But maybe not wanting to embarrass or piss off a judge would be enough to convince him.

Allarth nodded. "All right. Let me call her."

#

Ms. Velarth agreed to meet Hank in Micah's Junction the next morning. Hank informed Nahz and his officers, then set out for the port city to see if he could find the mysterious Otis. If his visits coincided with those of the *Blake's Ransom,* he was likely known around the port.

As he cruised down the mountains, he admired the forest falling away below him. The planet had a more dramatic beauty than Granville Station, with its gentler hills and valleys. His mom would love to photograph it, but he still hoped not to be posted here long enough for her to consider the trip out from Mars worth it.

About fifteen minutes out of Lothian City, his personal comm beeped. He keyed the mike. "Tremaine."

"One of Brek-Hathra's neighbors had video footage that showed a male Rorlan walking out of the fields and into Brek-Hathra's building around ToD. Never came out, at least not in range of the man's camera. But the neighbor who reported seeing a cloaked Rorlan leave the building said the picture looked like the guy he saw. Placed the departure about forty minutes after the video showed him entering the building. He didn't see Jarel."

"Where was the guy when this neighbor saw him?"

"Walking away from the building, about halfway to the street."

But Jarel had met the guy earlier. That was probably why the neighbor didn't see her. "Please tell me you can see the Rorlan's face."

"A wedge of it inside his jacket hood. Enough to see there's no nose. Three fingers on each hand. Also, there's a scar on the left side of his mouth."

"Is he a resident?"

"Not according to the records."

Well, hell. This case was one step forward, one or two back. "How hard is it for someone to make an unauthorized landing from orbit up in those hills?"

Silence crackled over the comm while the public safety officer considered. Finally, she replied, "There are a couple of plateaus where a small ship would fit, about the smallest you could go interplanetary on. You'd have to time it just right to penetrate the traffic zone unnoticed, and you would need to hide your ship from the satellite sweeps."

"Which you could jam," he noted. Planetary defenses were designed to spot larger ships. The ones out here, if they were as old as the other equipment, were probably calibrated for the very big craft that had dominated travel two decades ago. The small interplanetary landers had been common for only a dozen years or so.

"Yeah." Now she sounded glum. "But it could be done."

Great. Just great. "Regardless, Krista, you did good, solid work there. Shoot me the best image you have."

"Transmitting. We gotta nail this bastard, Hank."

"Right." He told her about Azra Velarth. "Do you want in on the interview?"

"Thanks, but I have other cases to work." But she hesitated. "Hank, the marshals service is unlikely to accept an alibi, especially from a lover, unless we can hand them the real culprit."

By *marshals service*, she meant Winslow. But she wasn't saying anything Hank hadn't already figured out. "Working on it. If you find anything else good, let me know."

#

Hank landed the runabout at HQ in Micah's Junction but didn't step out immediately. They'd reached the old-fashioned legwork part of this case. When it came to that, feet on the pavement were invaluable. Especially with the window around the *Blake's Ransom*'s stay on-planet opening day after tomorrow and lasting only thirty-six hours. He needed more feet.

Unfortunately, being the newest badge on the post, not to mention the whole *boss's shit list* thing, meant he had no idea whose feet he could trust.

The spooks would know. If they were trustworthy. He was going to have to trust someone, though, or risk time running out. The Lothian officers had no jurisdiction here.

Mulling that, he strolled up the aptly named Ocean Drive toward the mountains and Jory's Bar & Grille.

The manager, a young man built like a rail but with intelligence bright in his eyes, looked at the Rorlan's picture. "Never seen him before. Sorry."

"How about someone named Otis?"

The man frowned but slowly shook his head. "I think I might've heard the name at some point, but I couldn't put it with a face. We get a lot of people through here."

Considering the naked beings of several species and genders dancing in cages above the tables, Hank could believe that.

A few more questions and answers confirmed the almost-monthly visits from Brek-Hathra and the poker players.

Hank thanked the man for his time and started making the rounds. The Rorlan looked familiar to three of the bar owners. But the owners weren't the best place to start. The wait staff and bartenders were. Covering all of them alone in the time available was impossible.

At the corner of Ocean and Port, by HQ, Hank

paused. Might as well see if the spook squad could help him. Ryerson and Lang had seemed forthcoming enough.

He walked into the building, his current cloak of imaginary invisibility shielding him from notice or greetings, and back to the psi squad office on the ground floor.

The door stood open, and Brad Ryerson sat behind one of the two desks in the room. He kicked back and smiled. "Back from exile so soon?"

"I wish. Got a minute?"

When the psi officer nodded, Hank closed the door and took a seat in front of the desk. He explained the dilemma to Ryerson, who listened with grave attention.

"You definitely need more people," Ryerson said. "Lang's off tonight, but I can come up with a few others who would do."

He drew a paper pad and a pencil out of a drawer and started listing names. "To be honest, though, there aren't that many I can recommend. Few of the deputies would shoot off their mouths, but most of them aren't really acquainted with the concept of diligence. They would agree to help you and then not get around to it."

"Does this post follow the custom that a marshal can ask anyone he wants for help? Or do I have to go through Chief Deputy Winslow?"

Ryerson tore off his list and passed it over. "He doesn't want to be bothered with things like that, so you can proceed. Until you're no longer on the shit list, however, you can't be sure what he will or won't take an interest in."

"Figured." Hank glanced over the list. Dree Barnet

was on it. So were Ryerson and someone named Reeth, both with the Greek letter psi by their names. Three other names were there.

Shrugging, Ryerson said, "Yu is solid. As are Shandy and Paltron, if someone stays on top of them. But it's a place to start."

"It is that."

"Shoot me your data. Since the other marshals know me better than you, I'll see about bringing them on board. Then I can go back to Jory's and talk to the staff."

"Thanks." Hank went back out to work his way down the street.

When he walked outside, though, the smell of warm bread from the diner across the way made his stomach rumble. He could break for dinner, talk to Addie, thus killing two birds, etc., and then make his way down Port.

Addison's was busier than he'd expected. The tables and bar stools were mostly occupied. A couple more freighters must've made planetfall.

He found a small corner table and ordered.

In due course, Addie made her way to him. "Back so soon?"

"Everybody keeps saying that. I'm going to think I smell or something."

She grinned. "Not so far. Have you ordered?"

"A little while ago. Got a minute? There's something I need to talk to you about."

Her eyebrows rose, but she said only, "Sure. My office is behind the bar."

She led him behind the long, wooden counter. The Grog hustled up and down behind it. Addie waited to catch its eye, then signaled to the office.

As Hank followed her in, she said, "Chrriikk will bring your food in here if we're not done. We can't hold the table for you."

"That works."

They sat together in front of her desk. When Hank pulled up the Rorlan's image, she frowned at it. "I think he might've been in here, but I couldn't say, Hank. We get a fair number of Rorlans, being so close to the port."

"Location, location."

"Yeah. Gotta give my dad points for picking a good one when he opened the bar."

"Anybody come in here who's named Otis?"

"Not regularly. I can ask my staff, though." Nodding at his comm, she asked, "Can I keep that photo?"

She'd been helpful. Maybe she deserved to be trusted. But he didn't know her well enough to turn over the photo of a murder suspect. "I need to hold onto it. Sorry."

"Well, a Rorlan with a scar will be memorable. Most of them are so quiet, but that guy looks dangerous."

Now that Hank thought about it, the guy did. "If either this guy or anyone named Otis comes in, Addie, don't let on there's anything unusual. But call me ASAP." He passed her a card with his contact number.

"I'll do that."

"Someone'll be around to talk to the staff later."

She nodded, but he would've bet real money that she would talk to them first. Her employees, her choice, and he couldn't stick around to stop her. "Be careful," he ordered.

"Always. What did these guys do, anyway?"

Hank hesitated. "It's better for now if you don't

know."

His meal arrived, and Addie sat behind her desk, working on her terminal while he ate. She apparently wasn't going to trust him in her office after he withheld the photo, but it was her space, so she set the rules. He would finish his meal and hit the rest of the bars still on his list.

#

Hank changed into street clothes before heading to the small conference room on the second floor of HQ for the meeting Ryerson had set. Dree waited there with deputy marshals she introduced as Reeth, Shandy, Yu, and Paltron. Ryerson walked in a moment after Hank, reporting nothing definite from the staff at Jory's. Everyone wore street clothes with stunners under their jackets. If their quarry came into the city early, a uniform would be like a red alert siren. Everyone listened as Hank explained the situation.

"We have to nail down the identity of this Otis before the *Blake's Ransom* lands day after tomorrow. If we don't, we won't have another shot at him until the freighter returns in six to eight weeks. I've talked to the managers of the bars but not to the wait staff and bartenders yet. I've flagged the places where something about either of these two people seemed even vaguely familiar, but they all need to be followed up."

He transmitted the list of bars to everyone. Comms pinged as the list hit them. "I'm the new guy, obviously," Hank added. "If anyone knows anything that could help, please share."

"Warrants?" Ryerson asked.

"We don't have enough evidence to get them," Hank said. Unfortunately, warrants applied only to arrests or searches and seizures, not bringing people in for questioning.

Reeth, a stocky woman with dark tan skin and graying, close-cut hair, raised an eyebrow. "I don't see Mother Mary's on here."

"What's Mother Mary's?" Hank asked. That place wasn't on the orientation app. He would've remembered a name like that.

"You wouldn't have seen it yet," Shandy, a short, stocky, balding guy told him. "It's on Whistler, but it's private, so it doesn't have a sign. Or show up on the orientation app. You have to be a member to go in."

"Okay. Can anybody here do that?"

No one volunteered. Paltron, a solid, blond woman with keen, black eyes, said, "I'll see if I can bull my way in."

They divided up the bars and restaurants and headed out. Hank had the half of Port Street closest to the spaceport, while Yu, a tall, rangy woman, had the other half.

She started two doors up from HQ at The Asteroid Belt while Hank hurried to the other end of the street to work back.

He'd reached the door of the first place, Pirates Haven—a name that, out here, might not be all in fun—when his comm chimed. Stepping to the side of the doorway, he clicked his mic. "Tremaine."

"Hank, it's Addie. I talked to my staff, and we've got a lead for you. Marlis, one of my waiters, remembers a woman named Otis who came in with a Rorlan."

A woman. Well, that was a surprise. "On my way."

#

Addie showed Hank into her office again. Marlis, the waitress who'd served him a couple of days earlier, was already seated in one of the chairs by the desk. Addie closed herself in with them. Hank said, "This is marshals service business, Ms. Addison."

"And this is my place, marshal. My employee." She sat behind her desk, folded her hands, and looked directly at him.

Ousting her would take time he didn't want to waste, so he turned back to Marlis. He pulled up the Rorlan's image and showed it to her. "Is this the Rorlan you remember?"

She frowned at the picture, studying it, before she nodded. "I think so. That guy had a…whatchacallit, the hair that sticks up straight down the middle of his head with none on the sides. That. Can't see this guy's hair."

Addie opened her mouth, but Hank shot her a warning look. "A Mohawk?" he asked Marlis.

When she nodded, he asked, "What color?"

"Black with green stripes."

Awfully conspicuous for someone who was sneaking around. Unless he was actually bald and the hair was a disguise.

"When was the last time you saw him?"

"About six weeks ago, give or take. He was waiting in the back corner table when that woman came in. I was coming up from the side when she said something about she was 'tired of being Otis,' or something like that, and they needed to 'retire that name.' I remembered because it was just so odd. He hissed at her, so I took a couple steps back before they spotted me. I pretended like I hadn't heard anything. We don't want customers complaining about us eavesdropping or any of that."

"Of course not," Hank agreed. From the corner of his eye, he saw Addie nod.

Marlis continued, "Since they seemed kinda edgy, I apologized for keeping them waiting. I just had a feeling, the way he hissed and all, and Rorlan gills sure do make that loud, she'd spoken when she shouldn't have."

"That's good thinking, Marlis," Hank said. "Can you describe this woman?"

"She wasn't that remarkable, you know? Hair was a deep, rusty brown, but her face looked older, like maybe in her forties, so I figured that was dyed."

Hair a deep shade of rusty brown? On a woman who looked to be midforties? "Did she have any distinguishing marks on her face?"

"Nuh-uh." Marlis shook her head. "Just some freckles. On her nose and cheeks."

That sounded like Kendra Jarel, the field worker from Lothian. Could her irritation have been a cover to throw him and Nahz off?

"Hang on a second." Hank sorted the ID photos of everyone they'd interviewed, pulling out the women. Handing the tablet to Marlis, he said, "Scroll through these, please, and tell me whether you see her."

Marlis scrolled past Jarel. A moment later, she scrolled back. "This is her. She looks a little thinner, but

I'm pretty sure it's her."

"How sure is 'pretty sure'? Would you swear to it?"

The waiter hesitated, studying the picture, before she nodded emphatically. "Yes. I would. It's her."

Finally, real progress. "Do you know the Rorlan's name?" he asked.

She shook her head. "They paid cash, too, so there wasn't a credit slip."

If Jarel was Otis and worked on-planet, though, why did the *Blake's Ransom* come into the business at all? Did they have a contact aboard her? Or were they using the ship's schedule as a cover? "Marlis, do you know anything about a ship with 'Ransom' in its name?"

"No. Sorry, marshal."

"Don't be sorry. You've been a big help." No wonder Brek-Hathra's neighbor hadn't seen Jarel when he spotted the Rorlan. Her entire earlier statement was a lie. "Thank you. But please don't mention that you knew anything useful. It's for your safety."

Addie demanded, "Do you think she's in danger? If so, I can—"

"If she were in danger for what she heard, they would've done something the night she spotted them. The important thing now is that no one knows she had any info to share with me."

Marlis went back to work. Hank sent his team her information via text and photo mail rather than calling.

"I need to talk to the rest of the staff," he told Addie. "See if anyone else noticed anything."

"I told you they didn't." She raised an eyebrow. "I need my staff on the floor tonight, marshal. We're busier than a buffle stampede."

Nancy Northcott

"I understand that, and I'll be as brief as I can, but—"

His comm chimed. He pulled it off his belt to read the message. The *Blake's Ransom* was early. She'd just cleared traffic control and was inbound.

"Fuck," he snapped, and Addie shot to her feet.

"Hank? What is it?"

She wasn't authorized to know what they were investigating, but her waiter was their only witness. With the *Blake's Ransom* arriving tonight, the Rorlan and Kendra Jarel might already be in town.

"Keep an eye on Marlis," he advised. "Be sure she's never out of your sight."

"But—"

"No time. Gotta go now." And set up an op with limited personnel and no advance notice, to spot people who might or might not be here as well as their mystery contact from the ship. Assuming they had one. All without alerting, and thus possibly enraging, the chief deputy marshal, who did not want Allarth's arrest challenged.

Yeah, Hank thought, rushing out the door. Good luck with that.

CHAPTER TEN

Who could he trust to monitor the street cameras? Dree and Ryerson seemed the best choices. The others, he barely knew, and Ryerson's endorsement of a couple of them hadn't exactly been stellar.

Striding toward the street, Hank clicked his mic. "Barnet. Where are you?"

"Coming out of Jazz Planet, on Orleans. I got your message."

"Good. I need you in the surveillance room at HQ. We need to know whether that Rorlan or Kendra Jarel is in Micah's Junction. And if so, where they are."

Silence came back to him for a long moment before she answered. "Hank, getting into that room when you're not assigned requires clearance from the Officer of the Day."

Which meant Winslow would be informed. Shit. Scowling, he clicked the mic as he reached the street. "Roger that. I can take the surveillance room." Leaving the street right now sucked, but letting her take any heat from the top was a poor way to repay her help.

"No, I got it. The OD is Walak, and he's more likely

to listen to me than a newbie."

"Yeah, but—"

"I got this. Really. Where are you going to be?"

"Watching the port to see who comes off the *Ransom*. I'll have everyone else continue what they're doing until you have info for us."

"Okay. I'll let you know when I'm in place."

Heading toward the port, Hank sent a message to the rest of his team. Three doors down from the port was the Brew and Buffle bar, with outside tables. The evening chill had driven most customers indoors, but a few hunched over the tables.

One long table had six people gathered around it. The two-top behind it was empty and partially shielded from the street by people's bodies. Perfect.

Hank went in, ordered a beer, and claimed the little table. While he waited, he updated the alert on the *Ransom* to notify him when she landed.

Minutes ticked by. One of the men at the big table had boyfriend problems. His friends sympathized, and the conversation turned to trashing everyone's sleazoid exes. Each of the group at the table, it seemed, had one.

Hell, even I do. But Belinda Suzerenn had been two posts and seven years ago. Since then, Hank hadn't been with anyone long enough to risk being made crazy.

"Hank?" Dree's voice sounded in his earpiece. "I'm in. We're feeding in the photos of Jarel and her Rorlan buddy now."

"Roger. Thanks."

Shandy reported a possible sighting of the pair at a pool hall. Reeth had a sighting at The Golden Rooster, on Dali Street. Paltron was still trying to get into Mother

Mary's.

"I'm not a member," she reported, "so they're stonewalling me."

"Isn't that interesting," Yu replied before Hank could.

Hank smiled into his beer. "Great minds."

Paltron added, "I'm giving them about one more minute to produce the manager before I call stonewalling obstruction and play the arrest card."

"You," Hank replied, "are a woman after my own heart."

"Careful. I might hold you to—Here we go." She signed off.

The muted whine of atmospheric engines and the swirl of air over the port—held back from the town by the force fields—heralded a ship arriving. A long, shadowy shape with four stubby engine mounts amidships came down toward the rear of the landing field. Before it dropped out of sight behind ships in closer slots, the field's lights hit the hull. The *Blake's Ransom* had arrived.

A moment later, the preset alert on Hank's comm chimed.

Because the ship had landed so far back in the field, he couldn't be completely sure who came off her and who came from other ships. How would he know which one to follow?

"Tremaine? You there?" Dree's voice. She must've chosen the more formal hail because she had an audience.

"What do you have, Barnet?"

"Kendra Jarel is in town. We picked her up coming

from the Depot. Tracking her now."

"Roger. If you—"

His comm beeped. He put Dree on hold. "Tremaine."

"Paltron. I hit pay dirt. Kendra Jarel is here."

"At Mother Mary's?" Hank asked, sitting up straighter.

"You betcha. The manager has grudgingly agreed to let me plant my not-a-member butt on a stool at the bar."

"Tremaine, it's Reeth. I'm not far from Mother Mary's. I can be there in about two minutes and watch the back door."

"Great. Do that." Hank paused, considering. Jarel might not be meeting the Rorlan or anyone from the ship tonight. Or she might be.

Still, following her could lead them to the Rorlan at least. It was also a better bet than hoping he could pick out the right random spacer coming out of the gate. "Yu, report."

"I'm down by the water. No one here has seen either of the suspects. I can get to Mother Mary's, but not fast."

Dree chimed in, "I can get there, Tremaine. Deputy March, here, the monitor officer, will let us know if… Stand by."

Jarel would recognize Hank, but maybe she didn't know the others. Much as he wanted to dive in, hanging back was smarter.

"The Rorlan just walked into town from the woods," Dree informed them. "He's west of the port, about a ten-minute walk out."

Hank asked, "What's in the area he's coming from?"

"Nothing. Supposedly. But there's an abandoned,

overgrown tract that's supposed to become a park someday. You could land a flitter there if you were avoiding the Depot. And if the heat from your engines didn't start a fire."

"What's the shortest way to Mother Mary's from there?" Hank eyed the foot traffic on Port Street. This was where knowing the ground better became important. Damn Winslow and his arbitrary assignments.

Ryerson broke in, "If he takes a right on Whistler, it's a straight shot."

The Rorlan couldn't turn left because that would put him up against the spaceport's right of way, so if he turned at all, it would be to his right. Whistler was three blocks in from the edge of town, with Mother Mary's in the second block down from the port.

"Nope," Dree reported. "Turned right on Dali. He could be zigzagging."

"Making sure no one follows him," Hank agreed. He dropped a couple of credits on the table, picked up his beer, and sauntered across the street. "Keep us posted."

"Roger that," a gruff, male voice said. "This is March, taking over so Barnet can go have fun. Suspect is still on Dali, now taking a left on Orleans."

Hank loitered in front of the bookstore. At least there were enough people on the street that he wasn't conspicuous. "What's the foot traffic like on Whistler?"

"Moderate," Dree announced. She sounded out of breath. "I'm there, watching the front of Mother Mary's from about a block down."

"I'm coming up on her," Ryerson said. "I'll back her up and make her look less conspicuous."

So Paltron was inside, Yu out of range, Barnet and

Ryerson on the front, Reeth on the back. That left… "Shandy," Hank said into his mic. "Report."

"I'm up by the woods, Tremaine. It'll take me some time to work my way to Mother Mary's."

Hmm. "How far are you from the land that may be a park someday?"

"Coupla minutes' walk."

"Go check it out."

"You got it."

March's voice broke in. "Our boy's turning onto Whistler. Heading toward Mother Mary's."

Hank thought fast. "Let him go in." Only then could they get a definite link between the suspect and Jarel, and one from them to anyone else. "If he goes past the club, follow him."

Of course, if they lost him, Hank's ass would be Winslow's grass. Never mind that the chief deputy had officially closed this case. He would jump at the chance to rub Hank's nose in a failure.

Paltron spoke softly. "Hey. Guy just came in and sat with Jarel. Trying to get a photo."

A few moments later, it flashed onto their screens. An unremarkable, middle-aged human male with a beer belly and a wiry build sat with Kendra Jarel.

"I'll see if I can get closer," Paltron said. "There's a table open, and the manager has forgotten to hover around giving me the evil eye."

Hank bit back his *Be careful.* So far, at least, these particular deputy marshals were performing well. Not like the fuckups they were supposed to be. Of course, neither was he, so their competence shouldn't be such a surprise.

"On my way," Hank informed the others. "We'll see what Paltron can get before we move in."

"They're not going to just let us in," Ryerson noted. "Even if we had warrants, they'd stall. Not everyone in there with our suspects is an upstanding citizen."

"Imagine my surprise," Hank replied. "Still, we don't want anyone hurt. Might be safer to take them when they come out. That place doesn't have any hidden exits, does it?"

March's gruff voice said, "Checking. Stand by."

Hank turned off Port into an alley that connected with Whistler. People loitered there, chatting, drinking, and in the case of a couple of happy women, necking. The crowd made great cover.

As he emerged from the alley, the Rorlan walked past, heading for Whistler. Hank strolled on down the alley and cut left to the building's rear on Dali.

"No other exits," March reported. "At least, not on the official plans."

Everyone acknowledged. Hank found Reeth in the shadow of a parking port under the building across the street. Less foot traffic here than on Whistler. They would be more conspicuous, but there was no help for it.

"How's it going?" he asked.

She shrugged. "So far, one spacer, who definitely needed to bathe, wanted to party. Three drunks reeled by, but I resisted the urge to arrest them. The usual."

"Right."

"Uh-oh," Paltron said. "The Rorlan came in, sat down for about a minute. The wait-droid came over, and now they're all getting up. Being a bit too casual. Heading for the doors. The Rorlan and Jarel to the front, the other spacer to the rear. Crap. I bet that whiny-ass manager tipped them."

"Roger," Hank replied. "Move close so we can take them as soon as they come out."

Everyone acknowledged. With stunners out, he and Reeth took positions against the wall on either side of the rear exit.

A minute passed. Then another. No sound came from the front. At least nobody had opened fire. A stunner made a distinctive whine when used.

"Hey!" somebody behind them said.

Hank and Reeth wheeled. At the corner on Reeth's side of the building, a square chunk of the road's surface was rising. A hidden hatch. Pedestrians glared at the man emerging from it.

"You," Hank shouted. "Freeze. Everyone down!"

The man who'd been with Jarel and the Rorlan wheeled and fired blindly toward Hank. Pedestrians hit the ground, some screaming and all with hands covering their heads.

"Go," Reeth told Hank. She fired, grazing the man, who fired back.

Letting out a choked cry, Reeth dived to the side. Hank lunged right and fired. Dodging his bolt drove the man into the path of Reeth's. He dropped and lay still. Hank restrained him and patted him down, pocketing not only his stunner but two knives and a pocket gas can.

With the prisoner secure, Hank knelt by Reeth. "Let me see." Her leg was raw and bloody halfway between the knee and thigh.

"A damn lucky shot," she ground out. "Would you believe it?"

"No. Aggravating," he said. "Tremaine to dispatch. We need a medic and a wagon behind Mother Mary's."

"The wagon is on its way already. Medics heading out now."

That likely meant Barnet and Ryerson had the Rorlan and Jarel. Hank clicked the mike again. "Barnet. Status."

"Two in custody," she said. "Who's down?"

"Reeth. Meet us at HQ." So they had their suspects. What they didn't have was anything beyond the circumstantial. Somehow, they had to flip one of these assholes.

#

An hour later, Hank met the others outside the interrogation rooms. "I got nothin'," he admitted. "Anybody else nail anything?"

Headshakes answered him. Damn.

"We have the Rorlan, Darge Nelarth, at the scene but no connection between him and the victim," Hank mused, thinking aloud.

"He claims he'd come to see Jarel but had the wrong building," Paltron said. "The fact that he's not on the security cams is, as far as he claims to know, just one of life's little mysteries. Bastard."

Hank shook his head. "We don't have enough to get a warrant for a DNA sample yet, even if we knew the crime scene prints contained enough for an identification. There's nothing on this other guy with them at all, except Paltron heard them discussing moving goods."

"Smuggling," Dree muttered. "But he claims they were discussing taking packages of local goods out for sale next year."

"Somebody tipped them," Reeth noted. "But who?"

Hank checked his tablet. "Comms from the bar are clean. The techs found no record of the droid warning them or doing anything beyond its job, and its records show the manager nowhere near that group. So *who* is a very good question. We can't impound the Rorlan's vehicle until we arrest him, so Shandy got a couple of others to stand guard over it tonight."

"Well, now what?" Paltron said.

"We let them stew overnight," Hank answered. "I have an idea, but it depends on what happens tomorrow."

#

The next morning, Hank met Azra Velarth at the front door of HQ. She wore a lightweight cloak with the hood up. Around a wide sun visor, lines of worry in her face were visible. Only when Hank showed her into an interview room did she remove the visor.

"Will this take long?" she asked. "No one must see me here."

"Not too long, ma'am, no." He engaged the recorder, read off the pertinent data, and asked, "Were you in Cartwright's Creek the night of September 8?"

"Yes." She cleared her throat. "I went there to see an old friend, Dex Allarth."

"Tell me about the evening."

"I arrived there about 2038 and remained until early morning. Dex and I are childhood friends. We seldom see each other. We were meditating together."

That was one word for it, he guessed. "Was Allarth with you the entire time?"

"Yes. Between the rites, we talked. Caught up." She toyed with her visor. "Marshal, what do you know of our Arthgalrigan faith?"

"Not much, I'm afraid."

"Meditation is…it's intensely personal. Something friends share until one or the other…your word for it would be marriage. When one marries, meditation is not to be shared outside the wedded dyad."

"Yet you went to Cartwright's Creek to meditate with Allarth?"

"We have long been friends, and I missed sharing that with him."

Hank nodded, but whether she was meditating or committing adultery—and maybe they were the same in her culture—didn't matter. "Did Allarth leave you alone for any reason?"

"No. We were within sight of each other at all times."

"Did you go anywhere? Outside his place, I mean."

"No."

He believed her, but a few things still didn't add up. "Why use assumed names to rent your flitter and to land at the Cartwright's Creek Depot field?"

"My husband." Swallowing hard, she looked down at the sunglasses. "He is a fine man but very…you would say traditional. He would not understand."

When she lifted her face again, it was tight with anxiety. "Please, Marshal Tremaine. He must not know. I swear on my life that my meetings with Dex are only for meditation."

Maybe so, but nobody would risk the displeasure she so obviously feared except for deeply emotional reasons. Hank took her through the evening a couple of times, pushed the button to have her statement transcribed, and had her sign it.

Next up, Kendra Jarel.

#

The woman lounged in her chair, her face bored despite the shackles holding her hands close to the table. Hank sat down and studied her silently.

After a couple of minutes, she said, "You got something to say, then say it."

"Oh. Sorry." He shrugged. "I was just wondering how you'd do on Styx Station."

"Never heard of it. Either charge me with something or let me go. That's the law."

"Yep. But I have about 18 hours before that kicks in." Copying her pose, he leaned back in his chair. "Styx is a hot, arid world they're terraforming now. Pretty soon, they'll be wanting a test population. You know, to see how well the terraforming sustains human life."

"That's nothing to do with me." But she fidgeted in her chair.

"Not this minute, no. But your identification of Allarth doesn't stand." Playing a hunch, he added, "We also have you on video coming out of the shed behind Allarth's house early in the morning before the weapon used to murder Abner Brek-Hathra mysteriously turned up there. So you're looking at a perjury charge."

"I was nowhere near that shed. What I said's not perjury. I told what I saw, best I could."

"Yeah, you were very definite. Very. If we get trace DNA off that bat and it matches yours, well, it's not just perjury."

Her face blanched before she looked away. Maybe she hadn't had her gloves that night.

Hank continued, "Really, you should hope you only end up with perjury. Shorter sentence for that. But it does happen to be one of the crimes that get people conscripted for terraforming tests. You'll have a nice little hut out on the plains of Styx, maybe a chance to grow a garden. That is, when you're not doing grunt work for the terraformers. No climate control in the on-planet housing, though, because that would screw up the experiment."

She looked away from him, scowling, but her eyes were tight at the corners.

"Temperatures on Styx swing pretty widely. Gets up to 110 degrees Fahrenheit in the shade during the day. All year. Goes down to about 100 at night in the summer, 27 in the winter."

"You're bluffing," she snapped.

"I'm not." Hank leaned in. "The bat is being tested as we speak. We have you on video." Not really on the video, but the truth wasn't a requirement in interrogations. "And Dex Allarth, unfortunately for you, has an ironclad alibi."

Jarel said nothing, but her throat worked in a hard swallow.

He waited a few minutes before pushing out of his chair. "Your funeral, babe. That kind of heat ages a person. You'll probably look twenty, maybe thirty, years older than you are when you come out. Going to be tough, getting a job that's not grunt work with a felony on your sheet."

"What if...let's say I knew something. What would it get me?"

"Depends on what you know." When she opened her mouth, he cut her off. "You spill it all, or you get nothing."

"Fuck." She slumped at the table. "I want a guarantee of no work crew."

"If your info's good, I'll put in that word."

"That stupid bitch, Alice, found the box of Abner's things, stuff he'd culled from shipments. We'd been smuggling in stuff for a while, me and Abner. Then he decided he was going out on his own. Why, I have no idea." Jarel blew out a heavy sigh. "The people we work for, they couldn't have that. Not the stealing, not the independent selling."

"What part did Darge Nelarth play in that?"

"He's the enforcer. Has a base on Layton's World, coupla places to land here. Abner and me reported to him."

"Who paid you?"

"Nelarth did. He's been sticking close to help with the latest shipment. Someone higher up set up the fake bank account for Allarth."

"Uh-huh. What's Boxton's role?" That turned out to be the guy from the *Blake's Ransom.*

"He carries the wine and wool and leather goods out for us."

So they'd been stealing from the demesne, too.

"How does he manage that?"

"You'd have to ask him."

"Who made the call to get Allarth arrested? You had to know we'd look for another Rorlan if Allarth had an alibi."

"Yeah, well, he wasn't supposed to. Guy's snooty. Keeps to himself." Slumping, she said, "Nelarth made the call. With a voice scrambler. All I did, I swear, all I did was to plant the bat in Allarth's shed and claim I saw him come out of Abner's place."

"It was enough to frame an innocent man," Hank said. "Who actually killed Brek-Hathra?"

"Nelarth, when Abner wouldn't fall in line. He tried to wipe his prints off, but Rorlan skin chemistry…you can't wipe it all." She shook her head. "He wasn't supposed to kill him, but no, he had to lose his temper. Damn idiot. He wasn't sure he'd jammed all the video, and then I learned my neighbor'd been looking out the window—nosy bastard thinks he's the neighborhood monitor or something—and seen a cloaked Rorlan. So we had to set up another Rorlan, and Allarth, that sanctimonious snot, was handy."

So he'd been right. She'd completely invented her statement.

He took her through the sequence a couple of times before she said, "That's everything. Now do I get my deal?"

"I'll put in for it. I just have one more question." Based on a hunch that might or might not pay off. "Who's making the drug Abner had in his system the night he died?"

"I don't know. Swear I don't."

"You helped make it, though."

"Oh, no. I don't deal in drugs. Stuff, yeah, but not drugs." She shook her head emphatically. "Some tourist wanted some bacca roots to study. I sold him some from a field we were plowing under to plant a new crop. That's all. Never saw the guy again." She twisted her hands. "Next thing I heard, there's some new drug that comes from bacca. I figured it was him, but I swear, all I did was sell him some roots."

"What about the acid in the marshals service runabout?"

"Nelarth had that done. I don't know who did it or how."

So that was a loose end that wanted tying up.

"Why did you all suddenly leave Mother Mary's?"

"Nelarth carries a silent alarm. And before you ask, I don't know who it's connected to. I don't want to know."

He studied her, but his gut said she was telling the truth. Anyone behind a smuggling operation would limit the circle he trusted. "You willing to have a telepath verify all that?"

"If I have to." She eyed him warily.

"It's that or Styx." When she nodded, he said, "Then we're good."

Hank walked out of the room. With what he'd just gotten, they could flip the spacer. The pieces were falling together. Everything but anonymity for Azra Velarth. There was only one way to get that. He just hoped it wouldn't blow up in his face.

#

Hank stood at something very close to attention in front of Winslow's desk. "Thank you for seeing me, sir."

The chief deputy frowned at him. "I've given you enough rope, hotshot. You hang yourself with it yet?"

"No, sir." Hank took a deep breath, then laid everything out. The longer he spoke, the more Winslow's frown deepened.

When he finished, the boss grilled him on every point. By the second time through, Hank's ankle ached, and his temper was steaming.

Winslow leaned back in his chair. He studied Hank for long moments, likely trying to find some way this could blow up in Hank's face.

Hank set his jaw. He would not give this asshole the satisfaction of showing his distrust or his physical discomfort.

At last, still scowling, the chief deputy said, "Well, this'll satisfy that woman up in Lothian, anyway."

He could've been happier about that, but Hank would settle for not enduring a rant. "I had help, sir. Marshal Barnet flipped the spacer." The guy had named an employee at the Cartwright's Creek Depot as the runabout's saboteur. Unfortunately, the man had vanished. So had any trace of the guy Jarel had described as buying bacca roots from her.

They could find those guys later. For now, Hank could take satisfaction from knowing Brek-Hathra's murder was solved.

Winslow scowled at him. "You've made the case. Done a great job of kissing up to the bitch in Lothian. Why are you still here?"

"There's something else." He explained about Azra

Velarth. "Doing a favor for her, keeping her name out of it, could help the service down the road. It's always good to help a lady, especially a judge's wife." He'd saved his best argument, the one Winslow would most likely swallow, for last. Casually, Hank added, "Besides, we might need a favor someday."

Winslow rocked back and forth for almost a full minute. "Here's a thought. We help her, she owes us. Handy to have a judge's wife owe us."

"Yes, sir." If Winslow wanted the credit for that idea, he could have it. What mattered was protecting the woman's identity.

"All right, Tremaine. I'll approve confidential source status for her. Scrub her name from the record and send the source ID number to me only. Now get back to work."

"Yes, sir."

When he walked out of the reception room, Dree, Ryerson, and Shandy were waiting. Ryerson looked him up and down. "He's still in one piece."

"No blood," Dree commented.

"So far," Shandy added. "What do you say, New Badge? Want to go get lunch?"

"Sure."

The group ambled out of the main doors and swung left.

"Where are we going, anyway?" Hank asked.

Ryerson replied, "Addison's, where else? Food's above average and, when you're not on duty, it's one place that doesn't water the beer."

"I could go with that," Hank said.

While he and his comrades ate, he would tell them

what he hadn't shared with Winslow. He was saving that news until the documentation arrived.

His friend on Calliope had pegged the drug in Brek-Hathra's system and in that of the guy who died in the bar as a derivative of bacca, as suspected, but it was a new compound, produced by fermenting the roots, which had different chemistry from the leaves. The process altered the hallucinogen in the drug so it produced only euphoria in most species. Except in Telinganans, like the guy in the bar. In them, it produced anaphylactic shock, fatal if it wasn't treated fast.

Now the marshals service had a new problem to track down. If he could interest Winslow. Far better to try that with data to back him up.

Walking up Port beside Shandy, he asked, "So how long until someone else transfers in and I'm not the new guy anymore?"

Ryerson grinned at him. "Around here, you never know when some new asshole will turn up. Meanwhile, we have you."

Everyone laughed, Hank with them. He'd lost the cloak of invisibility that came with being on the boss's shit list. He'd also survived the chief's attempt to make him look like a screwup, busted a smuggling ring, and solved a murder.

Maybe three years here wouldn't be as bad as he'd feared.

The End

From the Authors

Thank you for reading *Welcome to Outcast Station.* We hope you enjoyed it. If you would like to know more about our books and new releases, sign up for our newsletters on our websites.

www.JeanneAdams.com

www.NancyNorthcott.com

We will never spam you, and we don't sell or share our subscribers' addresses.

We return to Outcast Station this fall with *Christmas on Outcast Station.* It will be available in both ebook and print formats. We hope you'll enjoy the holidays with us.

About Jeanne Adams

Jeanne Adams writes award-winning suspense, paranormal, mysteries and urban fantasies who specializes in thrills and suspense. Even her paranormal and urban fantasies have a suspense element, so be prepared! She loves football, baseball, dogs, Halloween and the weird. She's also a sought-after speaker, who knows a thing or two about getting rid of the evidence... (She teaches classes for writers on body disposal, plotting suspense that sells and marketing!)

Jeanne lives in DC with her husband and two growing sons, as well as two dogs – a Lab and an Irish Water Spaniel. Don't tell, but she's prone to adopting more dogs when her husband isn't looking.

Featured in Cosmopolitan Magazine, and other publications, her books have been consistently hailed as "One of the best Suspense Books of the Year!" by Romantic Times. You can find her at her newly redesigned website: www.JeanneAdams.com, on Twitter at www.twitter.com/JeanneAdams or at www.Facebook.com/JeanneAdamsAuthor

Also by Jeanne Adams

Paranormal Suspense:

The Haven Harbor Series:

The Witches Walk – Event Planner Mari Beecham doesn't believe Haven Harbor is really a town of witches…but it is. Murder and old magic come calling in this intense story of love, betrayal and passion.

The Halloween Promise – A novella of Haven Harbor at Halloween!
A Yule to Remember – A novella of Haven Harbor for the Yule Ball!

Historical Paranormal Suspense:

Behind Enemy Lines – It's 1939 and the world is on the brink of war. Hitler is rounding up arcane artifacts and the experts who understand them. He wants English wine expert Lady Grace Corvedale for the magical pendant she wears. Can American agent Lt. Robert "Dix" Dixon find her before the Fuhrer does?

Urban Fantasy:

The Tentacle Affaire – He doesn't believe in aliens. She doesn't believe in magic. They're both wrong.

Suspense:

Dead Run – A woman and her son, hunted by a brutal drug lord…who happens to be her ex-husband. An undercover agent who must decide whether his duty is to catch the bad guy or save the woman who rocks his world.

Capitol Danger (with Nancy Northcott, Suzanne Ferrell and JD Tyler) A novel in four parts. What happens when a home grown terrorist cell decides that the first woman president shouldn't live to take office? An action packed story of an attempt to kill the president at her Inaugural Ball.

Deadly Delivery – A Suspense Novella – One night stands can be killer! When real estate developer Deirdre Shercroft helps out with deliveries for her parents' business, she doesn't bank on running into drug dealers. Or the one-night-stand fling she can't forget.

About Nancy Northcott

Nancy Northcott's childhood ambition was to grow up and become Wonder Woman. Around fourth grade, she realized it was too late to acquire Amazon genes, but she still loved comic books, science fiction, fantasy, history, and romance. She currently enjoys attending and volunteering at science fiction conventions.

Nancy has written freelance articles and taught at the college level. Her most popular course was on science fiction, fantasy, and society. She has also given presentations on the Wars of the Roses and Richard III to university classes studying Shakespeare's play about that king. A sucker for fast action and high stakes, Nancy combines the elements she loves in the books she writes.

Reviewers have described her books as melding fantasy, romance, and suspense. Library Journal gave her debut novel, Renegade, a starred review, calling it "genre fiction at its best."

For more information, visit these sites:
www.nancynorthcott.com
Twitter: @NancyNorthcott
Facebook:
https://facebook.com/nancynorthcottauthor

Also by Nancy Northcott

<u>Fantasy</u>

The Boar King's Honor Trilogy - A wizard's fatal mistake, a king wrongly blamed, a bloodline cursed:

The Herald of Day
The Steel Rose (forthcoming)
The King's Champion (forthcoming)

<u>Paranormal Romance</u>

The Light Mage Wars - Mages fighting ghouls and demons in south Georgia near the Okefenokee swamp. The series encompasses three books published under the series label The Protectors.

Sentinel (an extended-length novella)
Renegade
Protector (a novella)
Guardian
Warrior
Nemesis (forthcoming)

<u>Suspense</u>

The Lethal Webs - Romantic spy adventures set in the United Kingdom. The series features two spies, a series of adventures, and one steamy romance.

The Deathbrew Affair (forthcoming)
The Runway Murder Affair (forthcoming)
The Deadly Cargo Affair (forthcoming)
The Christmas Village Affair (forthcoming)

The Arachnid Files - Romantic suspense feature spies and law enforcement officers

Danger's Edge, a novella in the anthology *Capitol Danger* (with Suzanne Ferrell, Jeanne Adams, and J.D. Tyler)